To Mary

So who is Mary?

The Boat House Café

With warm wishes! Linda Cardillo

Linda Cardillo

BOOK ONE OF
First Light

BELLASTORIA PRESS
Books that nurture the soul

ISBN: 978-1-942209-00-3

The Boat House Café

BELLASTORIA PRESS
P.O. Box 60341
Longmeadow, Massachusetts 01116

For Judy Murphy

Some come to Chappaquiddick Island to hide;
others come to heal.

PROLOGUE

Herald Tribune
March 15, 1941

For Sale
Former fishing camp on Cape Pogue Bay. Includes dock, boat house, cottage and shed. Waterfront property bordered by Shear Pen Pond and Cape Pogue Bay, adjacent to East Beach. Land includes 25 acres of meadow and woods. Spring-fed well. No electricity. Accessible only by boat.

I read the ad and saw not someone's abandoned shack—the kind of isolated place a beleaguered man goes to get away from a nagging wife or a mind-numbing desk job.

No, I saw a small café, scrubbed and welcoming, the aroma of fresh-baked pie wafting out the window.

I saw my own salvation.

Chapter One
Innisfree

The wind at Innisfree talks. Late at night, just outside the rear windows of the house, the voices rise up from the beach below the sea wall, slither through the grass and whisper around the eaves. Sometimes it is the low murmur of lovers under the filmy curtain of the Milky Way. But often, it is the conspiratorial rumble of those whose only purpose on the shore in the middle of the night is secretive, furtive. The words are indecipherable, but the voices rise and fall with inflection. The wind converses—with the house, with the sea, with itself.

The first time I heard the voices, I froze in my bed, silent and still, straining to understand what they were saying, convinced they were men arguing about breaking into the house. I am a woman alone with a cash business. Everyone knows that. Easy prey.

I keep a gun in a wooden box under the bed. No one knows that, except perhaps old man Lyons who runs the Edgartown Hardware where I purchase my ammunition along with my nails and buckets and garden tools.

I mentally prepared myself to unlock the box and load the pistol, when I realized the voices were continuing in an endless, monotonous loop accompanied by the shushing and high-pitched whistle that I recognized as the voice of nature, not of men. I let down my guard and lowered the window by my bed. Enough of that disturbance. And then I slept.

After that night, the murmuring of the wind no longer disturbed my dreams, and became one more confirmation of the wisdom of leaving New York to set up housekeeping at Innisfree. Another is the afternoon lull between lunch and supper customers, when I sit with my cup of tea on the porch of the Boat House Café, overlooking Pogue Bay.

A tangle of wildflowers—daisies, beach roses and thistle—climbs up the bank and quivers in the wind, beckoning the finches and the monarch butterflies. Beyond the flowers and the birds, the water dances and the sun spreads a covering of silver lace upon the bay, not unlike the tablecloth my granny tatted for my mother before she and Da left County Kerry for Martha's Vineyard. Sunday after Mass in Edgartown, my mother spread that cloth on our dining table and my sister Kathleen and I set out the dishes.

Ma left a cold lunch at the Knolls for the Bradleys, who always went to dinner at Rose Jeffers' place on Sunday evenings, leaving her free to cook us dinner. She taught me to cook, Ma did. Roast chicken, beef stew, colcannon, pound cake, pies. Were she here now to see the Boat House and how it has flourished, she would recognize her recipes and her careful kitchen management. I know to the penny what it costs me to serve a meal at the Boat House. I don't skimp on the quality of the food I put on the table, nor do I let the Connors Market Store on Main Street, where I get my provisions, overcharge me. But I also am not timid in setting a fair price for what I offer, and my customers come back for more.

If it was Ma who gave me the skills to cook for a living, it was the Jordan Marsh bakery in Boston that taught me how to serve a customer with respect and grace. When I took my waitressing job in New York, many of the girls didn't understand that at all. If they got orders mixed up or had trouble in the kitchen that caused delays, they never apologized to their customers or soothed the displeasure with another cup of coffee or an extra cookie on the dessert plate. I knew there were rewards to treating people well–financial rewards in my pocket, introductions when the time came for me to make my move and buy this place.

If anyone were to ask me why I came here (although no one does), I would tell them, "This island was my childhood home and the source of the only happy time in my life."

My brothers and sisters and I were free to roam the beaches and woodlands and moors of Chappy because our parents were caretakers of the Bradley mansion on North Neck that everyone referred to as the Knolls. As little ones we saw no distinction between us and Ned Bradley–we all played together by day and then everyone in the neighborhood went home for supper–we to the caretaker's cottage, Felicia and

Ellen Bellamy to their house down the road and Ned up the hill to the Knolls. The food was plentiful, the pace of life unhurried and the cares of the adult world blissfully unknown to us.

That I had to leave that idyllic existence was not my choice. Bad times hit the Bradleys when the market crashed in '29. They lost the Knolls and everything else. Without the Knolls, they had no need for a caretaker and cook, and Ma and Da picked up and moved us to Boston soon after it became clear they'd not find any other work on the island. I was seventeen at the time. Old enough to understand our misfortune–and our dependence on people like the Bradleys. When the full force of the change in our lives hit me, it was like the wallop of a monster wave at Katama that emerges out of nowhere and catapults you into the hard, wet sand.

We lived in a tenement, with the only light a dim gray sliver that seeped in through dirty windows facing a shaft. The odors of rancid cooking oil and unwashed bodies permeated the stairwells. We were assailed by wailing babies and the voices of angry men who couldn't find work and desperate women struggling to put food in their children's bellies.

That place robbed my Ma of her soul and her voice. On Chappy, she'd sung, especially in the evenings when the moon rose over East Beach and her work at the Knolls was done. Kathleen played the piano and the little ones—Daniel and Patrick and Maureen—gathered at Ma's feet, exhausted from a day in the open air. She sang all the tunes she had learned in the old country, holding on to that piece of her life as best she could.

We had no piano in Boston, but Ma knew the songs well enough to sing without Kathleen's accompaniment. But after a few months she was too tired one night to sing, and the little ones, no longer free to run in meadows and climb apple trees, were too agitated to sit still and listen.

I think Ma's silence was the hardest part for me. Her voice could have drowned out the suffering that shouted at us, not only from the dank hovel that had become our home but from every corner of the city. Without her voice, we slipped farther and farther from everything we had known and loved on Chappy.

When we left Chappy I took a bag of stones with me. I had collected them over the years, wandering along the beach. They were all perfectly smooth and rounded, their rough edges worn away by the sea. At night in bed I emptied the sack and held them like talismans in my hand. Rubbing the stones as if they were Aladdin's lamp, I made a vow to myself that I would escape the sadness that engulfed us and return to Chappy. I didn't know how long it would take me, or what I'd have to survive, before I got back.

Chapter Two
Home

How do I tell you about myself when I have spent nearly half a lifetime hiding who I am from others? Like the Carmelite nun I should have become—the second-born daughter of a devoutly Catholic Irish family—I've maintained a vow of silence. Not out of sanctity, but out of shame.

I returned to Chappaquiddick Island in the early spring of 1941. I had taken the train from Pennsylvania Station in New York to Providence, Rhode Island, and then a ferry to Vineyard Haven on Martha's Vineyard. Everything I owned fit neatly into a small valise. Although my childhood had been expansive, its boundaries extending as far as my ten-year-old legs could carry me along the beach or my eyes could embrace of the sea and the sky, my adult life had been contained, folded neatly into well-defined compartments–shop girl, waitress, boarding-house resident, and finally, as I disembarked from the ferry at Vineyard Haven on a rain-soaked April day, potential businesswoman.

In addition to the valise, I clutched in my hand the business card of Marcus Gardner, Realtor and Associate Justice for Dukes County. He and I had been corresponding about a parcel of land on Pogue Bay with a dock, a boat house and a cottage, all in considerable disrepair and therefore within my price range.

My imagination had been captured by the ad Mr. Gardner had placed in the Sunday *Herald Tribune* a few months before. I knew Pogue Bay. I had splashed in its waters, dug up clams on its tidal banks and set sail on Ned Bradley's skiff back when we still reveled in the freedom of island children before the impact of the world beyond Martha's Vineyard and our own rash decisions altered everything. Mr. Gardner's description of the peninsula reached across the miles and the years between my childhood on Chappy and my life in New York City.

It pulled at my heart in a way no man had ever spoken to me—not even Ned before the tragedies that changed me from an earnest and good girl into the woman I am today.

As soon as I read the ad I *knew* that the land on Cape Pogue was my salvation. I am no romantic, who thinks that island life is a balm. But my city life–a necessity, not a choice—had nearly broken me, and I understood that I was the only one I could depend on to release me from the downward spiral my trust in others—especially men—had set in motion.

I was able to respond to Mr. Gardner's ad with more than wishful hope because I had money. Money I had earned and saved. When I arrived in New York in 1934, I found my first job at the Horn & Hardart Automat, filling rotating compartments with slices of lemon meringue and coconut custard pies. It was a lifetime away from serving customers at the Jordan Marsh bakery in

Boston, where personal attention was offered along with the blueberry muffins. But I was more than happy to be behind the glass carousels, out of sight of the customers at Horn & Hardart. For all they knew, the pies were being baked and inserted into the compartments by a robot.

But I realized soon enough that robots and invisible servers don't receive tips, which is more than likely what appealed to the Horn & Hardart customers. Grateful as I was for a job in the middle of the Depression, my meager wages were not enough to dispel the fear and despair into which I had plunged after I had fled Boston and Ned Bradley.

So one day after my shift at Horn & Hardart, I pulled off my hairnet, changed out of my gray-with-white-piping uniform and into my best dress and pumps and applied for a waitress position at Delmonico's Steak House. I'd watched the restaurant from a coffee shop in the neighborhood that allowed me to linger over my cup. The clientele were well-dressed, arriving in cabs or well-cared for cars with drivers—women with fur collars snug around their slender necks and men who commanded notice. Men who would appreciate the kind of attention I knew how to give and be rewarded for.

I got the job. Every night, I returned to my room on West 33rd Street and, despite my aching feet and the tension in my jaw from smiling nonstop for eight hours, I sat in the middle of the rose-colored chenille bedspread I had bought at

Woolworth's with my first paycheck, and I counted up the reasons I was willing to act the part of solicitous servant to the wealthy. The tips were erratic at first—I was the new girl and often got assigned tables with out-of-towners, businessmen from the Midwest in New York for sales conventions or New England college professors who were seemingly unfamiliar with the practice of tipping. But no matter how meager, I set aside a portion, tallied it up and filled out a deposit envelope that I dropped off at the bank on my way to work the next day.

As I gained seniority among the waitresses, my tables got better. A few of the girls left because they married customers—or were set up in uptown apartments with every comfort except a wedding ring. But that wasn't what I was aiming for. I had figured out long before I got to New York that the only sure way out was money in the bank that I had put there myself.

And when I had enough, I contacted Marcus Gardner, packed my valise and closed the door on city life.

I found Gardner's office in Vineyard Haven a short walk from the ferry terminal. I shook out my umbrella, left it in the stand shaped like a pelican just inside the door and introduced myself to the gray-haired woman who appeared to be either his wife or mother, based on the nameplate on her desk, "Mrs. Gardner."

Her brow wrinkled when I gave my name.

"Keaney?" She seemed confused, almost startled by my appearance on her doorstep. Had they not been expecting me? I had clearly written that I was arriving that day to inspect the property. I had no intention of basing my purchase on the flowery description of Gardner's ad or my own memories of Cape Pogue, filtered through the prism of childhood idylls.

Mrs. Gardner's finger ruffled through a group of files on her desk and pulled out a manila folder clearly marked "M. Keaney—Cape Pogue."

"We weren't expecting a woman, especially one so young." She still seemed not quite convinced that I was, indeed, the M. Keaney who intended to buy the property. She looked behind me, as if expecting a husband or father following up the rear with the heavy luggage.

I had purposely used my initial, rather than my given name of Mae, to forestall exactly the response Mrs. Gardner now had. I hadn't wanted to damage my chances of being taken seriously, or increase the likelihood that people would question too closely the reasons that a young, unmarried woman would be seeking a spot so wild and remote. Better to deal with those questions in person, cash in my hand, than by post, where I could easily be dismissed.

"Is Mr. Gardner available to take me to see the property, as we arranged?"

"Oh, you wouldn't want to go out there now, in the rain!"

"But of course I would. Better to see it under those conditions so that I understand fully what its drawbacks might be."

She was about to continue her resistance when the door to the office in the rear opened and a man of about fifty emerged, pulling on a Mackinaw.

"I'm heading down to the ferry to meet this fellow Keaney, Aggie. Frank Bennett said he has time to run us over to Pogue in his catboat to take a look at the place."

Aggie (whom I now took to be Marcus' wife) raised her eyebrows and nodded toward me.

"Keaney's already here, Marcus."

As soon as he saw me, Marcus Gardner's face blanched and his features tightened briefly into a profound expression of pain. Whatever disquiet my arrival had triggered, I didn't think it was because he was expecting me to be a man. But he recovered quickly and stuck out his hand. I took it, gripping it securely so that he'd know I was here to do business and not indulging in some childish fantasy. I pushed aside my curiosity about his shock at my appearance, and asked outright, ignoring Aggie, "Shall we get going then?"

He nodded and held the door for me while I retrieved my umbrella. We retraced my steps down to the waterfront. Marcus hailed the boatman, Frank Bennett, and I look my place in the rear of the catboat. We skimmed out of the harbor and around East Chop toward Oak Bluffs and then Edgartown harbor.

As Bennett slowed to navigate the Gut, the narrow channel that connects the harbor with Cape Pogue Bay, I cast my eyes along the bluffs of North Neck and the beach below. The Knolls still stood there, its windows boarded up and paint peeling from its porches. The stairs leading down to the beach were rotted and missing several risers. I turned away. This wasn't why I had come. Instead, I aimed my sight in the direction Bennett was steering the boat, through the channel and across Cape Pogue Bay to a peninsula. A weathered cottage and a boat house stood at the end of what appeared to be a still serviceable pier.

He tied up and Marcus climbed up to the dock first, stretching a hand down to help me disembark. I had changed on the ferry from my city traveling suit into woolen slacks and Wellingtons, so I was well-prepared for exploring whatever the land offered up, woman or no. The rain was a fine drizzle, coating the brambles and the wind-twisted trees with a slick coat of beaded water. The gray clapboard that covered the boat house and cottage was soaked to nearly black, tinged with green on the northern side.

Marcus pulled a key ring from his Mackinaw pocket and unlocked the boat house. It was apparent from the overgrown brush outside and the state of neglect inside, that no one else had been out here either to view the property or care for it. I felt a smile twitching at the corners of my mouth at my advantage, but controlled it. I didn't want Marcus to think I was too pleased with what I saw.

I inspected both buildings carefully, well aware of the work that would need to go into them to make them habitable, but holding back my tears when I gazed out the windows with their views of water on three sides. Even in the rain, the place was far more than I had hoped—far more beautiful, far more full of possibilities and far more of a comfort to the wounds in my soul.

After the buildings, which were close to the water's edge, we trudged over the remaining acreage—meadows, marshes, groves of cedar and pine. It took my breath away. As far as the eye could see, the only neighbors were the hawks and plovers and foxes. But I wanted confirmation beyond my own senses.

"Any folks live out here on the Cape?"

Marcus Gardner stopped on the path to consider his answer. He may have thought a positive answer was important to me—a woman alone, in need of reassurance that human company was close at hand. He hadn't been prepared for a woman, although he had adjusted easily enough back at the realty office. A customer is a customer, as long as she has money to spend. But I watched him ponder that a woman's needs might be different. Finally, he spoke.

"Oh yes, Miss Keaney. You'd not be entirely alone out here. Joe DuBois lives at the lighthouse, just up the path to the north of the cedar grove. Used to be a whole family – the keeper, his wife and children. But when the last keeper retired, only Joe replaced him."

Marcus Gardner could not have known that more than Joe DuBois within walking distance might have caused me to get back into Bennett's boat and begin my search again. Especially if there'd been children. But a lighthouse keeper on his own more than likely would leave me to myself.

"I'd like to take one more look at the buildings, if you don't mind." And I turned briskly back to the cottage.

Despite the rain, both the cottage and the boat house were dry inside, and although the clapboard was soaked, I didn't see any sign of rot.

I began making mental notes of what I'd need, especially in the boat house. I had no intention of using it to keep a boat. I had other plans, which hinged on the answer to my next question.

"Fisherman still come out here much? As I recall, stripers and blues used to be plentiful some years back."

"Although some things have changed, the fishing hasn't. The bay is quite an attraction for anyone with a boat and a fishing rod. You fish, Miss Keaney?"

I shook my head. "I've done some clamming in my day, and caught some herring down at the dike as a child. But I've never even held a fly rod."

But I was pleased to hear that many who did cast their lines still fished in Pogue Bay. I was satisfied. From the moment I set foot on the dock, this place had spoken to me in the deepest core of my being. But I couldn't let my longing for a refuge overwhelm my ability to sustain myself here. If this were to become my life, I needed to know it would be so for the rest of my life. I had saved enough to buy a place and outfit it, but not enough to provide for myself for longer than a year. The place had to be livelihood as well as sanctuary, and now I was sure that this spit of sand with its overgrown beach roses, stunted trees and weathered but sturdy buildings could do just that.

After years of masking my emotions as a shop girl and waitress, I'm pretty adept at presenting the face that will get me what I want. I saw no difference in my negotiation with Marcus Gardner.

"I think I've seen enough, Mr. Gardner. I'm ready to go back."

I kept my peace on the boat ride. It was too rough to hold much of a conversation as the boat bounced from one swell to the next. I saw Gardner motion to Bennett to take it easy, probably worried that his one viable buyer might be too green in the gills by the time we got back to Vineyard Haven to contemplate a repeat this journey anytime soon—let alone on a regular basis.

I'd weathered much worse than seasickness, however. And the salt spray on my cheeks both masked my tears and reminded me all too well of the island childhood that now seemed within my grasp.

By the time we returned to the realty office, Aggie Gardner had recovered well enough from her skepticism to brew us a cup of tea and offer me a towel to dry my face. Most likely she had wired my bank in New York and gotten a reply that, indeed, I had the wherewithal to buy the property.

I accepted the tea and the towel, laid out my observations on the weaknesses of the place and made my first offer. Gardner made a few mumbles about needing to pass it on to the owners—heirs of some off-islander who had used the place as a fishing camp. The heirs were a niece and nephew living in California. That piece of news gave me greater hope that I'd be able to wrap this up without too much agitation. They had no sentimental ties—had probably never even been to the island. The property to them was no more than an albatross they'd be happy to exchange for my cash.

"Well, then, if you can direct me to a hotel where I might find a comfortable and respectable room, I'll go get settled and wait to hear from you."

I thought it best not to appear too anxious or eager for an answer from the far-flung niece and nephew. Besides, my clothes were soggy and I was ready for a hot bath.

Aggie was clearly prepared for such requests and handed me a card for the Vineyard Haven Inn, down the block on Main Street. I took my valise and found my way.

I waited two days for Marcus Gardner to contact me. Longer than I had anticipated, but not so long that I wavered and made the first move. I kept busy. The first night I ate a plain supper in the dining room at the inn—pot roast and boiled potatoes, some cherry pie with a canned filling that probably hadn't been baked in the hotel kitchen. I was curious about that kitchen—what equipment they had that could be easily serviced on the island—but as a stranger it would have done me no good to ask right away. I'd seen enough restaurant kitchens in my waitressing days to be well schooled, and the weekend chef at Delmonico's had taken a liking to me without an expectation of reciprocation. He'd written down manufacturers and catalog numbers for me. But that was a high-end shop in the financial district of Manhattan—not the sort of clientele or cooking I'd be expecting in the middle of nowhere.

That night at supper I chatted up the waitress, an older woman in her forties with the posture of someone who has carried a lot of heavy trays or borne some heavy sorrows in her day. The dining room wasn't busy on a Wednesday in April, so I knew I wasn't harrying her by engaging her in conversation. I noted her name on the brass tag pinned to her apron.

"Have you been here long, Betty?"

"On the island or here at the inn?"

"Both."

"My whole life, to answer the first question, and what feels like my whole life, to answer the second."

I smiled in sympathy at her description.

"How about you? Just passing through at an odd time of year for a tourist, or planning to stay for some unfathomable reason?"

"Whether I stay or not depends on an answer I'm waiting on."

"From a man? You aren't one of those mail-order brides, are you? If you are, let me tell you, get on the next ferry out of here."

I laughed out loud at her vehemence, which unfortunately drew the attention of the dining room manager, who raised her eyebrows.

Betty hurriedly made herself look busy at my table, despite the fact that the dining room was nearly empty.

"You couldn't be farther from the truth. The last reason I'd come here would be for a man. In fact, the main reason I'm coming here is to get as far away from men as possible." I surprised myself at how much I revealed, but something about her invited the revelation. She seemed to share the same opinion, if not experience, of men's behavior.

She clucked in agreement.

"Well, good luck to you. I wish I'd made a similar decision when I'd been your age, but I got too caught up in what I thought was love."

She picked up her tray and disappeared through the swinging doors of the kitchen.

I left her a nice tip and retreated to my room, with its third-floor view of the harbor. The last ferry had docked for the night, so it was too late to take the waitress' advice—not that I intended to. The dream I had held onto through all my years of loss was tied up in my staying and following through on the one thing that I believed would be my salvation.

And so I waited for Marcus Gardner to come back with the answer that would set me on my final course home.

By the time he sent word to me at the inn, the rain had subsided and I had rented a bicycle to get me to Edgartown. As the closest port to Cape Pogue, I knew it would be most economical to do my provisioning there, and I wanted to know what was available as well as who was running the store. I had mixed feelings about whether it might be someone who would remember me or my family. My name had meant nothing to Marcus and Aggie Gardner, but Vineyard Haven was far enough away from Chappy and its insular community to account for that. I had gotten used to the anonymity of New York, for better or worse. I didn't hold out much hope that the news that Mae Keancy had purchased the fishing camp on Cape Pogue would remain within the confines of the Gardner family. Aggie struck me as the kind of woman who enjoyed being privy to information that gave her status in a community where gossip was the primary currency.

I decided to pedal along the beach road to Edgartown, rather than take the inland route. The sun had risen in a cloudless sky, and after my waterlogged first day it felt good to have light and warmth surrounding me. As children we hadn't spent much time on the main island of Martha's Vineyard, so there were no familiar tugs to distract my thoughts as I pushed on to my destination.

In Edgartown center the grocer Ma had used was gone, but I found another on Main Street, Connor's Market Store. I wandered through the place, looking over the stock and assuring myself it would be ample for my needs. It being off-season, not many customers were in the aisles. My presence was noted, but the young girl behind the counter didn't recognize me. I bought some bread and sandwich meat to make a lunch and took it down to the harbor to eat. Down on the dock I discovered the icehouse was still in operation and inquired about prices and delivery. I planned to order furniture from Sears.

Not much to see at this time of year. The yacht club basin was still empty; a few fishing boats headed out toward Nantucket Sound. A small ferry was tied up on the Edgartown side. I folded up the paper wrapper from my sandwich and strolled to the ferry landing. Across the mouth of the harbor was the familiar sandy shore of Chappy.

Seized by a sudden whim and the freedom to do as I pleased, I asked the ferryman when he'd be leaving.

"Whenever I have a passenger," he answered.

"Well, then, I guess it's time!" I pushed my bicycle on board and stood at the railing as he pulled out. The voyage across is a scant three minutes, but the difference between Edgartown and Chappy can feel like a lifetime.

All the indifference I felt when I'd pedaled along Beach Road disappeared as the ferry touched the bank and I stepped across the gangplank. My eyes searched for signs of the ghosts that had populated my dreams—the memories of my last trip across the harbor when I'd left with my family twelve years before.

Our belongings had been piled into Luther Johnson's wagon as if we were some pioneer family heading west to new opportunity. But Ma's face was pinched, her lips pressed tightly together. I saw no anticipation in her face, only fear. Da stood by the helm with Mac Brown, the ferryman at the time. A cigarette hung from his lips, his back to Chappy. He never once turned around.

"Good riddance," I heard him mutter as the engine started up and we rolled across the harbor.

But I had faced back at Chappy the entire ride. It was all I knew of the world, and if I'd had my choice, all I ever wanted to know. I wasn't a girl looking for adventure or sophistication, like Felicia Bellamy. A year older than me, she had left Chappy with ambitious dreams to act on stage, live in a city and fall in love with someone like Fred Astaire. It was an irony to me that I, who wanted nothing more than to cling to my childhood on the beach at North Neck, had become a twisted version of Felicia's dream. I was an actress on the stage of Delmonico's, conjuring up the accommodating, ever gracious servant. I lived in a city, albeit not in the penthouse Felicia had envisioned. And although Fred Astaire had not fallen in thrall at my feet, many an imitation in an elegant tuxedo had made their way into my heart.

Approaching Chappy again on that sunny April morning, I stared ahead at my lost innocence. Not with any illusions about recapturing it. That was not what this decision to return to Chappy was all about. But somewhere on this island was the soul of the girl I used to be, and I intended to find her, or at the very least, console her that she was home again.

The wind whipped at my hair as I mounted my bike. I had no program when I set foot on the ferry, but now that I was here, my feet pedaled directly to North Neck, past rusting mailboxes, grazing cows and the Pease's apple orchard. I turned down the all too familiar lane and arrived at the caretaker's cottage. Like the Knolls I'd seen from the water the day before, it was boarded up. Here and there, slates were missing from the roof above the bedroom I'd shared with Kathleen. Ma's vegetable garden, so carefully tended and abundant with potatoes and kale and leeks and pale green cabbages with tightly wrapped heads had disappeared amidst a nest of matted crabgrass and emerging dandelions. The fence that had stood guard against the rabbits and opossums was rotted and leaning aslant. Ma hadn't had time to harvest the last of the Hubbard squash and pumpkins when Da had announced we must pack up and leave.

I leaned the bike against the sturdiest part of the fence and picked my way carefully around the poison ivy that had overrun the once tidy yard. Ma had been ready at the end of every day with a bar of soap to scrub down our bare feet and legs after our roamings.

There wasn't a single pane of glass to press my face to and peer into the house. But, truth be told, it wasn't the house I'd been drawn to. I kept going out to the bluff where the Knolls sat like the prow of a ship. Remembering the sorry state of the stairs to the beach, I made my way carefully, testing each step to see if it would hold my weight. The stairs stopped short a few feet above the sand and I jumped down. It was high tide, with just a couple of yards of dry ground before the water advanced and receded. The shore was scattered with shells smashed by seagulls from the air, their method of choice for opening quahogs. Ned and I had tried it ourselves from up on the bluff, but by the time we got down to the beach to retrieve the succulent morsel inside, a gull had swooped in and snatched it. After that we'd pried open our precious catch the human way. We'd worked too hard to dig up the clams to lose them to clever birds.

I took off my shoes and stockings and walked along the water's edge until I came to the vantage point I was seeking. I shielded my eyes and looked across Pogue Bay until I could make out the silhouette of the dock and two structures on the promontory above the water.

I watched a flock of mergansers skim across the surface of the water.

"Home," I thought. Not here, where I stood, full of memories, ghosts, regrets. But there, across an expanse of brilliant blue teeming with life. One of Ma's songs filled my head at that moment, the words from a poem of her countryman William Butler Yeats.

I clambered back up the decaying stairs, retrieved my bike and pedaled back to the ferry landing and the future awaiting me.

That was a year ago. The California heirs wired Marcus Gardner their acceptance of my offer and the Hibernia Bank in New York forwarded my down payment the following day. I moved from the Vineyard Haven Inn to a rooming house in Edgartown until I had fixed up the cottage enough for it to be habitable. I am not above scrubbing and scouring—Ma had taught me well how to keep a place clean. But a cottage that has only been used as a fishing camp and then is abandoned for God knows how long was not fit to live in when I first crossed its threshold as its owner.

I filled crates with the debris—rusted tackle, broken pottery, moth-eaten blankets—and paid the boatman Bennett to haul it all away in his catboat. I bleached and whitewashed the walls that were spattered with grease and mold. I replaced shattered windowpanes and missing door hinges. I had a privy dug and lay new linoleum in what was to become the dining room of my café.

When the cottage was finally free of the last remnants of its former life, I left Edgartown behind and took up residence.

I had flyers printed up advertising my café and I traveled around the island, posting them on message boards and leaving stacks at the places frequented by fishermen and boaters—tackle and sail shops and boatyards.

Word spreads, as it tends to do in island society. Cape Pogue is an unlikely place to find a cup of tea and a cream-cheese-and-olive sandwich. My first customers were the merely curious, the skeptics and the dismissers. People like Aggie Gardner, who told everyone—at the Grange Hall, at church suppers, at the post office—of the odd woman from New York who had the hare-brained idea she could open a sandwich shop way out on Pogue Bay.

"How ridiculous is that! I bet she doesn't last through the summer and Marcus will be back trying to sell that godforsaken piece of property yet again!"

I dropped off two pies at Olson's store near the ferry landing in Edgartown and asked him to tell folks if they were out on the water they could get a slice and a cup of coffee at the Boat House any afternoon.

I called my place the Boat House not because I have no imagination, but because that was what people knew it to be. If someone said "We tied up at the boat house over on Pogue Bay," a listener knew immediately what was meant. I found myself a good-sized stars and stripes and hung it from a pole close to the water's edge. It was visible as far as the Gut, and in the beginning, that flag caused people to wonder.

"What's that over by the boat house?"

The flag, Aggie's disparaging gossip, the pie samples at Olson's—whatever prompted people, they puttered over to my dock, tied up and stepped into the Boat House to satisfy their curiosity.

I did not disappoint.

The curiosity-seekers left with full bellies and more gossip to fuel the mill.

"She's not got much to say, but bakes a damn good pie."

"She's cleaned out that abandoned fishing camp so you wouldn't even recognize it. She's even planted what looks like a vegetable garden out back."

"Who knows why she chose to be out there, but it's the only place to stop for a bite to eat when you've been fishing since dawn and the belly is hollering to be filled up."

The trickle of first timers turned into a stream about July, when summer people started to arrive and found it more convenient to stop at the Boat House for a sandwich rather than go to the trouble of packing a picnic when they were out for an excursion at the beach.

When I sat down in the evenings at the cottage and tallied up each day's receipts, I was bone-tired, my hands rough from washing dishes and tending to the garden. But I could breathe.

By October, I had earned enough to tide me over the winter. I ordered a load of coal for the stove, canned the last harvest from the garden and settled into my solitude.

Winter at Cape Pogue was everything and nothing like my childhood at North Neck. The caretaker's cottage was inland, not at water's edge, and so we had been protected from the brunt of wind and rain and snow. But we had also been cut off from the harsh beauty of ice-edged beaches and frozen marshes, shimmering as the sunlight flashed on reeds coated in a thin layer of ice. I realized how accustomed I had become to the grayness of urban snow and the bustle of New York during the holidays as I blinked at brilliant white patches scattered across the empty beach… and reveled in the silence.

I attuned myself to the rhythm of the natural world, keeping pace with the daylight. I had taught myself to be a solitary person, but in the cacophony of Manhattan my solitude was, of necessity, also containment. I had closed myself off, bound within the dingy walls of my room.

At Pogue, I found my solitude to be exhilarating. Even the frigid temperatures and fierce winds of a New England maritime winter did not deter me from charging across the moors each morning. I had ordered a pair of Maine boots from L. L. Bean and laced them up over heavy wool socks. With a watch cap on my head and a sailor's pea coat on my body, I'm sure I cut an odd figure as I roamed the outer reaches of the island. But there was no one to remark on my strange appearance or my driven pace. People like Aggie Gardner were snug in their homes in town, and fishermen out in the bay or on Nantucket Sound were too far away to identify the dark figure moving with a singular intensity across the landscape.

Were I a more religious person, I imagine I would consider these morning walks a meditation, a contemplation of my sins. Examination of conscience, I had learned to call it when I had memorized my Baltimore Catechism, the book of doctrine used in every Catholic school in the country. The prelude to a good confession and the hope of absolution.

But I had no desire to confess.

Instead, I spent my walks in close observation of the life around me, even in the depth of winter. For many creatures it was a time of repose and restoration.

Occasionally, in addition to the doe or fox whose path crossed mine, I would see in the distance another solitary figure, a man. It was always early morning and he was always on East Beach in what appeared to be a stance of reverence or even a trance facing the water and the sunrise.

At first I thought he might be a soldier. A contingent of National Guard signalmen were stationed on Peaked Hill in Gay Head on the western side of the island. After Pearl Harbor, the number of military men on the island increased, and they had begun to use East Beach as a firing range to test weapons. The isolation of the beach and its distance from the more populated parts of Chappy made it the most likely choice for target practice. I had encountered some of the soldiers in Edgartown. I wondered if one of them might be the man on the beach, but dismissed that idea. The soldiers were too raucous, too filled with the agitation of those who have felt the recoil of a weapon in their hands and find that they crave it.

But even if I had recognized him, I had no desire to disrupt the peace that had settled itself on my life. In fact, I had every reason *not* to establish a conversation He was a man. A man who shared my inclination for dawn walks on winter mornings, but who nevertheless represented for me what I had come to Chappy to escape.

When I saw him, ramrod still, his breath a visible cloud moving in and out of his body in rhythm with the ice-capped waves pounding the beach, I turned and headed in another direction.

But in May, when the fishermen returned and I reopened the Boat House, I discovered who he was.

Chapter Three
Tobias

Fog comes in fast here. One minute I've got my head down peeling eggs for the egg salad and the next I look up and can't see the end of the dock, let alone the other side of Pogue Bay. It's not good for business. Customers already here, instead of lingering for a slice of cake after their sandwich or another glass of ginger ale, they hurry to get in their boats, eager to make it back to Edgartown before they completely lose their bearings. Anyone heading here for a bite to eat gives up on that idea as soon as they see that veil of mist starting to blow in from the east.

Sometimes the fog lasts for days, muffling the elbow of the peninsula in cotton batting, cutting me off from human contact. Most folks think that's why I'm out here—that I can't abide other people. They assume I'm odd, troubled, maybe that I've suffered some great tragedy in my life or committed some egregious act and am hiding from retribution. The truth is somewhere in the middle, but no one ever bothers to ask. They think, everyone has secrets; Mae Keaney perhaps more than most.

My isolation does mean that folks don't bother with me much, especially the women. When Frank Bennett fetches me in his catboat to take me to Edgartown, they watch me and then quickly look away when I glance up from my market basket and meet their eyes. No one asks me to stop for a cup of tea, not even the wives of the men who come by regularly for my sandwiches when they are out to the Gut to fish.

But the fog brought me unexpected company one evening. When it rolled in swiftly around five, I noticed that someone had just tied up at the dock. I thought he'd slip away again when he saw the fog behind him, but instead he came on up to the Boat House and knocked on the door.

"Would you be closing or might I get a sandwich, Miss Keaney?" he asked me politely. He was a stranger to me. I don't get too many Wampanoag as customers.

I had planned to close when I saw the fog. I'd been on my feet all day. But I still had a bit of chicken and some rhubarb pie, so I let him in and made him a thick sandwich with lots of white meat.

"Don't you want to be heading back? Most folks pull up anchor as soon as they feel the mist on their cheeks."

"That would most likely be summer folks who don't remember from year to year how quickly weather changes around here. I've got too far to go and too heavy a catch to risk running aground where I don't want to be. I learned from my granddad, and he from his, that you pay attention when the winds at Cape Pogue speak. If they tell you to be still and wait, you listen."

"You superstitious? Like that boy who claims he heard ghosts down at the Dike Bridge?"

"Superstitious? No, I wouldn't call it that. Superstition in my book stems from fear. I'm not afraid of what I know, and I know the weather around here well enough to stay put."

And stay put he did, while I washed up in the kitchen and swept the sand out of the dining room that accumulates every day. Something about his presence was a familiar comfort. I did not feel compelled to put on my display of hospitality as I did during the day with most of my customers. He seemed genuinely grateful for the food and the shelter from the weather, and appeared to appreciate the solitude of an empty restaurant as much as I do at the end of a busy day. I thought at first that was why I felt so at ease, but it was more than that.

I was bringing it out the rhubarb pie when I realized who he was. He had gotten up from the table and was standing at the window. It was his stance and his stillness that revealed his identity.

"What brought you to the Boat House this evening? You haven't been here before."

"I don't often fish this side of the bay. But I'd heard from other fishermen of your place—the good food, generous portions. When the fog set in, it just made sense to pull up and find out for myself. Word gets around, good or bad, in this place. People talk about more than your food, as you probably know. But you strike me as the sort of person who doesn't care much about what people think. I've seen you, winter mornings, out on the beach. Wasn't sure it was you until I came in here this evening. But even without your cap and your boots, you stride across this dining room in much the same way."

"What way is that?"

"Purposeful. Observant. You don't miss much, do you?"

"It appears that you are equally observant, and as recognizable looking out my window as you are watching the sun rise on East Beach."

"So we aren't really strangers to one another."

"Except that you know my name and I don't know yours."

"It's Tobias. Tobias Monroe."

"Mr. Monroe, I've got some whisky in the cupboard. Fog looks like it'll be here awhile. Would you like a drink?"

He stayed for a glass of whisky and we talked about what kept us here in this wild place—that both of us maybe were too wild for the civilized places, the cities where rules were defined by people not like us. We talked about being "different"—he a Wampanoag among white people, me a woman alone running her own business. I asked him outright why he wasn't in the military. Since the war began, most of the young men had either enlisted or been drafted, and it was unusual to see an able-bodied man of Tobias' age on the island who wasn't in uniform.

He might have acted insulted by my directness, but perhaps the whisky and the honest conversation up to that point made my question less of an affront. He did not answer with words.

Instead he held up his left hand, which had rested in his lap most of the evening, and which, I admit, I had paid little attention to.

It was missing a thumb.

"I can manage as an island fisherman, but the Army, in its wisdom, requires all ten fingers."

The fog cleared around eight in the evening, with a full moon casting a cascade of light all the way to North Neck.

He took his leave then, with a tip of his cap.

"I'll be back for more," he said. And I knew he didn't mean chicken sandwiches.

Chapter Four
"It will be revealed with fire"

I was rolling out pastry dough for the weekend's pies, the slap of wood against the cushion of shortening and flour accompanied by the boom of the mortars on East Beach. The mergansers had fled as soon as the guns started firing, a black cloud of wings lifting as one and escaping to the west. Unlike the birds, I couldn't rise up and leave when the army disturbed my solitude with its testing.

We were at war. Nothing but the Atlantic separated East Beach from Hitler, and I understood the necessity of the guns. But the lack of an imminent enemy and the boredom of hours spent staring out to sea seemed to have infected the soldiers with a constant need to make sure the guns still worked. Days of quiet, when one could forget that civilization lurked just the other side of the dunes, were then punctuated by the deafening scream of shells arcing over the sand and landing with reverberating thuds that shook the pottery stacked in open shelves above my head.

I glanced out the window at the sky above the beach, darkened with smoke that hung briefly and then started to drift. The winds were normally westerly and carried the noxious clouds out to sea. But today I could see the edges of the smoke wafting toward the cottage and the Boat House. Despite the heat, from both the July morning and the oven, I leaned across the counter to pull the window closed.

Had I not done so, I might have smelled the fire sooner.

It was only after I had taken the first batch of pies from the oven and gone out to the coop to gather eggs to hard boil for sandwiches that my nose detected something different. Not the metallic odor of the exploding mortar shells, but something more reminiscent of Christmas than summer. My brain recognized quickly that it was no celebratory Yule log in a fireplace but the pine woods bordering the lighthouse that were on fire. My woods.

I left everything—the egg basket, the pastry board dusted with flour, the remaining dough I had yet to pound into submission. I ran across the meadow and cut through the cedar grove toward the lighthouse and the help of Joe Dubois. As I got closer to the woods, rolls of choking grayness billowed toward me. I heard the fire as well as smelled it as I approached the clearing—the hiss of pine sap and the crack of brittle wood as weakened limbs fell to the ground. Despite the stillness of the day, I felt the heated air pummeling skyward as if driven by a furious wind.

I emerged into the sandy yard surrounding the lighthouse and the keeper's cottage. The buildings themselves were intact, although the whitewashed clapboard of the lighthouse was coated with soot. The source of the fire appeared to be beyond the clearing, close to the beach, and moving away from the lighthouse.

I called out for Joe. I couldn't imagine he was inside, but I pounded on the door of the cottage anyway. No answer. I tried the handle and found it unlocked, as I expected, but there was no response within to my shouts. I ducked back out, continuing to call Joe's name, and thought to check the buoy below the cliff where he kept his boat tied up. The boat was gone. Not unusual during the day for him to be off fishing or patrolling the beach. But he would have to be quite far off not to see the smoke. I looked along the beach for the soldiers, but they were nowhere in sight. I could see the imprint of their Jeep tracks in the damp sand, leading south toward the Dike Bridge. Had they left, not knowing that one of the mortars had misfired and landed in the woods?

The realization that I was completely alone hit me like a punch. I struggled to catch my breath. I was on my own. The Chappaquiddick fire truck couldn't reach Cape Pogue, and there was no way to put out the fire.

My eyes were stinging from the smoke, and I pushed away tears that were the result of both the irritating air and my fear. I knew I had to take control of myself and the situation. I summoned the voice of my mother, long forgotten. "Go back to the cottage; grab anything that can cut down a tree or dig a trench. You're going to build a fire break."

I don't know what possessed me. A memory perhaps of some newsreel I'd seen of a forest fire out west. My pine woods were a pitiful excuse for a forest, and I realized I couldn't save it. But I was damned if I was going to let the fire take my home and my livelihood. If I could create a break, if the wind didn't pick up, if…

As I skirted the western edge of the woods I felt waves of heat emanating from deep within. My pace quickened along with my heartbeat. Up ahead I could see the weathered shingles of the Boat House, lit only by the early morning light creeping up the outer wall. Relief washed over me, even if it was only temporary. There was still time.

I ran to unlock the shed and rummaged in its dim interior for whatever tools might be of use. The ax hung from a high hook, and as I reached for it I heard a voice behind me.

"Let me help you with that, Mae."

I spun around. The long brown fingers of his good hand reached above my head and lowered the ax.

"Tobias! What brings you here?"

"The smoke and flames. I could see them from the other side of the Gut. Thought you might need some help. "

"I do. More than anything." I realized how desperate I was to tell *any* man that I needed him. A flicker of recognition passed between us and I quickly hooded my eyes.

"Come on, then. There isn't much time, but if we can create a break at the edge of the woods, we may be able to save your home." Tobias spoke gruffly, turning away from me. He had come up from his boat without a shirt, and the muscles of his back flexed as he hoisted the ax over his shoulder.

Despite my reluctance to depend on a man ever again, I was overwhelmed with relief that he was there. I grabbed a hand saw and a shovel and followed him out of the shed.

I thought I had understood—and welcomed—the wilderness that was Pogue. As close as Edgartown was via the water, I was living in the eighteenth century. But until I felt the heat of the flames on my cheek, the price I was paying for my solitude had only been an abstraction, a vague risk that I had been willing to accept in my eagerness to make a home here. The risk was no longer vague, and I felt the shiver of gooseflesh as my body registered the reality of the danger.

Tobias and I crossed the meadow beyond the cottage to the edge of the woods. He began hacking away at the shallow roots of the trees while I took up digging a trench. The ground was soft, layered with dead pine needles that had the potential to be an explosive fuel. I scraped away furiously, trying to concentrate on clearing a wide enough strip that the fire could not breach. I did not have to look up to judge the nearness of the wall of flames. I could feel it.

Neither Tobias nor I spoke. It was not our nature, but it was also impossible to be heard over the roar of the fire. Besides, all our energy was being poured into hacking and scraping. We worked for hours, methodically, silently, the only sounds the thwack of the ax or the rasp of a cough. By mid-afternoon we had scratched and gouged a strip of sandy turf that bordered the meadow.

"Nothing left to do now except hope."

Tobias and I stared at the southern edge of the fire from the far side of the break. It seemed less ferocious to me than earlier in the day, but my eyes were bloodshot from the smoke, and I was too tired to assess the danger. We stood leaning on our tools, well back in the meadow, watching the creep of the flames. I held my breath as a finger of what looked like liquid orange slithered along the ground from a fallen branch. It flared up as the pine needles beneath it turned to ash. But then, with nothing more to fuel it, slowly faded to a few embers. All along the break the same thing was happening—a burst of flame and then a slow diminishment of the ravenous maw of the fire.

I was so focused on watching the flames, willing them to sputter and die, that I did not notice Tobias had left the meadow until I turned to thank him. We had scarcely said a word to each other in the frenzy of the work, our throats raw from the smoke.

I felt rooted to the sandy edge of the break, afraid that if I turned my back the fire would defy me and leap over the barrier. But I didn't want Tobias to leave without hearing my thanks. Reluctantly, I moved back, edging slowly away from the woods until I felt I could turn to look for Tobias.

At first, I saw nothing except the smoke threading its way toward the water of the bay. The shed and the cottage were still shrouded, obscured by the haze. In the distance, the back of the Boat House loomed, the dark roof shingles the only sign that it was there. Below the roof then I sensed movement, a figure moving back and forth. Tobias. He hadn't left.

As I grew closer, although still looking back at the fire every few steps, I saw what he was doing. He'd dragged the hose I used to wash down the dock to the back of the building and was soaking the clapboard, turning the weathered gray to black as if a rain cloud had dumped its contents directly on the Boat House.

He heard me approach, although I didn't call out to him. His face was smeared with soot; his eyes were rimmed with red. Despite the bandana he'd tied around his forehead, rivulets of sweat trickled down, leaving spidery paths through the soot.

He gestured toward the hose.

"Just in case," he said, his voice hoarse. "I think the break will hold, but best to be prepared.

I pumped a full tank of water so that I'll have enough to soak the cottage when I finish here."

He turned back to the wall. I saw that he had taken the precaution of closing the windows of the kitchen that faced the back, and I smiled. Not many men would think of that. Another thing to be grateful for, small as it was. Another thing to be beholden to him for, a small voice whispered inside my head. The man had saved my home, my livelihood, and yet, that dark, cold core gnawed at me.

Just say thank you, but don't let him in, it warned.

I was about to speak those thanks when I heard a commotion at the dock. I hadn't given a thought to opening the Boat House, and had neither the head nor the food to do so. Casting another glance back at the woods and judging that the fire, although still burning, hadn't moved closer, I made my way around to the dock to turn away whoever it was.

Tying up was the boatman Frank Bennett, who usually ran supplies and passengers out of Vineyard Haven, but also provided me with service when I needed to go to Edgartown for provisions. But instead of a group of fishermen out for bass or blues, a crowd of men climbed up armed with hatchets and shovels instead of fishing poles.

Marcus Gardner led them.

"Miss Keaney." He nodded to me after appraising my appearance, which I realized must closely resemble that of Tobias.

"A sloop passing by East Beach a few hours ago took note of the flames above the pine woods and reported the fire when they made port at Vineyard Haven. We tried to reach Joe Dubois at the lighthouse, but got no response."

"Joe's boat has been gone since this morning. He must be off-island."

"I rounded up as many men as I could who were not out to sea." He gestured behind him. At least a dozen stood at the ready.

"I thank you, Mr. Gardner. We've built a break on the western edge of the woods that seems to be holding, but whatever your men can do, I'd be grateful…" I waved toward the flames.

"We? You mean others have arrived already?" He looked up, only then catching sight of Tobias, who was moving toward the cottage with the hose. I think Marcus Gardner had expected to be greeted as the cavalry saving the day.

"Tob-, I mean, Mr. Monroe saw the fire from the Gut and got here shortly after it started."

Something ugly flickered briefly across Marcus' face and then was wiped away when he realized I was staring at him. I didn't know what it was—suspicion, resentment—but I did not want to acknowledge it. Marcus Gardner had always struck me as a man with a very high opinion of himself—fed, I'm sure, by his position in the island community. I'd learned soon after purchasing my property that his real estate business was only a part-time occupation. Marcus Gardner was the senior justice of Duke County; a man who sat in judgment on the criminal cases before the court on Martha's Vineyard. His opinion of me seemed to fall somewhere above the defendants who appeared before him, but not much. For some reason unknown to me, Marcus Gardner did not like me. However, I did not take lightly the fact that he was here with help, and I didn't want him to leave in a huff.

"I'm grateful to you, Mr. Gardner, for coming as soon as you did. The fire is holding for now, but we are by no means out of danger. We best get over to the woods."

I led the men off the dock and across the meadow. Tobias continued to soak the house and did not turn around.

Marcus took out a large handkerchief and wiped his face as we stood at the edge of the break, heat still emanating in scorching waves from the still-burning pine. He was a big man, but soft in the gut. I wondered how long it had been since he'd done any manual work.

"This side looks secure," he said, glancing up and down the length of the perimeter. "We should head to the other side, toward the lighthouse."

He shouted to the other men and herded them north. I hadn't checked the clearing by the lighthouse since the morning. The woods lay back from the structures, with nothing but sand surrounding it, and the wind was blowing away from them, so I had felt we could leave the lighthouse while we dealt with the far more imminent danger on my side of the woods.

It occurred to me as the men went tromping off up the rise that their primary concern had been the lighthouse, not my property. The debt I owed Tobias was growing.

I followed the men with my ax. If there was danger to the lighthouse, I would do my part.

"Any idea what started the fire?" Marcus asked when we reached the clearing. As I had anticipated, the fire was moving away from the lighthouse.

"I have my suspicions. The army was testing the guns this morning. I could hear the reverberations from my kitchen. My guess is that one of the mortars misfired and hit the woods. But the soldiers were gone by the time the fire caught. I'll give them the benefit of the doubt that they didn't realize what had happened."

"I'll be sure to put it in my report and mention it to the commander."

As a precaution, the men soaked down the ground around the lighthouse and the keeper's cottage with water from the pump. Unless the wind shifted or strengthened, the danger seemed past. In fact, the wind had died down considerably since the morning and the flag outside the lighthouse hung limp, not even its edge ruffling. A blessing, I thought.

There appeared to be little left to do on this side of the woods, and I was anxious to return to the meadow and reassure myself that the fire was no longer a threat.

"You seem to have things under control here, Mr. Gardner. I'll be heading back." I started to move away, but stopped and turned to him.

"I'm grateful to you for bringing help." I gestured in the direction of the Boat House. "I've got some pies just out of the oven before the fire started. Please have the men stop by before you return to the boat."

I slogged around by the trail that led back above the beach, keeping the woods to my right. The area where the fire had likely begun was a charred, smoldering cluster of skeleton trunks. Thick ropes of sap clung to them like coagulated blood.

My own blood, after racing through my limbs all day, was slowing, and I could feel an overwhelming fatigue knotting my muscles. I stumbled over a rock in the path and nearly sliced off a finger when the ax flipped over my shoulder. I was on my knees, sand and gravel digging into my outstretched hands. They had broken my fall, but just barely. I reached for the fallen ax and started to pull myself up. I was lightheaded, and despite the heat, felt the prickle of goose bumps on my arms for the second time that day. Just as I was about to fall again a cool hand, calloused but long-fingered, grasped my elbow and held me steady.

It was Tobias. He held onto me only long enough for me to balance myself. The girl I once was might have leaned into him, taken strength from him but given up something in return. I was no longer that girl.

I nodded in thanks, but did not meet his eyes, which he had already turned toward the fire.

"It's burned itself down on this side. Nothing left for it to eat. If our luck holds, those clouds over Hyannis could bring us a shower tonight."

He had said "us," not "you," and it reminded me that my land—all of Chappy, in fact—had not so long ago been Wampanoag territory. Is that why he had turned his boat away from the sea and come to rescue it? Not for me, but for the land itself? That was a relief. As grateful as I was for his help, my soul could not yield another inch to another. Better that he felt a sense of duty to the marshes and ponds and groves than to me.

I straightened myself and thrust my chin in the direction of the Boat House. "I'm going to make some lemonade and slice today's pie. Come have a bite."

I strode off, a little less shaky, not bothering to see if he would follow.

As I skirted the edge of the break I could see a bit of smoldering at the perimeter but no new flames. Up ahead a couple of the men Marcus had brought with him were dumping wet sand on the floor of the woods. They must have found the wheelbarrow at the lighthouse.

It was well past four by the time I was pouring lemonade and dishing out blueberry pie. Tobias did not stay, but cast off before Marcus' brigade arrived for their refreshment. He hadn't said good-bye. And I could not recall, despite my intentions, if I had uttered out loud the thanks that had been poised on the tip of my tongue ever since I had seen him striding toward me early in the day.

I took the flag down at sunset. Frank Bennett had returned to pick up the Vineyard Haven men and I was alone at last. I washed up the sticky plates smeared with congealed blueberry syrup, dumped the lemon rinds, and closed up the shutters of the Boat House.

The tide was high when I descended the cliff steps to Shear Pen Pond with a bar of soap, a sponge, and a towel. Last century, the shepherds had driven their flocks into the pond for a good wash before shearing. Rather than scour the tub after my bath, the pond seemed like a better place to scrub off the layer of soot that clung to me like a second skin. I pulled off my clothes and plunged into the water, only momentarily disturbing the mergansers that had returned to roost on the tiny slice of sandbar on the opposite side of the pond.

I stood knee-deep to soap myself, the gentle abrasion of the sponge kneading my arms and legs. Wielding an ax is not the same as handling a rolling pin or hoeing a garden, but my muscles had functioned for me when I needed them. Fear gives us strength we do not know we have.

I moved deeper into the pond and swam to rinse off, its lukewarm water sluicing away the blackness on my skin and reminding me why I had fought so hard today. It could not rinse away the blackness on my soul, but it was a comfort to me nonetheless. I floated, letting the water buoy me as I leaned my head back and my hair spread out, released from its taut braid.

It was twilight when I emerged from the water, my skin wrinkled but clean. I wrapped myself in the towel and climbed up to the house just as the rain began.

Chapter Five
A Woman of Quiet Grit
Tobias

He knew she had offered what she could, not only to him but also to the others who had come to help—thick sandwiches spread with her own mayonnaise and pickles put up from her garden; the berry pies for which she had already become known on the island; even her lemonade, made with water from the spring and a dozen lemons.

She expressed her gratitude with food, not words, her proprietor's smile arranged carefully on her face, its warmth sufficient to welcome anyone who crossed the threshold into the Boat House's dining room. But he knew that beyond those four walls the smile would fade, its heat chilled as thoroughly as the cream she kept in the icebox.

He did not wish to sit there among the others, listening to them relive the hours working against the fire while she served them, her mask in place. She had worn no mask when he had fought at her side. Under the soot and her bloodshot eyes, her face had been unguarded then, shaped by the quiet grit of determination—to save the land, to survive. It was in one of those vulnerable moments, when she had stumbled and he had set her to right, that he had sensed her willingness to trust him. But as quickly as she had yielded, she had stiffened and distanced herself.

That, more than his unwillingness to endure the buzz of men who thought they had come as rescuers, kept him from stopping at the Boat House as she had invited him to do. He had slipped away when she was busy in the kitchen and set sail for Pucha Pond and the fishing he had never gotten to that day.

It was nearly twilight when he returned, his basket heavy with fish. He had planned to head home, open a beer, and fry up some of his catch, the exertion of fighting the fire finally working its way through his limbs and across his back. But he cast a glance back at the promontory above Shear Pen. A few wisps of smoke above the woods were the only evidence of the destruction. But the woods were too far from the shore to be certain. She had taken in the flag and the Boat House was shuttered, but there was no sign of her in the cottage. She might have gone back to the break to assure herself that the fire was no longer a threat.

He felt the same need. Mae Keaney was only recently a steward of Cape Pogue—and she was a good one. He had witnessed her commitment to the land today and understood that she saw it as more than the place on which her business stood. Something more visceral than economic survival had driven her to fight the fire. But his ties to Cape Pogue were rooted deep within his blood and bone. His people no longer possessed it, but still it possessed him.

He turned the boat toward Shear Pen and skimmed quietly in on the tide. He planned to anchor the boat instead of tying up at Mae's dock. If she was in the cottage he did not wish to disturb her.

He was tacking along the far shore when he saw her.

The moon had risen above East Beach and its silver light illuminated the long curve of her back, bent over as she scrubbed what he realized was her naked skin. He sat stunned for a moment, unwilling to take his eyes off her, and yet, determined not to violate her with his presence. He loosened the sail and steered the boat away from her. The channel was wide and deep at high tide and he was able to move silently and swiftly around the point and out of sight.

He was not a green boy who had never seen a woman naked before. But the vision of Mae Keaney standing in the shallows at one with the moving water of the pond, the wind off the ocean rippling through her unbound hair and the light of the moon skimming her strong, pale limbs, left him without breath and with a hunger that rivaled the flames that had devoured the pines.

Chapter Six
Benediction

I woke early the next morning, before the birds, before the sun. Like a hunter tracking prey, I slid soundlessly from my bed and sniffed. Nothing. My bedroom was on the far side of the house, facing the bay and away from the woods.

I grabbed a sweater from the hook and moved toward the kitchen, where I could use my eyes as well as my nose. I saw nothing except a faint strip of light along the horizon, peaceful rather than voracious. It soothed my nerves, but I knew I would not be convinced until I could stand by the break and know that it had held.

I considered traipsing across the meadow in my nightgown, but thought better of it. I might not be the only one out early checking on the condition of the woods. I knew Joe Dubois had made it back to the lighthouse when the beacon had started rotating last night. And the soldiers might return at any time.

As I dressed, it occurred to me that Tobias might also come back. He had fought fiercely yesterday, and I knew he would not abandon the woods. He would come to assure himself that the land was once again safe.

I had been disappointed that he had not accepted my offer of something to eat, but I understood his reluctance to join the crowd from Vineyard Haven. I had not been blind to the undercurrent of suspicion that had greeted his presence and I knew he had detected it as well. Why else would he have barely acknowledged them and kept to himself as much as he did?

I wanted to thank him properly, and seized on the idea of bringing him breakfast. I made some scrambled egg sandwiches from the eggs I had never hard boiled and filled a thermos with coffee. With the rationing since the war, a sack of coffee was almost impossible to obtain and I no longer served it at the Boat House. But I had saved a small amount for those moments when I absolutely needed it, and I thought Tobias would appreciate a real cup of coffee. I packed everything into a basket that I brought with me as I crossed the meadow, the grass still soaked from the rain. I had no doubt I would find him, either at the break or at the water's edge on East Beach, where I knew he venerated the dawn.

I was not mistaken.

He was walking slowly along the break, stopping every few feet on bended knee, his hand pressed against the earth. Deep in the Catholic recesses of my past I recognized something akin to benediction.

I had come to reassure myself that our efforts yesterday had overcome the fire. That we had won.

Tobias had come to bless the earth that had protected us with its barrier.

I felt awkward in his presence and hung back. My meager basket of homely food seemed ridiculous at that moment. Lacking imagination and gravity. I had long ago given up the rituals of the church, but I had never sought anything to replace them. Prayers had failed me too many times in my life.

Tobias' prayer—if that is what he was doing—was unlike any I had heard at St. Mary's, but nevertheless rang with a deep familiarity. It was not some mysterious Latin muttered over a silver chalice as incense wafted out over the congregation. I glanced up to see a few wisps of smoke hanging over the blackened trunks of the pine grove, and the words Tobias chanted, while strange to my ear, were conveyed with reverence.

That solemnity surprised me. I didn't know much about the Wampanoag. For the most part, they kept to themselves or floated on the periphery as Tobias had done the day before.

I was standing on my own land, but had the distinctly unexpected and unwelcome sense that I was an intruder.

I set the basket down and returned to the cottage, agitated beyond understanding.

The only cure I know for such mental unquiet is physical labor. I threw myself into action, pulling out my bin of flour, a crock of shortening, and a rolling pin. The men had devoured all of yesterday's pies. If I knew anything about islanders, especially the summer folk, I could expect a slew of curiosity seekers later in the day coming to see the charred remains of the woods.

I hulled strawberries, peeled and sliced applies, and chopped rhubarb until my fingers cramped. I rolled out enough dough for a dozen pies, the sweat dripping down my forehead and between my breasts as if I were fighting that damned fire all over again.

When I took the last pies out of the oven, I raised the flag and unlocked the door of the Boat House.

Let them come, I thought. I'm ready now. I wiped down the table and the counter one more time, although I'd done it the night before. A thin layer of soot had settled again on the wood, somehow finding its way in despite the closed windows and shutters.

The familiarity and solidity of the café was a comfort to me. I knew what to do here, unlike earlier in the day on the meadow.

The bell at the door chimed and I put on my smile to greet my first customers.

I closed up finally at dusk. Not a single slice of pie was left. When I brought the last bag of trash out back to the bin I nearly stumbled on my basket, left on the stoop. The sandwiches were gone; the thermos was empty. But the basket still had some weight to it. I folded back the towel I had used to wrap everything. Tucked inside was a smooth white stone the size of a goose egg. I held it in my hand, tracing the faint striations of gold and gray that wound around it and absorbing the warmth of the fire held within it.

There was no sign of Tobias.

I carried the stone into the cottage and put it on the table in the dining room as I did my tally for the day. It did not surprise me that the day's business had more than compensated for the lost sales from yesterday. Even Frank Bennett had profited from the fire, ferrying boatloads of onlookers eager for a glimpse of the destruction. I imagine the story of the fire had made the round of the bars in Vineyard Haven and Oak Bluffs as the firefighters had slaked their parched throats last night. That fascination with disaster—the desire to smell the smoldering forest, feel the heat, see the blackness of death—was as predictable as the pull of the moon on the tides.

I closed my ledger and put the stone on a shelf in the corner cupboard, a memento of fear and hope.

Chapter Seven
The Hunter

The stream of curious onlookers dwindled as the charred gash of the pine woods cooled. My own fears of the fire reigniting were quelled as a heavy rain on Sunday night danced on the bay and turned the ashes into a sodden black quagmire.

Tobias did not return while the town folk descended upon Cape Pogue, pointing fingers at the skeleton trees and trying to keep their unruly children from getting filthy or burned. I had my hands full baking pies, chopping roast chickens into salad and waiting on tables. But despite the harried nature of my activities, I still was aware of his absence.

When the quiet of Monday morning arrived, I caught my breath and took stock. I don't often close the café during the summer, but the mist hung thick from East Beach to the Gut after the rain, and I'd made more than enough to compensate for a day off. I did not hang the flag and went for a walk instead.

I resisted the pull of the dead woods and went in the opposite direction, beyond the far shore of Shear Pen Pond to Drunkard's Cove. It was low tide and I took off my shoes to sink my toes in the wet sand.

Because of the mist I didn't see the boat until I was almost upon it, pulled up on the sand. Tobias' boat. I looked around for him and saw him emerging from the ridge above the beach with a large bag slung over his shoulder. Blood was dripping from it.

"You hunt as well as fish."

"Rabbit," he said. "My Aunt Agnes makes a mean stew. We've got relatives gathering for the Pow-Wow and I promised her I would help to fill the pot."

"My da hunted out here when we were young. Sometimes he took me with him to set snares. He taught me how to skin and gut the rabbits. Ma didn't want the mess in the kitchen."

"Then it won't make you squeamish if I do the gutting here on the beach?"

I shook my head. "I can help if you've got an extra knife."

He smiled, went to the boat, and rummaged around for a few minutes until he held up a small knife with a flourish.

We worked side-by-side on an old board he also retrieved from the boat. My hand was surer than I expected it to be as the memory of my father's rough and calloused fingers steadied me. Hunting had been one of the ways my father had provided for us, one of the things stolen from him in Boston. In the tenement where we lived, the only thing to hunt had been rats.

The mist had burned off by the time we finished, rinsing our bloodied hands in the rising tide. Tobias packed all but one of the skinned rabbits in a cooler in the boat and held out the last one to me.

"Thanks, Mae. Please take this one in exchange for your help."

I started to protest. "I didn't offer to help for that reason. Besides, it's far too much for me alone, and I don't think rabbit salad sandwiches will sell very well at the Boat House." I smiled. "But I'll take it if you'll join me for supper and help me eat it." I wanted to say, "I owe you that much," but held my tongue. I don't think he wanted me to be in his debt, but this seemed like a way to thank him.

"At the Boat House?"

I shook my head. "I closed the Boat House for the day. Come to the cottage. Around six?"

"I'll be there."

I watched him leave until the sail was just a speck of white against the clearing sky.

And then I asked myself, "What have I done?"

In the year and a half I had been at Cape Pogue, building my business and my reputation, I had kept the cottage separate. A refuge. I offered hospitality at the Boat House and *only* at the Boat House. Who I was to the island was the Boat House. When I closed the shutters, locked the doors, and walked across the yard to the cottage, I became the Mae Keaney who was known only to me. The Mae Keaney who no longer needed anyone, who was self-sufficient, who would not allow anyone to hurt her again.

The walls of the cottage were the barrier between me and the rest of the world. And now I had weakened those walls by inviting Tobias Monroe to supper. The fire had made me vulnerable.

I stomped back to the cottage with the rabbit, angry with myself. I spent the rest of the morning taking out my fury on onions, carrots and the unfortunate rabbit that had stepped into Tobias' snare.

By noontime everything was simmering in the oven and I went for a swim at East Beach to cool off in more ways than one. The water didn't help, even though I pushed myself far beyond the point I normally swam. By the time I returned to shore my legs were like jelly. When I got back to the cottage, I stood under the shower outside the kitchen, water dripping down my face and mingling with my tears. I hadn't known I could feel this lonely.

By six o'clock I had pulled myself together. I'd decided I could get through the evening with my Boat House manners. The cottage was just a building, not the armor around my heart, I told myself.

Tobias has a way of moving with the wind in the rushes, with the shadows caused by the clouds drifting across the sun. I sense his presence before I see him. He glides into my perception silently, without disturbing or startling me.

I was setting the dining table when I looked out the window and saw his boat at the dock. By the time I turned toward the kitchen, he was at the door.

"It smells delicious. Not at all like my Aunt Agnes' kitchen." He grinned. I think it was the first time I had ever seen him smile.

"We can sit out on the porch with our drinks, if you'd like." I handed him a glass of whisky and led the way. The porch faced the bay and the sunset, an expansive view that eased the discomfort of having him at the cottage.

He followed me out, but before sitting down he glanced at the wooden sign that hung above the door. My da had carved it and it had once had a place of honor on our house at North Neck. I had found it when I first arrived, on the day I visited the Knolls. It had fallen off the shingle and was buried under weeds in the garden. After I bought the Boat House, I went back and retrieved it.

"What does 'Innisfree' mean?"

"Many things. It's a small island in Ireland, a poem by the Irish poet William Butler Yeats, and the name my parents gave to our cottage at North Neck."

"It's a piece of your past."

"Yes, I suppose you would say that. A connection to a happier time."

"How does the poem go?"

I closed my eyes for a moment and called up the words. I hadn't recited them in a long time, although I held them close, like a candle flame in the wind. They were an incantation for me, words that had protected the part of me that had made it possible to escape my life and come home. For an instant, I considered demurring, denying that I knew them by heart. But I realized that Tobias of all people would understand the power of such words. I took a breath and began to speak.

I will arise and go now, and go to Innisfree,
And a small cabin build there, of clay and wattles made;
Nine bean rows will I have there, a hive for the honey bee,
And live alone in the bee loud glade.

And I shall have some peace there, for peace comes
dropping slow,
Dropping from the veils of the morning to where the cricket
sings;
There midnight's all a glimmer, and noon a purple glow,
And evening full of the linnet's wings.

I will arise and go now, for always night and day
I hear lake water lapping with low sounds by the shore;
While I stand on the roadway, or on the pavements grey,
I hear it in the deep heart's core.

Tobias listened with his eyes closed. When I finished, we were both silent. Then he spoke.

"It's a very fitting name. For this place, but also for you."

He looked at me, and for the first time, I held his gaze.

My intention to treat Tobias as I would one of my Boat House customers—cordial and gracious, but unapproachable—failed. He saw through the façade without calling me out. He accepted my reticence about revealing anything intimate about myself, all the while hearing what I did not speak, seeing what I kept hidden.

Despite my earlier fears, I allowed myself to lower my vigilance. His company was solace and acceptance, without demands. I had forgotten what it meant to have a friend. That night Tobias became my friend. Because he asked. Because I accepted.

Chapter Eight
The Book

The rest of the summer sped by. No more mortars went astray in the woods, but the war was never far from our minds, despite the isolation of the Vineyard. An airfield was built in the middle of the island to train pilots; islanders took up posts as plane spotters and patrolled the beaches watching for German U-boats; blackouts were ordered that kept the entire island dark.

Perhaps because of the heightened state of alert that the war demanded, islanders made an effort to maintain what they could of the familiar patterns of daily life. The fishermen and families spending a day on East Beach kept the Boat House busy enough to see me safely through the winter.

Tobias and I established an easy rhythm to our friendship, in harmony with one another. He had his fishing business and I the Boat House, both all-consuming in the New England summer, when one has to extract as much as possible from the warmth and the daylight before winter sets in. But we found ways to help one another. I added fish sandwiches to the Boat House menu and bought part of Tobias' catch every Friday; he repaired the cottage roof after a Nor'easter tore off several slate shingles. He brought me a side of venison when he hunted; I gave him a dozen Mason jars of my pickles, beets and green beans.

On Monday mornings he came for breakfast after a night spent fishing on Nantucket Sound.

Toward the end of August he brought me a gift.

"I have something for you," he announced. He handed me a small parcel wrapped in brown paper and twine. "Open it."

I undid the wrapper, winding the twine to save. Inside was a book, *The Collected Poems of W. B. Yeats.*

"The Grange had its annual bazaar last week. This was in a bin of books, mostly dime novels. I recognized the name and thought you might like it. I checked inside, the poem about Innisfree is there."

I ran my fingers over the stamped title and opened the cover. It was an old book, had probably been sitting in someone's attic. It was no wonder it had landed in a used-book bin. But the pages were crisp and clean. No one had scribbled in the margins or turned down a corner on a favorite page. But someone *had* placed a thin strip of beaded leather toward the end of the book. It marked where "Innisfree" appeared. I smiled.

"Thank you."

"I took the liberty of reading more of the poems before I wrapped the book. I found another I thought you might like. Perhaps you know it already." He took the book back from me and turned to another page, clearly familiar to him.

"It's called 'A Prayer for My Daughter.'"

My heart froze. My face turned to stone in order to conceal the searing pain that the name of the poem had called up. He could not have known. But why *that* poem, of the hundreds Yeats had written? His head was in the book, his eyes focused on the words rather than my eyes. If he had looked up he might have seen my struggle to contain the memory of praying for my own daughter. She was already dead when they handed her to me. Stillborn.

"Baptize her!" I had screamed at the nun, but she shook her head. Baptism was only for the living, she told me firmly.

I wouldn't let them take her from me until I had prayed over her. Named her Catriona, after Ma. It was the last time I ever uttered a word to God.

"It's a long poem, but this is the part that made me think of you."

I pulled myself back to the present as Tobias began to recite. I tried to listen without memory; tried to hear what it was he was saying about me.

May she become a flourishing hidden tree
That all her thoughts may like the linnet be…
O may she live like some green laurel
Rooted in one dear perpetual place.

He stopped.

"You have never struck me as a woman who cries easily. Even when you were threatened by the fire. This Yeats man—his words hold some power over you." He put the book down. "I didn't mean to cause you pain."

I pushed away the tears with the back of my hand.

"I'm sorry. Just tired. I don't think often about my family, but these poems . . . call up my mother something fierce." I grasped for an explanation that would justify my tears without giving up the truth.

"I'm truly grateful for the book, Tobias. Please don't regret giving it to me because of a few silly tears."

"No regrets. Maybe you'd prefer reading it to yourself instead of listening to me butcher the language."

"Oh, no! Poems should be spoken aloud. But why did you choose that one?" Maybe his reason for selecting "A Prayer for My Daughter" could help me distance myself from what it had awakened in me.

"It was the image of the tree with deep roots that made me think of you. When I see you, it's as if you take your nourishment from the land. From what little you say about yourself, I have learned that, if you could, you would stay here forever.

"I don't know much poetry. It surprised me to find so many of his ideas familiar to me. An Irishman who has never seen this place, and yet he can describe it as if had walked the beach or felt the salt spray or seen the moon rise over East Beach."

I smiled. "I think that's why my Da and Ma felt so comfortable here. It reminded them of Ireland."

"But you, you've come back because you *don't* want to be reminded of what you left."

He spoke quietly, without hesitation, a simple statement. He wasn't demanding to know *what* it was I wanted to forget, only acknowledging that he recognized that I *did* want to forget.

Despite his soft-spoken words, despite the trust that had accumulated between us over the summer, I was threatened by his discovery of what I thought was safely, deeply hidden.

"You assume too much, Tobias. And you are wrong."

My voice was cold; the walls of ice that thawed with our friendship were once again solidifying. The tears that his reading of the poem had elicited froze before they escaped, once again to betray me.

"I don't believe you, Mae. You may have succeeded in convincing everyone else that you're a strange duck who just wants to be left alone. But not me. I have come to know a beautiful, honest and determined woman whom I respect. You have brought a special kind of grace to this land, but you are incredibly sad. I don't know why, and I am not asking you to tell me. But don't lie to me. That is not who I know you to be."

"You don't know me at all."

"I may not know all of you. But what I do know, I care about."

We had been sitting on the porch steps, side-by-side, but not touching. Except for the hand he had extended to me when I stumbled the day of the fire, Tobias had not even accidentally grazed my arm. But I jumped up and moved away from him towards the water's edge as if he had tried to grab me.

I had my back to him, my arms folded tightly across my chest.

I felt, rather than heard him get up behind me—a slight shift in the air, then a breath let out in a sigh.

"I'm going. Enjoy the book."

When I turned around he was gone. I was still standing outside the house when I saw the gleam of his lantern reflected off the taut white sail pointed in the direction of Edgartown. I watched it until it disappeared through the Gut. Then I went inside, poured myself a glass of whisky and wept.

It was one in the morning when I heard the knocking on the front door. It took me a few moments to recognize that it wasn't the wind banging a shutter. Someone was calling my name.

I lit the lantern I keep by the bed, dragged the gun out of its box and went to see who it was.

I put down the gun and opened the door as soon as I saw Tobias.

"Is something wrong? Another fire?" I looked anxiously beyond him to the edge of the woods, while he looked just as anxiously at the gun.

"No. No. I didn't mean to frighten you. I came to apologize."

"And you couldn't wait until morning?"

"When I have something that needs saying, I don't want to wait. Are you willing to listen?"

I knew his question was a pointed reference to my turned back earlier in the evening.

"Come in." I was too tired and too spent to turn him away. I knew I would only toss in my bed the rest of the night if I didn't hear him out, wondering what was so important that he would come all the way back to say it.

"You want another drink or a cup of tea?" I could smell the whisky, and he looked worse than I had ever seen him.

"Have you been in a fight? Maybe you need some ice on your face as well as in your drink."

He waved away my offer.

"Sit, Mae." He pointed toward the sofa. I lowered myself into the cushion and he took a seat in the chair opposite me, his brown hands with their long fingers resting on his knees. The knuckles on his left hand, the hand missing a finger, were scraped and bloody.

I knew he had been angry when he'd left earlier. We both had been. But it was an anger contained. More than once I had seen him move away from confrontation rather than engage. Just as he had left me on the porch. I couldn't imagine what had happened in the intervening hours to cause such a change in him and drive him back here. Because driven is how he appeared.

"I came back to say I'm sorry for intruding on your privacy. I have no right to berate you for putting your past behind you. I overstepped the boundary between us, and I, of all people, should have respected those limits."

"Apology accepted." I remained still, reflecting Tobias' own posture. There had to be more. Why else set sail in the middle of the night?

He began to speak again.

"I don't apologize, however, for caring for you. I realized after I left you how much you have become a part of my life. You have filled a hole I didn't know was there. I don't want to lose you."

His face, which most of the time was an impassive mask, was now raw with pain. Not the pain that throbs after a physical fight when the fury has subsided, but the searing kind of pain that rips apart your soul when you are staring at the abyss of loss. I knew that pain.

And recognizing it, the bindings that had held me together, protected me from ever allowing myself to be open to love again, snapped.

I reached out and gingerly touched his cheek, trying not to hurt the swollen flesh that had already started to discolor. He flinched and I pulled back my hand. But he grabbed it, turned it palm up, and brought it to his lips.

And then we were on our knees and in each other's arms. When I could breathe again, I rose and took him by the hand to my bed.

I'm not the shriveled spinster the island considers me to be, but it had been a long time since a man had caressed me. And I had never had a man who took me with such tenderness or honored me with such pleasure. The hands I had watched over the summer setting snares and hauling in fish and repairing what was broken now roamed over my body with the same concentration. His hair had loosened from its leather thong and drifted across my breast. It smelled of the sea and smoke.

I fell asleep in his arms, his breath and his heartbeat obliterating the memories I had come to Pogue to forget.

The birds woke me in the morning. Tobias was gone. The emptiness beside me screamed its rebuke. *You stupid, stupid girl. Haven't you learned by now!*

I washed my face at the basin and pulled a brush through the tangles in my hair, its disarray another damning testimony to my stumble back to the girl I used to be. I could move away from the bed, but I couldn't leave my skin. I smelled of sex; I smelled of him. I would swim away those reminders, even on this chilled September morning. But I feared the waves of East Beach could not wash away the waves of memory coursing through me as I stood in front of the mirror.

I grabbed my towel and thrust my feet into my sandals. I had to get out of the house.

And then I smelled the Spam frying on the stove, heard the opening of a cupboard door, the fragment of a whistled tune. I moved toward the kitchen instead of the beach and then stood in the doorway, watching him. His back was toward me, bare and brown. I saw the scar on his shoulder that I had traced the night before in the dark. A black-and-blue mark had bloomed near the top of his jeans. It looked as if he'd been kicked, not pummeled with fists.

We hadn't talked about the fight. We hadn't talked about anything.

I reached out for him, circling him with my arms and pressing myself gently against his back.

"Good morning," I murmured.

"Good morning."

"I thought you had gone." The words were out of my mouth before I could censor them.

He spun around and held me by the shoulders.

"Did you really think I was one of those men who takes what he wants and then sneaks off into the night? If you only knew!"

"I didn't want to think it, but . . ." I stopped myself before completing the sentence with, ". . . I have only been with men who leave me." Instead, I seized on the last part of what he had said.

"If I only knew what?"

"Nothing. Doesn't matter. Just know I'm not that kind of man. Trust me to be here for you, as I have all summer. I'm not going away. Hell, I want to be with you now as much as I can." He ran his thumb over my lips. "I want to kiss you again."

After breakfast he left to fish and I spent the day harvesting what remained in my garden. I kept the Boat House open on the weekends in September, but during the week I used the time to prepare for the winter. I had already dug a root cellar for potatoes, squash and carrots, but I had a bumper crop of cucumbers still to pickle, beach plums to pick and preserve, and herbs to dry. I stayed busy, only occasionally finding myself drifting into a heated fog of memory from the night before. Despite Tobias' reassurances in the morning and the certainty he seemed to have of his own feelings, I questioned my own reaction to the precipitous change that a dusty book had wrought in my life. Why had I thrown off the constraints that had guided me since my arrival on the island? Why had I plunged so recklessly into his arms? He had asked me to trust him, but could I trust myself to know if I had chosen well, when so many times in my past I'd made disastrous choices? Had I made another bed that would only cause me pain to lie in?

The voice in my head that had taunted me when I found him gone from my bed reverberated with every thwack of my hoe. *Stupid, stupid girl.*

Late in the afternoon I was scrubbing the dirt from under my fingernails when I saw his boat skim into the dock. I watched from the window as he tied up and lowered the sail, every movement fluid, deliberate. He really was a beautiful man. And he had come back, I reminded the voice.

That night we ate the bluefish he had brought and then made a fire to dispel the chill of the evening.

"Would you pick a poem you love and read it to me?" he asked, handing me the book. "I want to know what makes you happy."

When I finished, he carried me to bed.

We spent the next three days like this, each one layering upon the one before. They did not dispel my doubts, but they cushioned me. The bed I'd made was no longer a simple frame with a ticking mattress and plain muslin sheets, but was now piled high with down pillows and an embroidered comforter that enveloped me in its muffled warmth.

Chapter Nine
Rumors

That peaceful cocoon split apart on the fourth day. Tobias left to fish as soon as the sun rose. Once a month Frank Bennett came out to Pogue to pick me up in his catboat and take me to Edgartown to do my provisioning. This time of year I needed Mason jars for the cucumbers and beach plums; flour and powdered milk; what sugar I could get with my ration coupons; kerosene for the lanterns and whisky for the long nights.

Frank arrived not long after Tobias had left, but he didn't mention seeing his boat. It wouldn't have occurred to him that Tobias Monroe might be sailing from Mae Keaney's place, and I was happy enough to keep people thinking I slept alone. As Tobias had said, the island thought I was an odd duck. I didn't need them also to think I was a wanton one.

After I had finished the marketing and ordered everything to be delivered to Frank's boat I stopped by the post office to pick up my mail. It was there that I overhead a fragment of conversation that I might have paid no heed, but I was standing in line and could not ignore what was being said.

"... body washed up at Katama...one of the soldiers...it was first assumed that he had drowned from foolishness. But I heard the sheriff is considering it a suspicious death."

"I wonder if it was the same guy who got in a fight with that Indian last week in Oak Bluffs."

"You mean Tobias Monroe? I heard about that…angry words and too much beer. Somebody had to pull'em apart before they killed each other."

"Always thought he had a violent streak in him—a real sullen guy with a chip on his shoulder about 'his people's' land."

"Did you need something Miss Keaney?"

I jerked my attention back to Owen Hapgood behind the counter and fumbled with my purse, trying to shake off the foreboding that was spreading its icy fingers through my gut.

I could not imagine Tobias as a murderer, but the perception of his silence as a deep-simmering anger was hard to dispute. What I saw as Tobias' reverence for the land could easily be construed as a fierce sense of ownership. I remembered how I had felt like an unwelcome interloper the morning after the fire when I had come upon him by the edge of the woods, even though Tobias had not said a word.

I left the post office and completed my errands. I did not want to hear any more rumors. Like the fire, spreading through dry tinder, the conjectures were going to leap from one monger to another, hungry for outrage.

The boy from Connor's Market trundled my packages down to the water's edge and loaded them onto Frank's boat, but Frank was nowhere in sight. I looked up and down the wharf, but saw no knots of men engaged in conversation or lone figures catching a smoke. I didn't really want to go in search of Frank, but could feel the agitation rising in me like bile. I wanted to go home.

I set my shoulders and marched up Main Street to the hardware store, where I knew Frank liked to hang out with the old men discussing the latest news circulating about the war. It was three in the afternoon. The days were getting shorter but it was still a brilliant fall day. Pushing open the door of Edgartown Hardware, I stopped to let my eyes adjust to the dim lighting and then scanned the room. Many of the men were the same fishermen who ate my sandwiches and pies. Some of them looked up and I nodded, but none of them was Frank. I checked with the clerk, who hadn't seen him, and turned to go. Only then did I hear the scattered words, "Katama." "Indian." "Dead soldier." They weren't talking about the war.

I ducked out again, my desire to be away from the murmurs and speculation of Edgartown now even more intense. Where was Frank? I looked further up Main Street toward the courthouse, although that was hardly where he might have gone. I reluctantly turned back to the wharf, resigning myself to wait. I couldn't fault him for not being at his boat. I normally spend more time in town, and neither he nor I could have anticipated that the news of the soldier's death would be rampant. Or that it would disturb me as much as it had.

I could not explain my uneasiness. The Tobias described in the furtive conversations was not the man I thought I knew. And yet, a voice within me warned, *He's a man. Why should he be any different than the others you have known*? Had I misinterpreted his stillness for peace, when it had merely been a camouflage, a deceit? A man in hiding, rather than a man forthright?

I shook off my foreboding, reminding myself that I don't fare well in town. The narrow streets, the watchfulness and gossip, the noise of machines, all these things encroach upon me.

I paced up and down the wharf. *I need to get my own boat*, I thought, and it was not the first time. But buying and refurbishing the property had left little over for such a purchase. I had thought it would be an extravagance that would sit at the dock for weeks at a time, need to be stored over the winter, require fuel and maintenance. A burden more than a necessity. Now I wasn't so sure.

Frank finally showed up, ambling around the corner of Daggett Street. I hailed him and met him at the slip. I bit my tongue to keep myself from demanding "Where have you been?" It was none of my business.

We pushed off and puttered out of the harbor, rounding the ferry landing and moving swiftly toward the Gut. I was glad his motor was too loud for conversation. No doubt he'd heard the news linking the drowned soldier and Tobias, and I had no desire to listen to more opinions about "that Indian."

When we reached the Boat House dock Frank carted everything to the kitchen. Normally I would have made him a cup of tea and offered him a slice of pie, but I was in no mood for the chat I knew would accompany the food.

"Frank, if you don't mind, it's been a long day and I'm worn out. I've wrapped up half a pie for you to take home."

I handed him the pastry, wrapped in wax paper and tied up with string, and paid him for the trip.

"Thanks, Mae. I'd like to get home myself." He nodded and started down the dock, but then stopped and turned around.

"I suppose you heard in town about the dead soldier."

"Yes." *Oh, God. Not now.*

"Take care out here by yourself. Lock up."

He tipped his cap, got in his boat and cast off.

I stood watching for a few moments. The bay was calm and empty except for Frank's boat. Then I turned back to unpack my provisions and settle in for the evening.

I'd been honest with Frank when I'd said I was tired, but the fatigue came from the battle going on in my thoughts rather than from the busy day in town. I put together a grilled cheese sandwich for my supper and sat with it and a glass of whisky, staring out the dining room window of the cottage.

Sunset at Pogue can be a majestic, soul-inspiring thing even for—no, especially for—a fallen Catholic like myself. Nature casts a brilliant shroud upon the day, obliterating the ugliness and cacophony of human interaction. I needed to bask in its fleeting beauty, feel the orange-red fingers of retreating light soothe my churning mind.

I remained at the window long after the sky had faded to purple and then indigo. Across the water, no longer visible, sat the blacked-out town filled with rumors and accusations. I wanted to believe that here at Innisfree I was safe.

I finally roused myself, cleared my plate and glass and lit the gas lamp by the sink to do the washing up. The familiar night sounds surrounded the cottage. An owl on the hunt. A mouse scrambling under the stove for the pea that had rolled there and I hadn't found the time to retrieve. The rustle of dry grass in the meadow.

When I retreated to my bedroom, Frank's words of warning intruded into my thoughts at first. I considered pulling out my gun box from under the bed and even got down on my knees. But I stopped myself. Even if Tobias were a threat to me—and I did not believe that he was—did I want to shoot him?

All I knew for certain—all anyone in Edgartown was sure of—was that a man had drowned at Katama. Anyone who had spent time on Chappy knew the devastating power of the current at Katama. That soldier was not the first reckless young man to die there. Why the town had rushed to accuse Tobias was more troubling than the possibility that he might be somewhere outside my cottage. The danger was in the town, not out in the wilderness of Pogue. I finally understood my disquiet. I was not afraid for myself. I was afraid for Tobias.

In the morning I was not surprised to find him on my doorstep.

"Are you a fugitive?" I asked, as I let him in the kitchen. A quick look at the dock told me that his boat was not there. He saw my glance.

"I landed the boat at Drunkard's Cove and walked over. I didn't want to bring suspicion down on you if they are looking for me."

"Why are you here?"

"To say goodbye."

"Did you do what they are saying in town?"

"Do you think I did?" We shared the propensity to speak directly.

"Do I think you killed a man? No. Do I think you got into a bar fight with him? If you had a damn good reason to, yes. I heard he was a soldier. Might he have had something to do with the mortar that started the fire?"

I surprised myself with my certainty, but I realized that face-to-face with Tobias, any doubts that I might have entertained in town were dispelled, like the mist burning off on a summer morning.

"I did brawl with him the other night at the Ritz Café in Oak Bluffs."

"But you didn't kill him." It wasn't a question. I *knew* Tobias wasn't a murderer.

"No. I was angry but not out of control. What he had done to provoke me wasn't deserving of death. There was a meanness, an ugliness to him. But it's not my place to judge him and pass sentence on him."

"Although plenty of folks in town seem quite ready to pass judgment on *you*."

"Not a surprise. They've never much liked me, and it's easy enough for them to push their impressions of 'that insolent Indian' further to 'that murderous Indian'."

"What are you going to do?"

"I don't think I have much choice. I'm going to leave. I find myself once again apologizing to you, Mae. I'm sorry. I told you I wasn't going to abandon you. But I don't see how I can defend myself when the town has already decided I'm guilty."

"But if you run away, that will only fuel their certainty that you're the killer. Where will you go? Do you really think you can disappear without them coming after you?"

"Do you really think I can get a fair trial with Marcus Gardner presiding as the judge?"

That stopped me. I wanted to believe that judges were above the petty antagonisms that festered in small communities. But I knew Marcus Gardner plainly did not like Tobias, and I doubted he could put aside his feelings to judge him on the facts. Marcus Gardner was the kind of man who never entertained doubts about himself, never questioned that he might be wrong.

"No one, least of all Marcus Gardner, will believe that I left that soldier at the bar and never saw him again."

"Where did you go after the fight?" As soon as I asked the question I knew the answer. "Tobias, you came here that night. Did you come directly?"

"Yes. Sam Peters actually pulled me out of the bar and shoved me into my boat. 'Get out of here before the rest of the platoon comes after you and kills you,' is what he said. I wasn't afraid. I felt as if I could take them all on, and I told Sam as much. But he literally pushed the boat away from the dock. By the time I was out of the harbor I had cooled down enough, and I knew all I wanted was to be with you."

"What was the fight about? I've watched you all summer turn away from confrontation. If you were ever angry, it was well below the surface. What was different that night?"

"You. The fight was about you."

I was stunned. What could that soldier possibly have said about me to provoke a violent reaction from a man as controlled as Tobias?

"He was describing you as 'that Indian's whore' who thinks she's too good for the white men who eat at her table. He didn't know I was behind him, listening to him describe how he'd teach you what a real man could do to you. I stopped listening and punched him in the mouth to stop his filth."

"Oh, Tobias! That's what you meant the other morning when you said 'If you only knew' how different you were from the men who wanted only to take from me. I'm the reason you're being accused of murder! It's my fault." I was sick to my stomach.

"No, Mae. You're not at fault. That pig of a soldier is at fault. For all we know, he may have been on his way to rape you when he got himself killed at Katama."

"I'm going to the police. I'll tell them where you were that night after you left the bar. Sam can corroborate when he put you in the boat."

"And if you tell them I was here, that will just confirm what the soldier was accusing you of—everyone will label you the Indian's whore."

"And I will tell them, no, I'm Tobias Monroe's *woman*. You were the only one defending me while the rest of the cowards let that soldier spew his venom."

"I can't let you destroy your reputation to protect me."

"Tobias, you should know me by now. First, I have no reputation to destroy, and even if I did, I wouldn't want to preserve it by hiding the truth. You were here, in my bed, when the soldier died. I will swear to that. My reputation is not worth losing you—either to your fleeing as a fugitive or being imprisoned for a crime you didn't commit. Don't try to stop me."

"You're a brave woman, Mae. But think about what your coming forward will mean. You'll be isolated, vilified. You could lose your customers, your business. Don't do it."

"If I don't have you, Tobias, my so-called good name and my business will not make up for the loss of you. I love you. I didn't know that until today. But I cannot do anything except tell the truth. Now take me to Edgartown."

He started to speak, ready once again to tell me "no" and the reasons I shouldn't speak up for him. But he must have seen how resolute I was, must have heard the anguish in my voice. He crossed the space between us in two determined steps and took my face in his bruised hands. He kissed me fiercely, defying whatever stood in the way of our sharing another kiss.

"Let's go," he said, and I followed him across the dunes to where he had hidden his boat.

Chapter Ten
The Arrest

It was still early when we reached the Edgartown dock, and no one was around to note our arrival. I helped Tobias lower the sail and tie up. We had agreed on the way over to stop at Henry Walker's office before I went to the police. Henry was the lawyer who had helped me with the paperwork when I bought Innisfree. Marcus Gardner had wanted to represent me, but I didn't trust him to have my best interests at heart, and I had hired Henry. He'd become a regular customer at the Boat House, and I knew he had sent business my way in the early days. I believed I could trust him.

As we walked up Daggett Street from the wharf Tobias was skeptical.

"I know I agreed to this, but are you sure this man will help me?"

"He's honest. And unlike a lot of folks on the island, he's not cowed by Marcus Gardner. You need someone who knows the law. I also think he'll do it for me. I think he remembers me from the time I was a scrappy little girl, although he's never admitted it."

We could see Henry through the front window sitting at his breakfast when we rang the bell. His wife recognized me, but without warmth. She rarely came to the Boat House, although she'd had Henry bring home whole pies when she was entertaining. I don't doubt that she passed them off as her own.

Her eyes swept from me to Tobias and she stiffened.

"What do you want? Henry isn't seeing clients yet."

I smiled my Boat House smile. "We're happy to wait."

"Not here on the porch. Go around the back."

She was about to shut the door in our face when Henry's voice called from the dining room.

"Who is it, Ruth?"

Before she could answer, I spoke up. "It's Mae Keaney, Henry. I need your help with something important."

He came into the hall, wiping his mouth with his napkin.

"Good morning, Mae. Come on in. Ruth, could you bring us some coffee?"

Ruth took Henry's napkin and stalked off to the kitchen as he ushered us into his study.

"I suspect I know why Mr. Monroe is here, although not why you are with him."

"Then you've heard the rumors about the soldier who drowned at Katama."

"That I have. And rumor is the right word to describe what others are taking as foregone conclusion."

He turned to Tobias. "I assume you know that suspicion has fallen on you because of the bar fight."

Tobias nodded, but did not speak. I could see that he was tightly wound. He had trusted me to come to Henry, but he wasn't ready yet to trust Henry.

"Do you want me to represent you if you are accused?"

I was relieved that Henry had not said "*when* you are accused." I looked at Tobias. I had convinced him to come with me into town, kept him from fleeing the island as he had believed he must. Now that we were here and Henry had confirmed that the suspicions were real and not just idle bar talk, I was afraid that Tobias' silence was a sign of anger. Did he think I had betrayed him? I wanted to reach out to reassure him, but both Tobias' stillness and Henry's sharp eyes assessing our relationship kept me paralyzed.

Then Tobias spoke.

"I want to know if you believe me that I did not kill that man before I place my fate in your hands."

"I know that Mae would not have brought you here for my help if *she* did not believe you, and that is the strongest endorsement you could have. You have my word I will defend you with conviction if it comes to that."

I could see Tobias ease out of the rigid pose that he had assumed since Ruth had answered the door. Although still watchful, he no longer looked as if he might leap across the desk at Henry.

"Then I accept your help. And just so we are clear, I'm no charity case. I can pay."

"Understood. And just so we are clear as well, I am not taking you on out of the kindness of my heart. I want to see justice served in this case. I'm not about to have this town make you a scapegoat and try you in the bars and on the street corners because they think of you as a glowering loner with a chip on his shoulder. But you can't pull the silent treatment with me if I'm going to defend you. You agree to tell me everything, or we don't have a deal."

Tobias smiled.

"I like you, Mr. Walker. I see why Mae trusts you."

"Good. Now tell me what happened that night and be specific about the time."

I sat holding my peace while Tobias recounted the events of the evening as he had explained them to me. When he was finished, Henry turned to me.

"Mae, can you confirm when Mr. Monroe arrived at your cottage and that he did not leave until after 9 a.m. the next morning?"

"Yes."

"Are you willing to make a statement to the police to that effect?" He asked me gently. He knew that my revelation that Tobias had spent the night with me would not remain within the police report. Word would seep through the town quickly, inflicting its own damage.

I nodded. "I want to see justice done as well, Henry. I'm not going to sit by quietly to protect my name while an innocent man is unjustly accused."

"I wouldn't expect any less of you, Mae. And if anyone can withstand the fury of the harpies in this town, it's you. I'm just sorry you have to endure it."

"I'm grateful to you, Henry, for believing in Tobias, and for not thinking less of me because I do as well."

"Mr. Monroe, I'm going to make some quiet inquiries of the coroner about the time of death of this young man. We should be able to put any questions about your involvement to rest with that information and Mae's statement. But if you are arrested before we have a definitive answer from the coroner, you are to go without a struggle, contact me immediately and wait for me before you say anything to the police. Understood?"

"I understand. And thank you. I have confidence in you." Tobias stood up and shook Henry's hand.

And then all hell broke loose.

The door burst open, with Ruth cowering behind Al Simms, the chief of police.

"Henry, I tried to stop him but he says he has a warrant for this Indian."

I flinched at her words, spoken as if she were referring to a feral cat. I didn't believe that she had tried to stop Simms. In fact, I was sure she had told him that Tobias was here. How else would he have known?

Tobias went rigid again, his hunter's stance, ready to spring, but Simms had pinned his arms behind his back and handcuffed him. When he slammed Tobias' head down on Henry's desk, I screamed and started to reach for him to pull him away, but Henry grabbed me and held me back.

"If you interfere, he'll arrest you for obstruction," he whispered in my ear. "Stay calm. I'll handle it."

"Al, I'm representing Mr. Monroe. He'll go quietly with you, but I'm accompanying him. And before he goes anywhere, I want to see that warrant."

Tobias had not said a word, his face a blank mask still pressed against the leather blotter on Henry's desk. Simms had to let go of him to retrieve the warrant, and Henry moved around the desk to place himself protectively in front of Tobias.

"I don't think it's necessary for Mr. Monroe to be subjected to this indignity, Al. While I read the warrant. I'm going to have him stand up since he is clearly not resisting arrest." Henry spoke deliberately and calmly, but with an authority that eased the pain that was crushing my chest.

I should have let him run away, I thought. *I can't bear that I have placed him in the hands of this brutal policeman. He's already suffered a beating from the dead soldier. God only knows what they'll do to him in the jail once Henry leaves.*

Henry took his time reading the warrant.

"Al, it seems to me you have some genuine suspicions based on the alleged bar fight between Mr. Monroe and the deceased that several people witnessed. But after Mr. Monroe left the bar, do you have any evidence or witnesses to confirm that he even saw the deceased again, let alone did him harm? This appears to be based on nothing but circumstantial conjecture. You can certainly take Mr. Monroe in for questioning, but I don't see enough here on which to base his arrest."

"I beg to differ, Henry. As you can see, Marcus Gardner has signed the warrant. You'll have to take it up with the judge if you think I can't arrest Monroe."

"You can be sure that I will, Al. But right now I'll accompany Mr. Monroe to the station."

Henry turned to me. "Mae, stay here until I get back." He squeezed my hand. "I'll take care of him. I promise you."

The three men turned to leave, Al Simms once again grabbing Tobias roughly and Henry firmly stopping him with his voice.

"That won't be necessary, Al. I'm here to assure that he won't run."

Tobias stared ahead, his head held high, not bowed either in shame or submission. He did not say good-bye or even acknowledge me with his eyes.

I sank into my chair after they were gone, but any respite I might have sought there was quickly dispelled by Ruth.

"You can't stay in Henry's study while he's not here, and I haven't got time to babysit you until he comes back from this fool's errand. I know he told you to wait here, but you'll have to go sit on the back porch."

I followed her through the house and out the kitchen door, numb with fear. There were no chairs on the porch, so I sat on the steps hugging my knees. I heard Ruth lock the kitchen door behind me. Only then did I cry.

It was late morning before Henry returned. I heard him first, the deep baritone of his voice questioning Ruth and then criticizing her.

"You left that young girl alone outside with not so much as a glass of water? Where is your decency, woman?"

I heard the door open and rose to greet him, my hours of solitude finally at an end and my head full of questions. But the first on my lips was, "Is he free?"

Henry shook his head. "Not yet. I've at least convinced them not to arraign him until we get the coroner's report. And they've agreed to take your statement." He shook his head. "I have to warn you, Mae. Marcus Gardner is out for blood. You may not be aware, but there's history between Tobias and Marcus. I think Marcus has been waiting for an opportunity like this."

"I suspected there was, but Tobias never told me what. Marcus has always treated him with disrespect any time he saw him around the Boat House. Even when Tobias saved everything the day of the fire, Marcus looked at him as if he were scum. Could Marcus stop his release, even if there's no evidence?" I felt my tears welling up again. "This is all my fault."

"Why, Mae?"

"Tobias got into the fight because the soldier had called me a whore and threatened to go out to Pogue to rape me. Tobias wouldn't even have been at the Ritz that night if I hadn't gotten angry with him over a stupid book. He left and must have gone straight to the bar."

"But if he hadn't been at the Ritz to defend you, you might have become the soldier's victim. I know you are adamant about your independence and believe that you can protect yourself, but the world is not a safe place for any of us any more, Mae. Tobias did what any man would do for the woman he loves. Don't blame yourself. Tobias certainly isn't."

"He wouldn't even look at me when he left this morning."

"That was to protect you. He didn't want Al to think there was anything between you that might jeopardize you."

"You're sure of that?"

"He told me so. And he told me he doesn't want you to make a statement unless it's absolutely necessary."

"We've already been through that. I don't care what people think of me if it means I can keep him out of prison."

"Mae, I don't need to tell you what a closed society this island is. You grew up here, but you'll be ostracized when word gets out that you've been sleeping with Tobias Monroe."

"Henry, as if I'm not ostracized already. Let them talk about me at their ladies' teas."

"Mae, they're talking about you in the bars as well. Isn't that what started this whole thing in the first place?"

"Which is why I have to speak up for Tobias."

"Look, my advice to you is find Frank Bennett to take you back to Pogue and wait there until I send for you. It could be another day before we have the coroner's report, and I'd rather you stayed out of sight. There's no need to feed the maw of gossip with your presence in town. I also don't want Marcus Gardner provoked. You came to me for advice. Now take it. If you truly want to help Tobias, you'll go back to the Boat House and do what you normally do on a Tuesday in September."

Henry's last words were gentle, and convinced me that it was not only for my sake that he wanted me to leave. I nodded reluctantly and left for the wharf, where I was relieved to find Frank alone scrubbing down his boat. I wouldn't have to go seeking him out and raising questions in the minds of folks surprised to see me in Edgartown.

The wind was brisk, hinting that the Indian Summer we had been basking in over the last few weeks would soon give way to a true autumn. I pulled my sweater tightly around me to fend off not only the chill, but my own sense of foreboding.

As the Boat House came into sight my heart eased. Henry had been right to send me home. My agitation would have been no help to Tobias. I needed to collect myself, and Innisfree was the only place I'd find peace.

Frank cast off again as soon as he had brought me to the dock. I walked up to the cottage and let myself in. For a heartbeat, I felt Tobias's presence in the house, a sense of joy and relief that assured me what I was feeling for him was right and true. He wasn't there, of course, but small signs reflected his spirit. The house even smelled of him—smoke and earth and worn leather. I shook my head. For so long this house had been my refuge, but it had been a lonely and barren one. I didn't want to go back to that emptiness, that false sense of safety.

I was exhausted from the upheavals of the day, but I knew that any attempt to rest would be futile. If I had to wait for news from Henry, the best way for me was in work. I had a bushel of beach plums in the root cellar that needed to be cut and sugared for preserves. That kind of mindless, repetitive work was exactly what the afternoon called for. I hauled the fruit up to the cottage and worked at the dining room table, where the windows wrapped around three sides of the room, affording me a clear view of the bay and any approaching boats.

By nightfall all the plums were chopped and layered with sugar in stone crocks, but no word had come from Edgartown. I lowered the blackout shades, lit the lamps, scrubbed the sticky plum juice from my stained fingers and built a fire in the living room hearth. I had no appetite for supper, just a hollow pain in the pit of my stomach. I sat in front of the fire with my glass of whisky and thought only of Tobias, confined in a cell. I could not bring myself to climb into an empty bed and fell into a fitful sleep in my chair.

Chapter Eleven
Alibi

I woke with the birds, stiff and cold. Wrapped in my afghan, I stumbled to the outhouse in the half-light of dawn and ran the pump at the well to fill the water tank. I hadn't pumped in over twenty-four hours, and the last thing I wanted was to run out of water when I desperately needed a bath. It wasn't just the residue from the plums that stuck to my skin, but the thin film of contempt left there by the disdain and suspicion of people in town like Ruth Walker.

Back at the house I lit the gas water heater and then made some hot Ovaltine while the bathtub filled. I was still soaking in the tub, easing the kinks out of my neck, when I heard my name called down at the dock. It was still early, which meant that it could only be someone Henry had sent with news. I rose out of the water, hurriedly toweled myself dry and pulled on my clothes.

I ran down to the dock to see Henry tying up his boat.

"I didn't expect you to come yourself," I said, shivering from the cool morning air, I told myself. Not from fear.

"I thought it best not to bring attention to you. Besides, it will give us time to talk on the way back."

"Tell me now. How is he? Has the coroner filed his report?" I chewed on my lip, an old habit. "I'm ready to go."

"Give an old man something hot to drink first. Nobody is available to take your statement at the jail now, anyway. Just the overnight shift getting ready to hand over the keys."

I reached my hand down to help him up to the dock.

"Come on. I've got some Ovaltine up at the cottage. It's not coffee, but it's hot. You can tell me what's happened while you drink."

Once he had a warm mug in his hand, Henry was ready to talk.

"The coroner finally issued his report late last night. He's ascertained two things. Time of death was between two and four in the morning…"

"When Tobias was with me."

"Right. The other important finding was that although his body had a number of contusions consistent with what a fist fight could cause, none was the cause of death."

"Does he know how he *did* die?"

"Drowning. In all likelihood the young man was drunk and tried a reckless stunt, like so many before him."

"Does this mean Tobias is cleared?"

"Not yet. I'm afraid you are going to have to make a statement that he was with you all night. I've also got someone asking around the barracks, quietly, if anyone else saw the man on the beach that night."

"Do you think he was not alone?"

"It wouldn't surprise me. Although it troubles me deeply that they wouldn't have tried to rescue a colleague in trouble."

"Maybe it wasn't another soldier. Maybe it was someone not strong enough to help a drowning man—especially at Katama."

"Someone who doesn't want anyone to know she was out in the middle of the night…"

"And is willing to let an innocent man be accused."

"I can hear the outrage in your voice, Mae, especially given your willingness to speak up for Tobias. But all we're doing here is making unsubstantiated assumptions, just like Simms did yesterday with Tobias."

He put down his cup. "Let's get this done and your man out of jail."

He had called Tobias "my man." I let that simmer in my brain all during the bumpy ride across the bay in Henry's boat. I had changed into my best suit and hat, saved from my days in the city. I had barely worn it since coming to the island, but Henry agreed I needed to look as respectable and upright as possible—the business woman Mae Keaney, baker of pies, fighter of fires, and proprietor of a thriving business who had turned an abandoned eyesore into an island destination. I held that image of myself all the way from the harbor to the police station, because I hardly thought people would see me like that on the way back. I held my head high as we passed

Henry's house, with Ruth hiding behind the curtain in the front parlor.

"Courage," Henry said, patting my arm that he had entwined with his own, leading me up the street. And I knew that he, too, had seen Ruth.

Once inside the station, my guard was up; my spine stiffened. I know how to do this, I reminded myself. It's no different from other situations in my past when men tried to intimidate me.

Henry had warned me that they'd probably make me wait, so I was prepared. I settled into a chair, folded my hands in my lap and bided my time.

It was nearly an hour before the police chief called us into a small, windowless room. It stank of cigarettes and the sweat of nervous men.

"I understand from Henry that you can corroborate the Indian's whereabouts on Saturday night."

"If you mean Mr. Monroe, yes. He delivered a book to me around 6 p.m., left at 7, and then returned to my cottage around 10."

"Around 10? Can you be more specific? Was it earlier or later than 10?"

"I have a ship's bell clock in the house. It chimed the quarter hour shortly after he arrived, so 10:15."

"And when did he leave?"

I didn't hesitate. I stuck out my chin and said, "Not till after breakfast the next morning. That would have been about 9 a.m."

He gave me a knowing smile, one that implied Tobias was not the only man I had entertained overnight at Innisfree.

"And can you swear that he never left your house during the night?"

"Yes, I can."

"How can you be sure, Miss Keaney?"

I was about to answer when Henry interrupted.

"She's swearing to his presence all night, Al."

"That's OK, Henry. I'll answer the question. It's what he thinks, anyway. Mr. Monroe spent the night in my bed, Mr. Simms. I'm a very light sleeper. I would have awakened if he left."

"Are you in the practice of providing your customers with more than pie and lemonade, Miss Keaney?"

"That's an irrelevant and gratuitous question and you know it, Al."

Henry had also warned me that Al Simms would try to bait me. His final instruction had been, "Keep your mouth shut unless I tell you it's OK to answer."

I bit my lip again. Not out of nervousness, but to keep my outrage in check.

I expected that my statement would label me as an unmarried woman with a lover, but I hadn't anticipated that I would be accused of running a bordello. I was furious.

"I think we're done here, Al. You have no reason to keep Mr. Monroe any longer. He clearly wasn't with the deceased after their fight at the bar. Combined with the coroner's report, I think we have enough to conclude that Corporal Carlson was a victim of his own foolhardiness in trying to defy the power of the waves at Katama."

Henry stood and motioned for me to do the same.

Al Simms scraped his chair back, his mouth a grim line.

"I warn you, Miss Keaney, I better not hear of any illicit activity taking place after hours at your establishment."

Henry led me out to the lobby.

"I want you out of here when they release Tobias. You don't need witnesses to what is probably going to be an emotional reunion for you two. Go down the street to the Captain's Table and have a cup of tea. I'll bring him down when we've got the paperwork done."

I nodded, reluctant to go when Tobias was so near, but understanding the wisdom of Henry's direction. This was going to be worse than I had feared. I could hear the buzz already. Mae Keaney the madam, enticing men with her sexual wiles as well as her key lime pie.

I marched down to the Captain's Table, my face as stony as the police chief's.

Once again I waited. I took a seat near the back, away from the windows. Henry had convinced me that the less the town saw of me, the better.

"Sooner or later this will all die down and folks will move on to the next scandal. But for now, let's not give them anything more to chew on."

Someone had left the newspaper on the counter, so I picked it up to occupy me while I sipped my tea. I realized too late what a mistake that was as soon as I smoothed it out and saw the headline on the first page.

"ARREST MADE IN SOLDIER'S DEATH."

I wanted to rip the sheet into confetti and toss it on Marcus Gardner's front yard. Instead, I carefully refolded the paper and put it back on the counter face down. Would tomorrow's headline be, "BROTHEL OWNER PROVIDES ALIBI FOR SUSPECT"?

There have been very few times since coming back to the island that I missed New York, but this was one of them. I longed for anonymity, the ability to walk down the street without having people whisper behind their hands or their curtains about who I was and what I had done.

I stirred my tea for the thousandth time and tried not to keep glancing at the clock, the door or the faces of the other customers. When I thought I couldn't stay for a minute longer, Henry finally appeared, alone. He made his way back to me, pausing to greet the waitress before he slid into the booth opposite me.

"Where's Tobias? Didn't they release him?" I tried to keep my voice under control, but wasn't succeeding. Henry patted my hand.

"He's fine, Mae. But we both thought it best if he went directly back to his place in Cove Meadow."

"He didn't want to see me." I wasn't asking. I knew, with that certainty that comes from understanding someone who has let down his guard and offered himself with honesty. Tobias was a proud man. I had witnessed his humiliation when he was arrested at Henry's office. Even though my testimony had exonerated him, I was the one who had convinced him not to run away. I was the reason he had been taken with such brutality. No wonder he didn't want to see me.

"I'll find Frank and see if he can run me back to Pogue." I pushed my cup away and reached into my purse for my wallet. Henry extended his hand across the table and stopped me.

"I'll get it. And I'll bring you back."

"You don't have to take care of me, Henry. I'm a grown woman. I'm grateful for all you did for Tobias, but your duty is done."

"Mac Keaney, did it ever occur to you that I acted not out of duty, but out of genuine care for you? You are a remarkable young woman—strong and capable and possessing a core of goodness that is a beacon as strong as the Cape Pogue light in a world filled with darkness and destruction. But dammit, you don't have to do it all yourself, especially when you are hurting the way you are right now."

"I'm not hurting. I'm fine. I understand why Tobias doesn't want to see me." I was willing myself not to cry in front of Henry. He was so damn solicitous, when all I wanted was to be alone.

"Come on then. I'll walk you down to the wharf. And if Frank isn't around, I'm taking you home."

He left a generous tip on the table and steered me out. The place was filling up for lunch and it was time to leave.

Frank's boat was not in the slip where he usually tied up, so I reluctantly agreed to ride back with Henry.

"May I offer you a sandwich?" I asked him when we arrived at the Boat House, trying to make amends for my stubbornness at the Captain's Table.

"I'd be pleased to accept, Mae. Thank you."

Keeping my hands busy slicing tomatoes, spreading mayonnaise and layering thick slices of my cold meat loaf on my home-baked bread calmed me. In the kitchen I had control and order and familiarity. I knew how to do this—prepare a good meal with care and serve it as if I were offering a gift from my heart. It gave me comfort, doing this well when I had botched so much else in my life.

Henry smiled with satisfaction when he took the first bite.

"You cook as well as Catriona, Mae. She taught you well."

"I didn't know you knew my mother's cooking."

"George Bradley sometimes invited me up to the Knolls for dinner in the early days. How is your mother?"

"I wouldn't know. I lost touch with my family a long time ago." The comfort of this meal was draining from me like the tide at full moon.

"I'm sorry to hear that. It was shame to see your family leave the island when they did. George Bradley's greed brought down a lot of folks. But it's good to have you back and building such a success."

Henry didn't press for the reason I was estranged. I was grateful not to have to explain. But his mention of my family, and my mother especially, reminded me that our reconciliation was impossible. My mother's expectation, from the time I had been able to understand the words of her prayers, had been for me to enter the convent. I had never questioned the path she had chosen for me—had embraced it, in fact—until we arrived in Boston and our lives were thrown into despair. From that moment I questioned *everything*, furious with a God that had allowed my family to suffer. My anger had made it easy to fall off my good-girl pedestal into Ned's arms; after that reckless act, every step in my life had been a step away from my mother's dreams.

Henry wiped his mouth with his napkin and picked up his plate to clear the table.

"Please, Henry, I'll get that."

As he left, he turned to me. "Just give Tobias a little time to lick his wounds. He'll come around when he's ready." He tipped his hat and climbed into his boat.

I watched until he was just a glint reflected by the sun and then went in to clean up. I still had the beach plums to can and that was going to take me well into the evening.

As I hoped, I lost myself in the repetitive, careful rhythm of putting up fruit. The air in the Boat House kitchen was soon moist with steam rising off my sterilizing kettle and heavy with the sweet aroma of plums. I moved swiftly and smoothly through the motions of cooking down and straining the fruit, filling and sealing the jars with hot paraffin and settling them out on racks to cool. You can't stop once you begin, nor can you let your mind wander, or you'll wind up with a batch of scorched fruit and a mess to deal with.

It was after ten at night when I finally finished. I wiped the sweat from my brow one last time after I'd washed the pots, the counters and the sticky floor. It's a good thing I don't keep a mirror in the kitchen or I'd probably have scared myself.

I locked up the Boat House and started across the lawn toward the cottage with a small flashlight, pulling off the bandana wrapped around my hair as I walked.

I smelled the man sitting on my porch before I saw him, his cigar a tiny ember in the dark night.

"Evening, Miss Keaney."

"What brings you here at this hour, Mr. Gardner?" I hadn't heard or seen his boat. It certainly wasn't at my dock, which meant he had moored it elsewhere to keep his presence hidden.

"Why, I'm here to protect you. Al Simms told me he'd released the Indian because you provided him with an alibi. Some people might be disturbed about that and take it out on you."

"I'm quite capable of protecting myself, Mr. Gardner. There's no need for you to stay."

"I don't think you realize quite how dangerous Monroe is, Miss Keaney."

It was Gardner I was finding dangerous, and a warning chill crept up my back. The only reason he was here was not to "protect" me but to lie in wait for Tobias. Al Simms had clearly shared with him not only that my statement had given Tobias an alibi. He must have told Marcus that Tobias had spent the night with me, and Marcus fully expected Tobias to return.

"I'm a good judge of a man's character, Mr. Gardner. Now, if you'll kindly leave my house, I'd like to go in. It's been a long day and tomorrow's the weekend. I expect I'll have customers early."

As I climbed the porch I could see the glint of steel in his hand. If he tried to stop me, there wasn't much I could do with only a flashlight in my hand. But I was pretty sure it wasn't me he wanted, and summoned everything that had driven me to this point in my life. I shined the light directly in his face, temporarily blinding him with its brightness.

"Get out."

I pushed quickly past him into the house, slammed the door in his face and doused the light. I went straight to my bedroom and dragged the gun box from under the bed. I had taught myself to load it in the dark, but my hands still trembled. When the last bullet clicked into place, I sat back against the wall under the window and waited.

I didn't think Marcus would leave, but I also didn't think he'd break into the house.

For the first time that day I hoped Tobias would stay away. But if he did come, I knew I would defend him.

The night passed slowly. I knew the sounds of Innisfree intimately, and strained to hear anything that was unfamiliar—a boot scraped across the wood of the porch, the snap of a branch or the raspy breath of a man who smokes too much. But I heard nothing. Soon the fatigue of a day spent first under scrutiny in Edgartown and then in the kitchen caught up with me, and I fell asleep, upright and gun in hand.

Chapter Twelve
Revelations

I woke abruptly a few hours later, the sky still inky black, and I knew someone was in the house. I crouched behind the bed, with my gun pointed at the door.

"Mae?" The familiar voice whispered my name. "Are you here?"

I lowered the gun. "Over here. Beside the bed. Don't say anything."

I rose and crossed the room, pulling him through the door and then into the closet, out of the line of sight from the windows.

In the dark I could make out the outline of his face and found his lips. The kiss, returned, was intense but brief.

"Marcus Gardner was here, lying in wait for you. He may still be."

"I know. I saw his boat beached at Drunkard's Cove. I've been waiting below the cliff. He was prowling around the cottage and finally took up a sentinel position by the flagpole. He's still there, waiting for me to sail in unawares."

"Why does he want you? He's acting like a vigilante instead of a judge. I knew he didn't like you, but now he's hunting you. You didn't kill the soldier, but that doesn't seem to matter to him. It's something else, isn't it?"

"Yeah, but there isn't time now to explain. We can't stay here as long as he's out there. My boat is on East Beach north of here. We can slip across the meadow and into the woods while he is watching the bay. But he'll start circling again soon. Put on some warm, dark clothes." He was holding me and could tell I was wearing only the thin cotton dress I'd been wearing all day. I slipped out of his arms, handed him the gun and grabbed a pair of dark wool slacks, a sweater, my pea coat and watch cap. I changed quickly while Tobias watched the flagpole through the window. Marcus' silhouette was still there, visible against the white of the pole.

We crept out of the cottage on the meadow side, keeping along the eastern edge of the shed and the back of the Boat House. At the meadow we dropped to our bellies and crawled till we reached the shelter of the woods. Then Tobias grabbed my hand and we ran.

By the time we arrived at the boat I was breathless. The fear I had managed to contain finally exploded as we pushed the boat into the water and climbed in. It was only when we were on the open water and the sail was up that I turned around to see if Marcus had followed us, but it was too dark to see if the beach was empty. I turned back to Tobias.

He handed me the tiller. "Hold this for a minute."

He rummaged in a duffle bag and retrieved a blanket, then wrapped it around me.

"You're shivering. You're safe now. Forgive me for putting you in danger."

I huddled in the blanket, comforted not only by its warmth but by Tobias' wood smoke and leather scent. I didn't speak until the faint pink light of dawn limned the horizon. We were heading north, away from Chappy.

"Where are we going?'

"To my cousin's for a few days. Mashpee. I thought it would be better if we got off-island. Marcus will figure out soon enough that you are gone, and he has too many friends on the island for us to remain hidden there. His power doesn't reach beyond the Vineyard."

"When are you going to tell me what this is all about?" I was still afraid, but I wanted to know what it was I had to fear.

Tobias went still and pressed his lips into a grim line.

"I didn't mean for you to be dragged into the trouble between Marcus and me. I didn't want you involved at all. I told Henry."

"But I dragged myself in. I couldn't stand by silently when you were being falsely accused. I *am* involved and I deserve to know."

Tobias turned his face toward the far shore and away from me. But he began to speak.

"Marcus' sister was my wife. He was furious when she defied him and we eloped."

"*Was* your wife? And now?"

"She died. And Marcus blamed me."

He kept his back to me, unwilling, I suppose, to see the look of betrayal and raw fear on my face. I thought I had been the one with secrets.

"Were you ever going to tell me?" I couldn't mask my anger.

This time he did turn around.

"Were you going to tell me the secrets you are harboring about *your* past?"

"I didn't kill anyone!" I screamed, but my denial was only half-true. I hadn't killed my baby, but I had never forgiven myself for her death.

Tobias turned away again.

"Neither did I." He spoke to the wind.

"Then why does Marcus hold you responsible?"

"Hannah was a wild and unhappy girl. She was much younger than Marcus. He raised her when their parents died. We were both rebellious, incautious. My family wasn't happy either. Wampanoag leadership passes through the matrilineal line. I was an only child. By marrying a white woman, I was essentially ending my family's role in the tribe, since my children would be outside the line of succession. Our marriage was volatile. Neither one of us knew how to compromise or temper our emotions. I was also too young and too ignorant to understand that Hannah was mentally unstable. Her moods began to swing to alarming extremes—wildly exuberant one day and numbingly despairing the next. I took a job on a fishing boat that spent six weeks on the Grand Banks to get away from her. I ran away."

"And that's when she died."

"Yeah. She was drinking a lot at the time. One night she went for a swim at Katama. Her body didn't wash up for a couple of weeks."

"So the circumstances were like the soldier's death, and Marcus thought he finally had a way to make you pay for Hannah's drowning."

"Except that you thwarted him."

I reached out for him, my anger dissipated by his revelations.

"Marcus isn't the only one who hasn't forgiven you. You haven't forgiven yourself, have you?"

He didn't answer or respond to my touch. But I didn't remove my hand.

"I understand something about guilt. Let me tell you my own secret—the one you knew I was keeping from you."

Tobias turned to look at me.

"Do you remember the Bradley family with the house on North Neck?"

"I knew of them. Everyone did."

"My parents were their caretaker and housekeeper. We lived in the cottage on the edge of the property, near the road. When George Bradley went bankrupt in the crash, we lost everything, too—our home, our expectations, our future. My da took us to Boston to find work."

"That is no secret to be ashamed of, Mae. Yours was not the only family to suffer."

"Our poverty is not what shames me, Tobias. I hated George Bradley for what he did to my family. And then I took up with his son."

"Took up?"

"I became Ned Bradley's lover. He showed up in Boston where I was working at the Jordan Marsh bakery. We had been childhood friends, in that way children have of ignoring the barriers that separate us as adults. I was lonely and angry. He was bitter. We filled a need for each other."

"Did you love him?"

I was surprised by the question—more by the implication than the asking of it. Tobias cared whether I had loved someone else.

I shook my head.

"I was seventeen and convinced that what I felt for Ned was love, primarily because what I was doing with him defied everything I had been raised to believe as a good Catholic girl. It was the beginning of what was to become a life of lies and deceit. First, I lied to myself. Then I lied to my family."

"I've never believed you to be a liar."

"Only a keeper of secrets? Isn't that the same?"

"You're not hiding anything now. Go on."

"I became pregnant soon after we became lovers. I thought Ned would marry me when I told him. But he didn't. He wanted me to get rid of the baby. I couldn't. But I also couldn't disgrace my family. So I ran away."

"Where to?"

"To a home in Connecticut run by nuns. I'd overheard one of the girls at the bakery talking about a cousin who'd gone there. They found adoptive families for the babies. I saved enough for bus fare and then left home one day as if I were going to work. I never went back."

"You gave birth to a daughter. That's why the poem upset you so much."

I nodded.

"Do you know where she is? How old would she be now? Ten?"

I held my hand up to stop his questions.

"She's dead, Tobias. Stillborn. The girl I had been died that day too."

He reached out for my hand and enclosed it in his.

"That's not the end of the secrets, is it?"

I shook my head.

"I left the home feeling punished by God, a sentiment the nuns did not attempt to dispel. If anything, they placed the blame for her death on me. I believed I had sinned so grievously that I could not be forgiven. I didn't go back home. I couldn't. I went to New York. I did what I must to survive."

I turned away from Tobias to stare back at the receding coast of Chappy. Al Simms hadn't been so far off when he insinuated that I might bc offering sex for money after hours at the Boat House. In New York, I'd kept from starving by finding men willing to spend money on me in exchange for my attention. Once I had gotten the job at Delmonico's, it had been easy enough to meet them, charm them.

"I discovered a talent for feigning tender feelings for men. I got to be very good at pretending I was in love."

"Are you pretending now?"

"I don't expect you to believe me after what I've just told you, but no, I'm not pretending now. I love you."

He pulled me toward him, and with one hand still on the tiller, enveloped me in a powerful embrace.

"I love you, too, Mae."

I spent the rest of the journey curled up in his arms, neither one of us speaking.

It was close to noon when we reached Cotuit harbor. Tobias called his cousin Sadie when we arrived at the dock, and a short time later we were on a bus bound for Mashpee.

Tobias was greeted with warmth by Sadie's husband, Ronnie. Sadie, on the other hand, offered little more than a nod to me and a questioning glance at Tobias.

"I'll explain," Tobias told Ronnie. "But we've been out on the water since before dawn. We need something to eat, some hot tea."

Sadie, a baby on her hip and one tugging at her skirt, stood in the kitchen doorway.

"Come on, then," she shrugged. "I've got some soup left over from lunch."

I helped her set the table while Tobias went off with Ronnie, apparently to explain why we needed shelter for a few days.

"Are you Tobias' woman?" she asked.

That was indeed who I had become in the last forty-eight hours. I nodded to Sadie.

She turned to the stove to stir the pot.

"I thought he had gotten white women out of his system after that crazy wife of his drowned."

"You don't think he should be with a white woman?"

"Not Tobias. He should be the next sachem when his father passes. We all grieved with him when Hannah died, but the family was relieved that his marriage was no longer an obstacle. He's a good man; the tribe needs him to lead."

She faced me again and demanded, "Do you love him?"

I had the sense that this woman was a force—direct, protective, willing to fight for something she believed in, and that something was her tribe.

My emotions were raw. I was exhausted from the night's disruption and the journey across the water. I was still in upheaval about the revelations I had made to Tobias and the fragility of his acceptance. I had expressed my love to him for the first time only a few hours before. I wanted to tell this woman it was none of her business. I wanted to believe that Tobias and I were two outsiders who had found one another on East Beach and who didn't need anyone else. But I saw that was not true. He had a history with these people. He was connected to them in ways that reflected sacred bonds. I remembered the reverence with which he had blessed the land after the fire.

"Yes," I said, as fiercely as Sadie had questioned me. "I *do* love him."

"Then don't stand in his way. He's not a boy any more, infatuated with a blond witch. He has responsibilities to his people."

Ronnie and Tobias came into the kitchen at that moment. Sadie cast a warning glance at me and then slammed the pot of soup on the table. The baby startled at the sound and started wailing. Sadie thrust a ladle into my hand and left with the baby.

"What was that all about?" Tobias asked, looking after Sadie in bafflement.

"Nothing," I said, focusing on dishing out the soup. "I'm sure our unexpected arrival is something of a burden for her, with two small children."

I addressed Ronnie. "I'll try to be as helpful as I can. We're grateful to have a place to stay, but we'll try not to be here long."

"She'll calm down after I tell her what's happened. We're in your debt for what you did for Tobias. The least we can do is provide you a safe haven."

"Please, you owe me nothing. I only did what was right."

"At great cost to you," Tobias insisted.

We ate in silence, the hot soup finally dispelling some of the chill that had settled on me since finding Marcus on my porch the night before.

I washed up after we ate. Sadie had put the baby down to sleep and returned to the kitchen.

"Thanks for cleaning up." She seemed surprised.

"I run a café. If I don't stay on top of the kitchen I couldn't stay in business. Look, whatever I can do to relieve the hardship of our staying here, just let me know."

"I already told you what you can do."

This woman was relentless.

"Is there somewhere I can lie down for a bit? I haven't had much sleep since Tobias was arrested."

"Come with me. I made you up a cot in the attic. Tobias can sleep on the sofa in the parlor."

I hadn't expected that we would be able to sleep together, but her comment was so pointed that it only added to my anger and confusion. I followed her up the stairs to the space under the eaves that she had prepared.

"Thanks," I murmured.

"The bathroom is downstairs at the end of the hall." And then she left.

I collapsed onto the bed and finally allowed myself to cry.

We stayed three days. Sadie stopped slamming pots on the table, mainly because I offered to cook. We did not have another conversation, as she barely acknowledged me. I said nothing to Tobias, and was not sure that I ever would. I had no idea what lay ahead of us as a couple when it was not even clear it would be safe for him to return to the Vineyard. We had little opportunity to talk in private. The house was small, and as welcoming as Ronnie had been, I could see how much strain we had placed on him and Sadie.

After breakfast on the third day, when Ronnie had gone back to work and Sadie was outside hanging laundry, I spoke to Tobias.

"I think we should call Henry to tell him what happened and find out what's going on with Marcus. If I know Henry, he's probably gone out to Innisfree to check on me and found the place abandoned."

Tobias agreed, and we walked into town to use the public phone at the drugstore, rather than Ronnie's party line. I made the call.

"Mae! Where the hell are you?"

I'm safe, Henry, off-island for a few days."

"Is Tobias with you?"

"Yes. Did you know Marcus Gardner came out to Innisfree and was lying in wait for him with a gun?"

There was silence on the other end of the line.

"I knew someone had been there, but not that it was Marcus. I went out in my boat on Sunday when I heard you hadn't raised the flag all weekend. The house was open, ransacked, as if someone had gone on a rampage. I've been frantic with worry for you. You should have let me know sooner." His voice was gruff. I heard genuine concern beneath his anger with me.

I was sick with the thought of Marcus Gardner pawing through my things, but I couldn't dwell on the violation I felt.

"Two questions: Is the Boat House secure, or did he wreck that, too? And is it safe for us to come back?"

"He left the Boat House alone, except for some broken windows. But you need to come back. Now that you've confirmed it was Marcus, we have to stop him. Come directly to Edgartown. I don't want you alone at Innisfree."

"I won't be alone."

"I meant, it isn't safe for *either* of you."

Tobias listened with me, his arm tight around me as he heard Henry's description of what Marcus had done. He nodded that he agreed with Henry.

"Is Tobias by the phone? Let me talk to him."

I handed the receiver to Tobias and heard Henry question him.

"This is about Hannah's death, isn't it? I've been compassionate to the man's grief. The loss of a sibling you've raised is like the death of a child—unbearable. But it's gone too far. I promise you I will put an end to his obsession."

"I appreciate that, Henry, but I don't think that is going to be possible. He'll find some other reason to come after me until he exacts whatever he believes is justice. He'll never understand that I've been paying for Hannah's death every day since her body was found."

He hung up the phone. The arm that had held me so tightly slipped away and slammed into the wall.

"I'll get you back to Edgartown, but then I'm leaving the island. I shouldn't have involved you in this."

"It's too late." I didn't touch him. I could see how tightly wound he was. Any tenderness on my part would only have been met with rejection.

"It's not too late. Once I'm gone, the rumors will die down. You'll be left alone. The way you wanted it when you first came back to Chappy."

I shook my head. "I meant, it's too late for me. I love you. You didn't force me into your life. I came willingly. I'm not going to leave now that you're in trouble."

"But your life is across the water." He thrust his chin toward Chappy, unseen but very much in our thoughts.

"So is yours. You can't allow one man to dictate where you belong, no matter how crazed with grief he is. Chappy is who you are. It's in your blood, your people. Now, let's go home."

Chapter Thirteen
Clean Up

We spoke little on the journey back. It was nearly dark by the time we landed in Edgartown and our arrival was barely noticed. We tied up on one of the more remote docks and walked silently to Henry's house. The porch light was on and the door opened immediately when we rang. I was relieved that it was Henry and not Ruth who answered. He ushered us into his office and immediately poured us drinks.

"This will warm you up. I've made arrangements for you to stay at Vernon Parker's down along the Beach Road. I'll fill you in on the last several hours as you finish your drinks and then I'll run you over in my car."

I slowly swallowed the whisky, letting its heat fill my belly. Tobias gulped his down, his stance wary, waiting for what he believed was Henry's futile attempt to stop Marcus.

"After I spoke to you I called the state police. I don't trust Al Simms when it comes to dealing with Marcus. There's a small garrison at Vineyard Haven. The captain is not an islander and therefore not beholden to Judge Gardner. Mae, he'll take your statement tomorrow morning about Marcus' trespass and threat to Tobias. I don't want either of you to so much as look out the window at Vernon's. I'll pick you up and take you to the garrison. As far as we know, Marcus is still hunting Tobias."

"Can we trust Vernon?"

"There's no love lost between Marcus and Vernon. He'll keep your presence under wraps."

"What then? Will Marcus be arrested? Won't he get out on bail or personal recognizance? He's a pillar of the community."

"He'll be arrested and arraigned off-island."

"It will take more than the law to stop Marcus."

"I know that, Tobias. But the law is where we'll start. I have some thoughts on what path we'll take next, but for now, get some rest."

He picked up a basket from a table near the door.

"Ruth put together some supper for you to take with you."

I raised my eyebrows. It was certainly out of character for her to show us some kindness.

Henry addressed my unspoken surprise.

"She only knew it was for clients who would be arriving too late to get a meal in town. Let's get going."

It had started to rain and the Beach Road was slick and deserted. Vernon Parker's cottage was at the far end of Trapps Pond. He welcomed us and led us to a snug room off the kitchen after Henry departed.

"If you need anything, holler. I'll be in my workshop in the back of the house for a while. No need to worry about intruders. The dogs'll let us know if anyone's about, and I've got my rifle at hand. Henry told me what this is about. It's time someone put a stop to Gardner's twisted ideas of justice."

We thanked him and bid him goodnight. The room was spare. A bed with a thin coverlet, a braided rug underfoot, a small table and chairs by the single window. A bachelor's place.

Tobias went immediately to the window, checked that it was locked, and drew the shade down and the curtains closed. He opened his duffle bag and withdrew both our guns and placed them on the table. As reassuring as Vernon's rifle was, I was glad we had our own.

"Hungry?" I started to unpack the basket. Except for some sandwiches we'd had at Sadie's, we'd had nothing else. I was famished.

Tobias picked at the food—some roasted chicken, biscuits and cucumber salad. But I ate ravenously, as if storing up energy for what lay ahead.

When it appeared he wasn't going to want any more, I repacked the basket and pointed toward the bed.

"Will you come to bed?" I asked him, as I turned down the covers.

He shook his head. "Not yet. I'll keep watch for a while. You sleep."

I knew I wouldn't sleep while he was sitting by the window, tense with anticipation.

"We're both going to need to be alert once daylight arrives," I said as I moved behind him. I reached out to massage the knotted muscles of his back. I hadn't touched him since our phone call to Henry. That had only been that morning, but felt days rather than hours away. He didn't push me away, but he also didn't respond with any warmth. But I didn't stop. Even if *he* didn't need my touch, *I* did. I needed to feel connected to him, if only through my kneading fingertips. I thought to myself, *I am as relentless as Sadie. I will not allow him to push me away, no matter how dangerous he thinks it is for me to be associated with him.*

It seemed that no one wanted Tobias and me to be together. Not the white community in Edgartown, not his own people, especially Sadie. And now, perhaps not even Tobias himself. I bent my head to his ear, my hands resting on his shoulders.

"I love you, Tobias Monroe. And I will not give up on you. Now come to bed with me and let me show you."

He still didn't acknowledge me, but I didn't move away.

After a few moments he spoke, still watching through the break in the curtains.

"I want you more than anything, Mae. But I've only brought violence and disruption into the peaceable life you had created for yourself. If I could wind back the clock I would respect the distance you so clearly meant to keep between us. Even now, if that is what you want, I will abide by your decision."

I moved around him and took his face in my hands.

"I thought we had resolved this when you agreed to come back. What I want is you, despite—no, *because* of the last several days. My "peaceable life" was a very hollow one until you filled it."

I kissed him. For a heartbeat he hesitated, and then reached around my waist to pull me toward him. Then he got up, took me by the hand and led me to the bed.

The exhaustion and vigilance that had been our constant state for so many days should have dampened our lovemaking. But the separation we had endured during Tobias' nights in jail, and the overt disapproval at Ronnie and Sadie's house, only heightened our hunger for one another. He took me the first time as if he might never have me again. When he came, it was with a ferocity that claimed me, marked me. And I answered him with my own intensity. My body fought against everyone and everything that might take him from me—Marcus, the tribe, the judgment of the town, his own doubts.

Exhaustion finally overtook us, but only for a few hours of restless sleep. Before dawn we were both awake again, attuned to the slightest shift in movement or breath. We moved toward each other, this time with a tenderness that acknowledged there was no turning back, for now we possessed one another.

The smell of frying bacon roused us. Henry would be arriving soon. The respite we had carved for ourselves in the darkness was over. I grabbed the clothes scattered across that threadbare rug and got dressed.

My interview with the state police an hour later was a sharp contrast to the sneering inquisition I had undergone with Al Simms. I was listened to with respect. No one accused me of being a whore. I was believed.

"What will happen now?" I asked as the captain slid my statement across the table for me to sign.

"We'll arrest Judge Gardner this morning and transport him to Hyannis for arraignment. As he's the only judge on the island, he can't very well arraign himself."

"But what's to keep him from exacting his revenge once he's out on bail?"

Henry answered me. "Not everyone on the Vineyard is afraid of or beholden to Marcus, Mae."

"We'll be watching him," the state police captain interjected.

"Each of you can request a restraining order." He looked at both Tobias and me. "If he comes within 200 feet of you or your homes, we can arrest him again. And for the next few days, I'm willing to put a watch detail at each of your places."

"That won't be necessary for me," Tobias said immediately. "I can defend myself. Put a double watch at Mae's cottage."

"Tobias, I'm sure you can take care of yourself. But this isn't the Wild West. It's

Massachusetts in the middle of the twentieth century. If, in defending yourself, you injure or kill Marcus, you're setting yourself up for a long and complicated legal process. Not everyone is going to believe it's Marcus who has the vendetta." Henry spoke quietly but sternly.

"Spare me the lecture, Henry. Marcus is the one trying to kill me and threatening Mae." His mouth had that hard line I'd come to recognize. He got up to leave.

"Mae, I'll take you home and help you clean up at Innisfree. I don't think there's anything else we need to do here."

"We'll have a detail out to Chappy within the next few hours. Listen to your lawyer, son."

Tobias had already turned to leave, but I saw his back stiffen at the word "son." He didn't say it out loud, but I knew he was thinking, *I'm not your son.*

"I'm grateful to you, Captain," I said, as graciously as I could, and then followed Tobias out the door.

On the ride back to the pier in Henry's car, no one said a word. When we arrived at the boat, Henry finally spoke.

"I'll come out later when I know they've arrested Marcus. Be prepared for the condition of the cottage. The state police were already there and took photographs and dusted for fingerprints. It's not a pretty sight."

For one more time in the last few days, I climbed into Tobias' boat. The wind was at our back and we made good time through the Gut and across the bay. Despite what awaited me, I was eager to be home again.

After we tied up at the Boat House dock, Tobias retrieved his gun from the duffle bag and slowly approached the cottage. I followed him, stepping carefully around the broken glass strewn across the dock and along the path. Behind the Boat House I could see that whatever had still been growing in the garden had been ripped out. A mounting sense of dread filled me the closer we got to the cottage. Marcus had not just been looking for Tobias. He had deliberately destroyed Innisfree as a message to me.

I steeled myself as we climbed the porch. Tobias stopped me from going in.

"Let me check inside first."

"No. I'm going with you. If he's here, I want to wring his neck." I surprised myself with the fury I felt. As I followed Tobias into the house my eyes took in the chaos—cabinets and drawers emptied and their contents scattered across the floor in the kitchen, cushions torn from the sofa in the parlor, books pulled from the shelves. The bedroom was the worst and filled me with revulsion. The bed had been stripped to the mattress and my clothing—underwear, blouses, stockings—had been dumped on the floor. I wanted to retch, and bent over the small porcelain sink tucked into the corner by the closet.

Tobias, sure now that no one was in the house, held my hair back from my face as I threw up. I stood up, rinsed my mouth and stormed back out of the house, grabbing the keys to the Boat House. Henry had said it hadn't been touched except for the broken windows, but I needed to see for myself.

I let myself in the back, through the kitchen door, and knew immediately that Henry had been wrong. Either he had held back to soften the blow, or Marcus had returned to do more damage. The first thing I saw was the worktable in the middle of the kitchen, where I had left the dozens of jars of beach plum preserves I had canned. That day now seemed so long ago. The kitchen was a mass of blood-red jelly and glass shards. The sticky substance had oozed down to the floor and was seething with bees that must have gotten in through the broken windows.

Flour had been dumped out of its bin; an open can of Crisco was smeared across the stove; the ice box door was open, its contents reeking from three days exposed to the warm Indian summer air.

I sat down in the middle of the floor and howled. Tobias found me there. He crouched down and took me into his arms. The anguish in his face matched my own. If this was the havoc Marcus had wreaked on my place, I could not imagine what he would do to Tobias. I couldn't fathom Marcus' purpose in destroying so much. I knew him to be a much more controlled man, so the rage displayed by this rampage was inconceivable.

"Why?" I finally choked out. "Did he suddenly snap? Or was this somehow calculated?"

"Oh, I think he was very deliberate. He meant to provoke me by hurting you. He wants me to come after him."

"I've made you vulnerable."

"In more ways than you know," he whispered, his lips brushing my forehead.

"Promise me you won't fall into his trap." I shifted and looked into his eyes. "I can clean this up, but I cannot bear to lose you, either to Marcus' bullet or his plot to put you behind bars again. *Promise me.*"

He did not speak for a moment. I could see in his eyes the struggle to reconcile my demand with his own rage.

"I have to protect you." His voice was grim.

"You will protect me best by not getting yourself killed."

"You said yourself I cannot allow him to dictate my life."

"But if you get into this dance of revenge with him, that is exactly what you will be doing."

"Where does it stop, then?"

"It will stop with you. With us. I'm furious with him, for what he did to me; I'm not denying it. But I know already what my anger can do—to *me*, not to the object of my anger. Better that I turn that energy toward rebuilding the Boat House. Because I'll be damned if Marcus Gardner has the power to shut me down. Come on. There's work to be done."

We scrambled to our feet. I kissed him, knowing that he hadn't promised not to go after Marcus, but trusting that he would at least think about what I had said.

I pinned up my hair, pulled an apron off the hook by the door and grabbed a bucket to empty the ice box.

"I'll start with the broken glass," he said, and headed for the shed and a broom and a shovel.

We had been at the clean-up for a couple of hours when I heard a commotion at the dock. I was in the dining room of the Boat House, stacking chairs on tables so I could sweep out the glass that had fallen inside when the windows had broken. I looked out through the gaping hole and saw with dismay what looked like a flotilla. Horns were bleating and at least four full boats were heading into the cove. Most of my regulars knew the Boat House was only open when the flag was at full mast on the point. I couldn't even make a pitcher of lemonade, let alone feed the number of people I saw on the decks of the boats now tying up at the dock.

I went out to apologize. At the head of the crowd was Henry, who certainly should have known I was in no shape to be open for business.

"Mae, these folks with me are here to help you clean up. They figure it's as if you got hit by a hurricane."

I looked at the people behind him, many of them with the familiar lined and weathered faces of the fishermen whose business had helped me get off the ground and sustained me over the last two summers. Men who, like me, didn't talk much but who understood what it meant to work hard. Some of them had brought their wives. Even Ruth had come.

I nodded, dazed by this unexpected outpouring.

"Just tell us what you need done," Henry said.

I struggled to understand my reaction to the arrival of all these people. I felt stunned and uneasy, unfamiliar with the kindness so plainly on display and unwilling to be the object of their pity. But I also saw in their faces an element of anger that matched my own. Anger directed at the injustice meted out by someone who, above all, was expected to be most just. That surprised me, and eased my initial sense of being intruded upon in the midst of my very private pain. I was however, all too aware that my life had been ripped wide open by the arrival of these witnesses. I couldn't send them away. But the thought of them picking through the debris of my life left me hollow…and afraid.

"I know you mean well, Henry. But I don't know where to begin to direct all these people." I threw up my hands, raw from scrubbing. I could feel myself starting to fall apart again, as I had in the Boat House kitchen.

Once again, Tobias slipped in beside me and propped me up.

"I can organize the men to start boarding up the windows. If most of the women can finish the clean-up in the Boat House, Mae can handle what's in the house with one or two helpers."

He turned to me. "Why don't you ask Betty to go up to the cottage with you? I saw her on Frank Bennett's boat."

I nodded, wiped my face with the rag in my hand and looked down the dock for Betty, the waitress from the Vineyard Haven Inn. She had sometimes come out to Pogue on her day off, and Tobias was right to suggest her. If there was anyone, other than Henry, whom I could trust with the cottage, it was Betty.

The industry of island folk was on full display that afternoon, as hammers reverberated on wood and brooms pushed piles of broken glass and crockery into trash barrels that Frank's boat would haul over to the dump in Edgartown.

Up at the cottage, Betty put her arm around me in unexpected affection as she surveyed the wreckage in the kitchen.

"Oh, honey, nobody deserves this!" She gave me a squeeze and then plunged in, sorting the broken from the salvageable with the calm demeanor with which she cleared tables at the inn.

"I can handle the kitchen until it's time to put things away, if you want to take care of more personal things." She seemed to understand that the violation I already felt would be compounded if someone else were to clean up the bedroom.

I braced myself to open the door I had slammed shut earlier when I was so filled with revulsion by the thought of Marcus' hands rifling through my clothing, my bed, the journal I kept in my bedside drawer.

The afternoon sun was pouring through the western window. Flies buzzed against the screen, which miraculously had not been slit. I took a deep breath and began to gather everything into a pile on the middle of the bed. I couldn't stand the thought of putting any of it on my body until I had washed it in the hottest water. I pulled the corners of the sheets up around the bundle and hauled it all to the bathtub to soak.

I went back to the bedroom and swept and scrubbed until my arms ached. I made the bed with fresh sheets that had been stored in the linen closet with lavender. Betty helped me tuck the corners in.

"Some of the women brought thermoses of tea and cake. You need a break. Let's go replenish our bellies." She pulled me away from the bed and led me back to the Boat House.

The transformation from the morning was hard to comprehend. The kitchen was gleaming, the dining room set in order, even to salt and pepper shakers filled and in place on every table. The dock was swept of glass and all the windows had been boarded up. Even the garden had been cleared and a basket sat on the counter in the kitchen with some squash that had been salvaged from the trampling.

Out on the porch in front of the Boat House, the fishermen's wives were slicing cake and handing out cups of hot cider. Someone put a steaming cup in my hand.

Henry and Tobias were sitting on the steps and waved me over to join them.

"The captain sent over two troopers as he promised, Mae. They'll be patrolling the grounds for the next few days. They also brought word that Marcus has been arrested."

He extended his hand in a sweeping gesture. "These folks heard what happened from Vernon and it struck a nerve. I am truly sorry that you were victimized and threatened, Mae, but this rampage of Marcus may have loosened the mortar that will bring down the whole wall."

"I didn't know that people would care so much about me. They hardly know me." I shook my head. Things were loosening up in me as well.

I walked around the clusters of people to thank them and promised I'd open the Boat House for a final fall weekend at the end of the week.

By sunset the last of the boats had pulled away. The state troopers began their patrol and Tobias and I made our way to the cottage and locked up.

He poured us both a drink from a bottle Marcus had missed. It had been tucked away in a far corner of the cabinet. He built us a fire in the wood stove and we sat wrapped in each other's arms as darkness eased its way across the sky. There was no moon and we did not light the lamps. The exhaustion that I had pushed away all day in the intensity of emotion and duty finally exacted its toll. Everything drained out of me until I was numb.

When the fire had dwindled to a few embers, Tobias lifted me, carried me to the bed and folded himself around me. The only sounds were the light flap of the curtains against the sill and the steady, unwavering cadence of Tobias' breath against my neck. I slept.

The next morning, I cooked breakfast for the troopers and Tobias. Then I was ready to tackle the laundry. The sky was clear and a brisk wind was blowing—good drying weather that I didn't want to waste.

"I need to head out to the Sound to fish," Tobias told me as I put away the last of the breakfast dishes. Marcus hadn't broken every piece of crockery, but he had come close.

Tobias didn't have to explain his need to get back to the water. He hadn't been out in over a week, and it was as much his livelihood as the Boat House was mine.

"You'll be OK? I'll be back before sunset."

"I'm fine. The laundry will keep me occupied, and between my own gun and the troopers, I'll be on my guard. Go!"

I watched from the porch as he loped down to the dock. I knew that we both needed a few hours apart to digest all that happened. I fired up the water heater, filled the tub and began to scrub.

By the time I got everything wrung out and hung on the line, the wind had picked up, lifting the sheets and shirts and nightgowns in a frenzied dance. Good, I thought. It will all be dry by the end of the day.

I made the troopers some tuna sandwiches and tomato soup for lunch. Thanks to Marcus I had very little that was fresh on hand, but at least my canned goods had survived. I sat down in the afternoon to inventory what was left and make a shopping list to take to Edgartown the next morning. We could eat some of Tobias' catch for supper.

I was taking in the laundry in the late afternoon when I saw the storm clouds, thick and rolling up from the southwest. By the time I had grabbed the last of the sheets the rain had begun—heavy drops pelting the water of the bay so hard it looked like it was boiling. The troopers had dashed for the covered porches—one in the front and one in the back by the kitchen.

I watched the storm from the shelter of the dining room as I folded the laundry. I wasn't worried. Tobias was an experienced sailor and had probably pulled into a cove to wait out the storm. But still I watched, waiting for the reassurance of his familiar sail.

Chapter Fourteen
Redemption
Tobias

He hadn't realized how much he needed to be out on the water alone until he was out of sight of land. The oppressive days in jail; the boredom, uncertainty and unveiled disapproval at Sadie's; and then the evidence of Marcus' uncontained rage at Mae's had stretched his endurance to its limits. He believed Mae was safe with the troopers guarding her. He had to believe it or he wouldn't have left. He needed to think without the tug of her encompassing presence. Her fragrance, her intensity, her eyes, always piercing and observant, all pulled at him in ways that kept him from facing the difficult choices now confronting him.

Despite Henry's assurances and the unexpected support of the fishermen, Tobias was skeptical that he would ever be free of Marcus' vendetta. The Vineyard was too small to hide if someone was after you; but hiding was not an option for Tobias. Neither was running away. Mae had been painfully right. Chappy was who Tobias was—his heritage, his world, the sacred land of his people. But in staying, how would he protect Mae? The troopers couldn't guard her forever. If it were only himself, he would defy Marcus. In the past, once Hannah was gone, he'd had nothing to lose. But now, Marcus had a way to hurt him, as he had already, through Mae.

He baited his nets methodically as he relived the past week in his mind. Although he was a man filled with regret for not being able to help and ultimately save his wife, he had no regret for his relationship with Mae. He had been the pursuer. He did not deny that responsibility. But was Mae sorry she had opened her heart and her past to him? She had been withdrawn ever since their return to Innisfree. No wonder! He chided himself. Everything she had worked to build over the past two years had been pulled down by a vengeful old man. It was no surprise to Tobias that she had made no objection when he told her he needed to get out and fish.

He loved her. From the moment she had welcomed him at the Boat House that foggy night last spring. Her frankness, her strength, her independence, her vulnerability when she finally allowed him into her heart and her bed. How could he leave her when her presence was the only thing that had brought him happiness since Hannah died? How could he stay, when to do so threatened everything she had worked for?

He leaned his head in his hands, eyes closed against the pain as the net drifted behind the boat.

By the time the net was heavy with blues the sun had disappeared, obliterated by massive black clouds driven by a furious wind. He hauled in the net, dumped the catch into the hold and raised the sails as the rain began to pelt him.

The sea was churning, the waves pushed higher and higher by a mounting wind. The visibility was barely a few feet as the clouds formed an oppressive barrier around him. He was soaked and physically miserable. It only compounded his mental anguish. He'd been at sea in storms like this before. He didn't relish this type of sailing, but he knew what to do. He kept his focus on the task and let go of the conflict tearing him apart. This was no time for thinking of anything but keeping the boat afloat and pointed in the direction of home.

Years of sailing had honed his reactions to the level of instinct. Every sense, every muscle, was attuned to the changes on the sea. So when he heard the sound he knew it was a man's shout and not the howling of the wind.

His eyes scanned the water for the source. He finally saw the overturned hull off to his left, barely visible and sinking quickly. Clinging to it, without a life vest, was the man whose voice Tobias had heard.

He maneuvered his own boat toward the other vessel, trying to get as close as possible without capsizing himself. He bent down to grab a line that he could throw to the drenched and exhausted sailor. When he lifted his arm to toss the rope and the other man turned to catch it, their eyes flashed with recognition.

Marcus lunged with one hand for the rope and missed, but still held onto the hull. Tobias pulled the rope in and threw it again without hesitation. This time Marcus grabbed it, tied it around his waist and pulled himself toward Tobias as Tobias maneuvered away from the capsizing boat and its potential to draw him down with it.

Marcus grabbed the edge of the boat with bleeding hands and Tobias reached to haul him over the rail. Marcus was a big man with the soft belly of someone who sits behind a desk, not a tiller. Whatever strength he had summoned to hold onto his hull was now spent, and he could not do anything more than put himself into the hands of the man he had intended to kill.

Tobias wondered fleetingly if Marcus would pull him overboard as he attempted to rescue him. But he saw the desperation and exhaustion etched on Marcus' face and made the decision to trust him. With all his strength he grabbed at the inert man and pulled him in. Marcus sprawled on the deck, vomited and crawled into a fetal position without a word.

Tobias slipped back to the tiller, tightened the sail and steered wide of the now barely visible hull. A break in the clouds gave him a glimpse of shoreline and he headed toward it, ignoring the lump of flesh huddled in the prow.

It was two rain-lashed hours before they reached the beach. Tobias dropped the anchor, hauled down the sail. Marcus had neither moved nor spoken since his rescue.

"Can you walk?" Tobias shouted to be heard above the wind.

Marcus opened his eyes and raised his head to peer over the rail.

"Where are we?"

"East Beach," Tobias answered, pointing toward the lighthouse beacon intermittently flashing to the north. "Come on, I'll help you ashore." He reached out to the shivering, disoriented man whom he barely recognized as his arrogant and vengeful nemesis.

Tobias felt only pity, despite his suspicion that Marcus had been out on the Sound today with the sole intention of evading the state troopers and coming after Tobias again.

He struggled to support Marcus as they sloshed through the shallows and climbed onto the pebble-strewn beach.

"Leave me here." Marcus attempted to push Tobias away, but fell to his knees on the sand.

Marcus had given up. He wanted to be left on the beach to die, not to escape from whatever awaited him with the law. There was a desperation about him that Tobias recognized. He had felt it himself when Hannah had died.

"I'm not going to leave you to die, Marcus. We've both suffered enough because of Hannah's death, and I have no intention of adding your death to my pain."

"Why didn't you leave me out there when you realized it was me?"

"I'm not a killer, Marcus. No matter what you think. I didn't kill Hannah by leaving her. I didn't kill that soldier who drowned. And I'm not going to let you die. Now get up. Mae's cottage is not far beyond the dunes. We both need dry clothes and a stiff drink."

Marcus stared at him. "I wanted to kill you. Why, knowing that, would you let me live? I could still try to kill you."

"I don't think so, Marcus. I finally understand what has driven you all these years and I don't hate you for it. I forgive you. And that frees me."

Marcus rose from the sand and Tobias once again reached out his hand to him.

"I don't understand."

"Maybe you will after you've dried off and had that drink."

Tobias put his arm under Marcus and led him across the beach and the meadow to Mae's. By the time they reached the house the rain had stopped.

Chapter Fifteen
Hannah

I'd been watching the bay for Tobias' boat but the clouds were so thick it was impossible to see anything beyond a few feet. It was a shout from the trooper on the porch that turned my attention to the other side of the house and the two limping figures making their way across the meadow.

We all ran out toward them, my feet flying over the sodden grass when I saw it was Tobias. I didn't recognize the other man until I was within arm's reach. He looked nearly dead, his face ashen and his eyes unfocused.

"I think he's in shock," Tobias croaked and handed the barely identifiable Marcus into the troopers' arms.

Then he pulled me toward him and held me in an embrace that was relief, want, acceptance.

"I think it's over," he murmured into my ear.

I kissed him through my tears and then we followed the others back to the house.

The men got Marcus out of his soaked clothes and wrapped him in blankets while I heated some soup. One of the troopers had radioed to the hospital that they would be coming in with a man in shock and suffering from exposure. The operator cautioned that a second front had formed in the storm and the Coast Guard station had ordered all craft to seek shelter.

"It's kicking up to a hurricane," I heard the raspy voice through the crackling of the radio.

“Looks like no one is going anywhere tonight. Our relief crew can’t get out here and we can’t leave,” the senior trooper said as he came into the kitchen.

“I’m sorry, Miss Keaney. I’m sure it’s not easy for you to have Judge Gardner under your roof. At least he’s too ill to pose a threat, but we’ll keep watch over him.”

“I’m not afraid for myself, Sergeant. But is he going to be all right?”

Marcus Gardner was not exactly welcome in my house, but I didn’t want him to die here.

“Once he’s warmed up and had some of your soup the effects of his time in the water should recede. He’s lucky it’s September and not April.”

I poured some of the steaming soup into a bowl and carried it to the parlor, where Marcus was stretched out on the sofa buried in my quilts. The shivering and muttering had ceased, but he still looked half-dead to me.

I set the tray down. It was clear he wasn’t capable of picking up a spoon and getting it safely to his mouth. I looked around, but the men seemed to have disappeared. Tobias had gone back to the beach to secure the boat when he heard the radio report about the hurricane. The sergeant had gone to the privy and the other trooper was down at the dock checking on their boat.

So much for protecting me. But Tobias had assured me that Marcus Gardner had lost his power over us. Not because he was weakened by his near-drowning but because Tobias had saved him. As we had made our way back from the meadow to the house earlier, Tobias had told me of his internal battle when he realized it was Marcus clinging to the overturned boat. At that moment Tobias had understood the bond he and Marcus shared in their despair over Hannah's death.

"I realized I could never expect Marcus' forgiveness if I couldn't forgive myself. I told him that. I think he faced something himself out on the water. Whether he accepted my words or not, I know I'm free of Marcus."

I hadn't been out on the water, so I was hesitant to believe that Marcus didn't have the desire to hurt Tobias or me. I doubted his physical strength at that moment, but in my experience a man doesn't lose a lifetime of arrogance and anger because he's a little waterlogged.

Nevertheless. As I said, I didn't want him to die in my house. I sat down by the sofa, filled a spoon with soup and lifted it to his mouth.

"Mr. Gardner, can you swallow some soup? It will help warm you."

His eyes fluttered open and took a minute to focus.

"Where am I?"

"You're in my house, Mr. Gardner. Safe. But you need to eat to get your strength back."

If not your mind, I thought.

He turned his head toward the wall.

"Go away."

"I'm not going to cajole you into swallowing this soup, Mr. Gardner. But I damn well will not allow you to die while you are in my house. Open your mouth."

He faced me again.

"You always have been a woman who speaks her mind, Mae Keaney."As soon as he had finished speaking, he closed his mouth firmly.

"As hard as I find it to believe, there are people in this world who love you and an island community that looks to you for leadership. You don't strike me as a man who wants to be known as a quitter, a man who disappoints those who depend on him."

He narrowed his eyes and appraised me.

"You are not one of those people who love me."

"No, I am not."

"And yet, you've taken me in and don't want me to die."

"My arm is getting tired of holding this spoon."

"You and your Indian are both the same. I don't understand you."

"You seem somewhat more coherent than when Tobias brought you in. Maybe you don't need this soup after all." I put the spoon back in the bowl and started to get up with the tray.

"Stay," he said, reaching for my wrist.

"Only if you intend to eat."

He propped himself up on one elbow.

"Give me the spoon. You don't have to feed me."

I handed him the bowl and the spoon and sat silently by his side. Neither of us spoke as he swallowed the warm liquid.

His eyes were focused on the bowl, concentrating on bringing the spoon to his lips without spilling. His hand shook noticeably.

"You remind me of my sister," he murmured between sips. "Not in temperament, but in looks."

That got my attention. I started to protest, "I'm not like Hannah at all," but I held my tongue and waited. Sadie's immediate dislike of me began to make sense in the light of Marcus' revelation. It wasn't just that I was a white woman, but a white woman who looked like Tobias' dead wife.

"When I first heard that it was you who had spoken up for Monroe and I realized you were his lover, I thought he was trying to replace my sister with a replica."

"Is that why you wrecked my place?" My voice was controlled, barely above a whisper. But Marcus' words had thrown me into turmoil. I told myself he was trying to manipulate me into thinking Tobias loved me because I reminded him of Hannah. But the words cut me. I was competing with a ghost who haunted both Marcus and Tobias.

"Other than your looks, you are everything that Hannah wasn't—strong-willed, independent, self sufficient. You don't *need* anyone the way

Hannah did. She was fragile, volatile." He pushed the soup away. "I hated you the minute I knew Tobias loved you."

""Do you still hate me?"

"I hate that you are alive and Hannah isn't. I hate that your face calls up my memories of her. I hate being reminded of my failure."

"Your failure?"

"I didn't protect her. From the time she was a child, even when our parents were alive, I was charged with looking out for her. In the beginning it was easy—hold her hand in the surf so the waves didn't drag her out, catch her when she climbed too high in the apple tree and couldn't get down. But when she turned sixteen and started drinking and attracting the attention of men, I couldn't stop her. She laughed at my rules, defied the curfews and locked doors. When she eloped with Monroe I broke off contact with her. I never spoke to her again, and didn't see her until I had to identify her body."

As I sat listening to him with the hurricane building around us, I realized that Marcus had been as tortured as Tobias by the guilt he felt. I saw a broken man in front of me, forced to face his demons when the sea was about to take him.

"Have you ever told anyone else?" I asked. I couldn't imagine his wife offering a sympathetic ear.

Marcus shook his head. "Never. But something happened out on the water. I was ready to die. I wanted to die. And then I understood what had driven Hannah into the sea that day at Katama."

"Despair," I said.

Marcus nodded.

"Why are you telling *me*?"

"Because I can forget I am talking to Mae Keaney. I am talking to Hannah."

I understood. I reached out and touched his clammy hand, his fingertips still wrinkled from the hours in the water.

"She heard you," I whispered.

A door slammed and the voices of the other men rumbled in the kitchen. I gathered up the tray and left Marcus to his memories.

I found three grim-faced men. Jim, the younger trooper, had a gash across his forehead that was bleeding into his eye.

I grabbed a towel and pressed it against the cut while they all spoke at once about what was happening outside. Debris was flying everywhere. Trees in the woods, already weakened by the fire in July, were being uprooted. The tide was surging and had already reached the dunes on East Beach and was washing over the Boat House dock.

"There's soup on the stove and a loaf of bread I baked this afternoon," I offered, once I had stemmed the blood from Jim's wound.

"How's the judge?"

"Awake and coherent. He ate." I didn't offer any more.

I joined the men in the dining room for supper and then made up beds for the troopers in the loft. The house shook in the roaring wind, but held tight during the long night. Innisfree is high enough on the promontory to be safe from flooding. It was the wind that was more of a danger to us than the sea.

The howling noise and my own unease at Marcus' words kept me from sleep. Tobias did not share my bed that night. He took a pillow and quilt and nested on the window seat in the alcove off the parlor by the front door.

Because I was awake, alert to every crack and shudder of the walls around me, I heard the moan immediately. My bedroom opens onto the parlor. I didn't know whose voice it was—Tobias or Marcus—because each of them had reason to be in pain.

I pulled on my robe and padded out to the parlor in my bare feet. I checked first around the alcove and saw that Tobias was sleeping soundly, his chest rising and falling in a deep, steady rhythm.

I turned to the sofa and knelt by Marcus' head. His face was beaded with sweat and he was muttering barely recognizable words. I felt his forehead. He was burning with fever. I rose and moved quickly to the kitchen, where I lit a lantern and filled a basin with water. I brought it to the sofa, wrung out a washcloth and mopped Marcus' fevered brow. He continued to mutter gibberish, tossing his head back and forth. Suddenly he opened his eyes and grabbed my wrist.

"Hannah! Hannah!" And then he started to sob.

I tried to pull his fingers away from my wrist so that I could continue to cool him down, but he held on fiercely, as if I were the spirit of Hannah, whom he could not bear to lose again.

I did not correct him. He was too delirious to believe that I wasn't Hannah, and I was too tired to fight his misperception. I switched the cloth to my free hand and placed the other hand, still encircled by Marcus' desperate fingers, on his chest. His breathing was shallow and his heart was racing. I was about to call out for help, when Marcus spoke again the midst of his sobs. This time his words were distinct, although barely above a whisper.

"Hannah, forgive me. Forgive me for abandoning you. Please" He begged. I believe if he had been strong enough, he would have thrown himself to his knees at my feet.

The fury I felt for this man welled up. All around me were the signs of his wanton destruction. In the alcove slept the man I loved, the man Marcus wanted to kill. I had the power in me at that moment to destroy Marcus Gardner because he thought I was his dead sister.

And then I felt a hand on my shoulder. Tobias was behind me, wordless, waiting, and I knew what I had to do.

"I forgive you, Marcus. I forgive you both, Tobias and you. Now rest. Get well. Don't fall into despair because of me."

His grip loosened on my wrist. I heard Tobias exhale the breath he had been holding.

I rose to face Tobias, and kissed away the tears on his cheeks.

Marcus' fever broke at dawn, just as the hurricane dwindled to a heavy but windless rain. He fell into a deep and apparently untroubled sleep. I didn't know how much he would remember of the night's events, but I hoped that the message of Hannah's forgiveness would linger deep in his heart.

I opened the front door to assess what the storm had wrought. On the horizon, across the pond and beyond the dunes, a thin sliver of dawn stretched along the eastern shore.

"First light," murmured Tobias behind me. He circled my waist with his arms and I leaned back into his chest.

A new beginning, I thought.

After breakfast the weather had subsided enough for the troopers to transport Marcus to the hospital in Vineyard Haven. They improvised a stretcher from a canvas deck chair and carried him down to the dock. The police boat had survived the hurricane with minimal damage and started up after a few sputtering misfires.

As he was lowered into the boat, Marcus turned to me and Tobias.

"Thank you. I owe you both my life."

And then they were gone.

Tobias and I walked back up to the house arm in arm.

"Come over to East Beach with me," he said, and we turned to cross the meadow. The waves were still high and white-capped, crashing with foam and force along the battered beach. Tobias took my hand as we stood staring out to sea.

"I should have told you how much you resembled Hannah, but I didn't want you to think that was why I wanted you. I wasn't sure myself at first, afraid that I was trying to recapture what I had lost. But it is *you* I love, Mae. Not some shadow of Hannah. I don't see a ghost, like Marcus did. I see *you*, Mae Keaney—strong, beautiful, loving and unafraid.

"Do you believe me?" He looked at me.

I saw reflected back in his eyes the woman he was describing. I saw myself, and realized it was not a fake Hannah who had forgiven Marcus and Tobias the night before. It had been me.

Chapter Sixteen
Sachem

After the hurricane, cold weather descended upon the island. I had little reason to open the Boat House, even after we had cleaned up the mess. All the summer people had packed up and left with the hurricane, and there was no point in replacing the broken windows until spring.

I had some unfinished business off-island before I settled in for the winter. I dropped the charges against Marcus for what he done to Innisfree and I made an appointment with a doctor in Falmouth to confirm what I suspected.

"You're pregnant, Mrs. Jones."

I had given a false name even though I was away from the Vineyard. This news was my business alone, to share or not as I absorbed it in my own time.

I left the doctor's office with a mixture of elation, awe and determination. I was no longer a frightened nineteen-year-old abandoned by a callow and selfish boy. I was loved. And as Tobias had described me that day on the beach after the hurricane, I was fearless.

I had errands to attend to before I returned to Chappy and I busied myself with shopping for items that I would need during the winter, when ice delayed or canceled the ferry.

I was picking through skeins of wool and rolls of soft flannel at the mercantile when a woman's voice broke through my reverie.

"Mae? I never expected to see you in a place like this. You don't strike me as someone interested in the domestic arts." The voice was brittle and familiar.

I looked up, erasing the secret smile that had graced my face since the doctor's confirmation earlier in the day.

"Hello, Sadie."

I hadn't seen her since that eventful week in September, although she and Ronnie had been to visit Tobias' family on Chappy in October for a harvest festival. I had stayed away—precisely because I didn't want to create a scene with Sadie in the presence of Tobias' family. I know Tobias was hurt that I wouldn't go, but the animosity that bristled between Sadie and me, even now in the middle of strangers in a store, assured me I had done the right thing to avoid her.

"I suppose you know that Tobias' father is dying." She flipped carelessly through a stack of remnants on the table between us.

Please God, I prayed silently. Don't let her notice that these are fabrics for baby clothes.

I nodded. "I'm sorry. I know he's been ill for a long time." Tobias had been spending most of his time with his father when he wasn't out fishing. He came to Innisfree for a few hours in the early morning before he went out on the Sounds.

"My aunt needs Tobias more than ever right now."

"Tobias knows that. He's there every day."

"The tribe is going to need him even more when my uncle passes. I know he's still seeing you, even though you didn't come to the festival. As long as you are in his life he's going to be straddling two worlds. I'm begging you to let him go."

Her last sentence was spoken without rancor. She really was begging me.

"Tobias needs to make the decision himself, Sadie."

"Don't think you can hold him by getting pregnant. The tribe won't accept that child as a Wampanoag with you as its mother." She was back to her adamant threats.

I kept my face impassive. I would *not* let her know she had wounded me, found the chink in my armor. I had to force my arms to stay at my side and not fold them protectively over my belly.

I gathered up the wool in my arms, nonincriminating colors that didn't scream "baby." I'd have to forgo the flannel for now. The last thing I wanted was for Sadie to rush to Tobias and claim that I was trying to trap him into marriage with a baby. I knew he wouldn't believe her. But I wanted to tell him when I was ready. His father's impending death was consuming him. I didn't know whether the news of a child—our child—would be a cause for celebration or concern, when he was so enmeshed in the needs of his family and, as Sadie reminded me, the tribe.

"I'll keep your words in mind, Sadie. I love Tobias and have no desire to burden him or trick him."

"If you love him, free him to do what he was meant to do."

"If you'll excuse me, I've got to finish my shopping and get back to the island." I moved toward the cash register in the front of the store. I wanted to get away from Sadie and the oppression her words had settled on me. The lightness and joy that the knowledge of my pregnancy had brought me in the morning had withered and faded, replaced by a gnawing worry.

I knew Sadie was obsessed with the viability of the tribe. Even though the Wampanoag had intermarried with islanders for generations, there was a growing belief among some of the younger members of the tribe, like Sadie, that they were losing their identity. I didn't believe her that Tobias' child would never be accepted as Wampanoag. Sadie might not, but I believed that Tobias' parents would welcome a grandchild from their only son. God willing, Tobias' father would live into the spring and hold this baby in his arms.

Nevertheless, I worried. Sadie could cause a rift between Tobias and his family, or Tobias and the tribe. Even though Tobias didn't agree with Sadie's extreme views, the tribe and his identity as a Wampanoag were important to him.

I finished my shopping and caught the bus to the ferry landing, leaving Sadie to glower in the fading November afternoon.

I tried to push her words out of my mind as I made the journey home, first in the warmth of the ferry and then in Frank Bennett's boat as he transported me to the Boat House dock with all my packages.

It was well after dark when I arrived, but a lamp was lit in the kitchen. Tobias often left his boat in the pond on the opposite side of the cottage rather than at the dock to forestall gossip. Knowing he was waiting for me at the cottage dispelled the pall Sadie's pronouncement had spread over my joy.

He opened the door as soon as I reached the porch and he lifted the packages from my arms. He said nothing as he deposited everything on the counter, but I could tell from his expression that this was more than an ordinary visit. My heart sank when I feared that Sadie had called his parents with her suspicions. They had installed a phone, one of the Chappy party lines, when Josiah had gotten ill so that they could summon an ambulance.

I kissed him and then drew back to question him.

"What are you doing here at this hour? Why aren't you with your father?"

"He died this afternoon. I needed to be with you, even for a little while."

I took him into my arms and held him.

"What can I do for you? A drink? Something warm to eat?"

"Just lie with me for a while and hold me."

I took him by the hand and led him to the bedroom. I sat him down on the side of the bed and took off his shoes. I slipped off my own, sat down next to him, and then drew him up into the bed, pulling the comforter over us.

For a long time we lay without moving or speaking. He didn't cry, just buried his face in my breast while I stroked his hair, which he had pulled loose from its binding. Like the mourners Ma had described from her Irish village who came to wakes to keen, their hair wild about their faces.

Finally he spoke.

"I thought I was ready for this. But even knowing how sick he was, how much he was suffering, I feel the blow as if he'd dropped dead suddenly of a heart attack, and I didn't have time to say goodbye."

"But you did say goodbye, in the best way you could, by being at his side every day these last few weeks." I thought of my own father. I didn't even know if he was still alive.

"He talked to me last night. He'd been silent for days, barely eating, just taking tiny sips of water. It was as if he knew his death was imminent."

"Do you want to talk about what he said?"

"He told me he was passing the oar to me. That it was time for me to take up the leadership of the tribe."

I grew very still, my hand no longer stroking him, just holding onto a strand of his dark hair.

"You'll be a great leader," I whispered to him, blinking back the tears stinging my eyes and sealing my fate.

Tobias didn't stay. He had promised his mother he'd spend the night with her and tend the bonfire that had been built and lit as soon as his father had passed.

"When is the funeral?" I asked, as he put on his shoes. "I'd like to come."

The hell with Sadie, I thought. I can at least do this for him before I let him go.

He looked at me. "I'd like that. It will be tomorrow, up island at the Indian church in Aquinnah." He used the Wampanoag name for the land the rest of the island called Gay Head. One night as we sat under a sky awash with the stars he told me the Wampanoag story of the giant Moshup, who shaped Noepe (their name for Martha's Vineyard) from the sea. It was a story this baby I was carrying would need to hear, as important as the Irish poetry I had learned as a child.

"I'll be back tomorrow to pick you up."

I walked him down the cliff steps to the pond with my lantern and watched as he glided across the still water and out to the Bay.

I did not sleep well. All the words I had heard that day replayed in my head. The doctor's straightforward announcement, Sadie's impassioned demand, Tobias' doubts as he told me of his father's dying wish. My certainty in the afternoon was seeping away with every reconsidered word. My choices and their consequences were troubling. Did I tell Tobias about the baby and hope that he would marry me? Did I tell him, but refuse to marry him so that he would take up the leadership of the tribe and be free to marry a Wampanoag woman? Did I not tell Tobias at all? That seemed the least likely option. I had no intention of giving up this baby. I would raise it myself if I must. But there was no way to keep the existence of the child a secret from Tobias, even if I were to push him away. The island was too small.

I had no answers. But I knew Tobias was too fragile to tell him anything now. He needed to decide whether to follow his father's wish and take up a role in the tribe without the complication of the baby. I knew he would turn away from the tribe if he learned I was carrying his child. His honor, his history with Hannah, would compel him to choose to stay with me.

And I wanted him desperately to stay with me. I had opened myself to love in a way I had once vowed never to do. I had defied the island's narrow-minded opinions to save him from prison, had placed myself in danger, and had risked everything I had built for him. Of course, I wanted him to turn away from the tribe and toward me, if the choice was as black and white as Sadie had presented.

But I knew I would keep my mouth shut for as long as it took Tobias to sort out his life. I only hoped it was before the baby was born.

I gave up on sleep and warmed some milk while I rummaged through my closet for something suitable to wear to a funeral. I pulled out my black suit and hung it on the porch to air out the smell of camphor from the mothballs. As I fingered the fabric I thought of the last time I had worn it in the city. Dinner with the married banker whose expensive presents had helped to finance my purchase of Innisfree. When I announced that I was leaving New York for good, his reaction had been a telling mix of pique and relief. The man was supposed to be the one who ended an affair. It bruised him that I was the one who was leaving. But the blow was softened by the knowledge that now I'd never demand that he leave his wife and marry me. It was all very civilized. He wished me well. I didn't tell him where I was going or that he had unwittingly helped me to get there with his bauble-filled boxes from Tiffany.

I bathed and plaited my hair into a single braid that I wrapped around my head. I didn't intend to wear it down my back the way I normally did. I wasn't trying to look like a Wampanoag woman.

When I put on the suit, I realized I couldn't button the skirt. I found a large safety pin to fasten the waist. The jacket had a peplum that would cover it. I stood in front of the mirror smoothing and tugging the jacket over my belly, hoping that the other mourners would be too distracted to pay attention to me. I didn't expect

Tobias to notice, but I wasn't sure about Sadie. It was cold enough to wear a coat over the suit and I resolved to keep it on as long as I could.

Tobias arrived at ten to pick me up. I had never seen him in a suit. It looked brand new, and fit his tall, lean frame in a way that made him look like a man of consequence. *Like a leader*, I thought.

We went to his house in Cove Meadow in his boat and then switched to his truck to drive across the island. We rode out to Aquinnah in silence. It's about as far from Chappy as one can get on the island, a world apart. When we arrived at the church a large gathering of tribal members was clustered around a tall, composed woman who was looking over their heads, clearly searching for someone.

"My mother," Tobias said quietly as her eyes found him and he nodded.

"You should be with her. Go. I'll be here, but in the background. Now is not the moment to introduce me." It might never be.

I watched him move through the crowd toward his mother, stopping along the way to take the extended hands and bend his ear to the murmured condolences. Except at Sadie and Ronnie's house, I had never seen him among his own people.

He meant something important to them. Everyone reached out to touch him, to get close to him. His mother was on the other side of the crowd, watching his approach as closely as I was.

In the midst of her sorrow and loss, her fierce pride in her son communicated itself in the expression on her face.

He embraced his mother and then gave her his arm. Together they entered the church.

"Do you understand now who he is?"

The voice was directly behind me. I thought I would have had more sensitive antennae by now, able to detect Sadie before she pounced on me. I was glad I had chosen to wear a hat with a short veil that covered my eyes. It camouflaged both the tears and the anger welling up within me. Tears for my recognition of Tobias' role here, a role from which I was excluded; and anger at Sadie's uncanny ability to get under my skin. I wasn't going to admit anything to her.

"I think the service is about to begin." I followed the rest of the group up the shallow steps to the sanctuary.

I'm not sure what I expected from the service—perhaps some unfamiliar ritual that the Wampanoag had been practicing for thousands of years as they buried their dead.

But it turned out to be a Baptist church and a very simple Christian funeral. I sat in the last row, unwilling to have Sadie hanging over my shoulder with her never-ending message of my status as an outsider. But she moved ahead of me with Ronnie at her side to what I assumed was a place of honor with the family at the front. Every seat was filled in the nine rows of worn pews in the tiny church. Josiah Monroe's casket stood in the center aisle.

From the back of the church I could see that I was the only white person in attendance. The Baptist funeral was familiar enough—passages from Proverbs and the Psalms; a wheezing organ to accompany a small choir of women; a sermon from a white-haired pastor who extolled Josiah's exemplary life and warned us that death and God's judgment awaited us all.

The thin November light filtered through the square, unadorned windows. Despite its simplicity and barrenness by the Catholic standard of gilded saints and stained-glass windows that had surrounded me as a child, I felt at home amidst this community that had come together to see Josiah home with genuine affection.

When the service ended I was one of the last to file out of the church. Tobias, supporting his mother with a protective arm, met my eyes as he walked past me behind his father's coffin.

Outside the church, people were organizing for the trip back to Chappy, where Josiah would be buried in the Wampanoag cemetery. Sadie and Ronnie found me on the steps.

"Tobias asked us to give you a ride to the cemetery," Ronnie explained. "He needs to take his mother and uncle, and there's no more room in his truck."

I understood, and climbed into the back seat of their car for the long drive. None of us attempted conversation, for which I was grateful.

Once we were across the harbor and on Chappy the cortege turned onto North Neck. As children, we'd explored every inch of the terrain there, but had always skirted around the Wampanoag burial ground. Ghost stories told around bonfires on the beach had always included at least one about the Indian cemetery, and we knew better than to provoke ghosts. As a result, I'd never set foot on this peaceful, hidden place overlooking the bay. It was on this tree-dotted hillside, where all the gravestones faced the southwest, that I sensed a shift from the traditional Christian rite that the congregation had been observing within the walls of the simple white church. The mourners parted for an elderly man, his black suit now covered with a worn deerskin mantle that flowed over his shoulders as if molded to him. The back was decorated with beads. His head was banded with a strip of leather, also beaded. He began a chant as he circled the grave, first in a strange tongue that I assumed was the Wampanoag language, and then in English.

"Our brother Josiah has entered into the cycle of life. We commend his body to the earth as we plant our seeds, knowing that his spirit will find renewal in the afterlife just as our corn rises up in the spring after the death of winter."

Before the coffin was lowered into the ground, Tobias handed his mother a fishing rod, a brilliant orange and gold fishing fly and a canvas knapsack, and she wrapped them carefully in a bundle that she placed inside the casket. Beyond the grave was a pile of dry wood—kindling and driftwood. At the foot of the pyre was a thick branch topped with an oil-soaked rag.

Tobias lit the rag and then moved around the pyre, setting it ablaze. He stood back from the flames, but they cast a glow on his face that accentuated the planes of high cheekbones. Pinpoints of light from the mounting flames were reflected in his dark eyes. He was not dressed as the shaman in deerskin, he wore no feathers on his head. But there was no mistaking that the man who stood over his father's grave, who had helped his mother prepare a prayer bundle containing symbols of his father's life, and who had lit the final bonfire, was a Wampanoag honoring a sacred tradition.

Murmurs of approval were rippling through the mourners. I heard snatches of whispered conversations.

"We haven't seen a ritual like this in a generation."

"Too much has been lost in the dilution of the tribe. So many leaving the island and severing the bonds of community."

"Josiah led the tribe as best he could, but we've been losing ground for generations—both literally, in the shrinking of the land that belongs to us, and in the loss of our young people to the war and jobs off-island."

"Naomi and Josiah raised that boy not just to lead the tribe, but to save it."

Across from me I saw Sadie, staring at Tobias as if he were the messiah of her people, and I understood with both exhilaration and extraordinary pain, that, indeed, he was.

I slipped away from the grave and found a stone wall that was not too overgrown with brambles. I was exhausted, both from a sleepless night and the crushing fatigue of early pregnancy. But I was also struggling with what I had just witnessed and its meaning for my relationship with Tobias.

I thought back to my first encounters with him, well before I had come to love him. Winter dawns on East beach, his stillness and reverence extending itself out to reach even me, a lapsed Catholic whose anger at God had me sometimes flailing with rage. The aftermath of the fire, when he knelt to express gratitude to the earth. The deliberateness of his hunting and harvesting, when he helped me in the garden. Everything he did was with a sense of oneness with nature. Even our lovemaking was tinged with awe and wonder for the gift of the body.

How could I keep him from fulfilling the purpose he was meant to carry out? I knew I was mourning and keening within myself for this unfathomable loss, and I needed to get away.

I looked around and was surprised to see another white face, hovering on the periphery of the mourners still circling the grave.

"What brings you here, Marcus?"

"I knew Naomi and Josiah. They were Hannah's in-laws, after all.

"Of course," I said. "I'm sorry for your loss."

"They were good people. They were kind to Hannah."

I was going to ask him where Hannah was buried, but I thought better of it. I wondered if Tobias visited her grave and if he had lit a bonfire or buried her with her most prized possessions.

The crowd of mourners was moving down the hill away from the grave. Thin wisps of smoke drifted away from the remains of the fire, carrying bits of ash over the moor toward the sea.

Tobias was still at his mother's side at the edge of the grave. Since our eyes had connected at the church we had not spoken to one another.

"Marcus, might you be heading back to Edgartown?"

"I am. Do you need a ride?"

"I'd appreciate it, if it's not too much trouble."

I could not bring myself to break the solitude and solemnity I saw in Tobias' posture at the grave. I had no place there, and turned with Marcus toward the road without even a gesture of good-bye.

On the drive back to Edgartown neither Marcus nor I referred to the troubled night he had spent at Innisfree. Each of us was buried in thought and I was grateful for the silence as well as the ride.

"How do you intend to get back to your place?" he asked when I indicated he could drop me off at the harbor after we had crossed over on the ferry.

"Frank Bennett is usually around to run me back." I waved him off.

He nodded, skeptical but apparently relieved that I could manage from this point. I imagine it was not easy for him to be confronted so directly with the reminder of Hannah that I presented. It was not easy for me, either. Before he left me, however, he had something to say.

"Mae, I'm grateful to you for dropping the charges. I already owed you my life, but now I also owe you my dignity." He didn't wait for me to respond, but drove off.

Frank's boat was bobbing near the ferry landing, so I knew he was around. It was too cold to wait at the dock, so I scribbled a note to him that I'd be up at the Captain's Table and stuck it by the tiller.

The Captain's Table was warm and noisy, the clatter of lunch platters being set on tables and the buzz of voices in conversation enveloping me as I opened the door.

I was famished as well as exhausted and more than happy to have someone else do the cooking for me. I slipped into a booth near the front windows so I could keep an eye out for Frank. I was biting into my BLT, my eyes closed momentarily to savor the aroma of thick bacon and well-made mayonnaise, and did not see the tall, somber man in the black suit who entered the restaurant and quietly took the seat opposite me.

"Why did you leave?"

My eyes flew open. I swallowed and put down the sandwich. I heard in his question not just "why did you leave the cemetery?" but "why did you leave *me*?" It was as if he already sensed the decision that had been forming in my head for weeks and been starkly confirmed by what I had witnessed that morning at the funeral. He knew I was leaving him.

"I didn't belong there. I'm not your family. I'm not your people."

"It was Sadie, wasn't it? Pushing you away with her fanatic ideas about tribal purity."

"She never used those words. But it wasn't Sadie at all. It was you."

"Me? When have I ever pushed you away? I *wanted* you at the funeral. I *needed* you there."

"I'm glad I was there for you at that moment, but the moment has passed." I could feel my voice tightening as I forced myself to say things my head knew I must but my heart fought with a mounting sense of pain and loss.

"Something happened to you at the cemetery, Tobias, that had nothing to do with Sadie and everything to do with you and your father."

I saw the flicker of recognition in his eyes. He had to have felt what I and everyone surrounding the grave had seen. Even if he was not ready to accept it.

My voice was gentle, not forceful, although it took all my emotional strength to get the words out.

"You became the sachem the moment you lit the torch. You took on your father's mantle, even though no deerskin covered your shoulders, no bead and feathers adorned your head."

"The sachem has to be elected by the tribe, and approved by the matriarchs."

"Not a single person who witnessed your actions today at the graveside would oppose you. I heard the ripples moving through the crowd. You are the tribe's hope, Tobias. It's future."

"What about *our* future?"

His voice was gruff, demanding, and yet reeling with pain. As if he knew the answer but was going to fight against it with as much energy as I was expending.

"You know the answer, even though you don't want to hear it. The only way you can lead the tribe on the path you set this morning is without me."

"If I'm the leader, I can make them accept you."

"If you make them accept me, you will not be their leader."

"I love you."

"I love you, too. But we have both lived through too much to know that love is not enough. That sometimes destiny supersedes love."

"You are my destiny."

I shook my head. "You once enumerated the reasons you love me—for my forthrightness and grit, among them. I'm going to be the woman you love, not pretend to be someone else. I cannot beg you to give up what I know you are meant to be. As much as my heart is shattering, I cannot ask you to stay. I would not be true to myself and I would not be true to you."

We looked at each other across the table. Throughout the conversation neither one of us had reached out for the other. I had not expected to have this discussion in such a public place, but in retrospect it was the right place. Had we been able to embrace, I do not believe I could have sent him away.

He stood up, pushing down on the table with his strong hands. A faint trace of ash limned his fingertips. He leaned across, putting his face inches from mine.

"You have helped me find my better self; I don't want to lose it again."

"You won't," I assured him.

And then he left.

I pushed away the half-eaten sandwich, the bacon now cold and congealed, the lettuce limp. I had lost my appetite, and I wanted to go home.

I left the money for my meal on the table, pulled on my coat and went to the harbor. There was no sign of Tobias and I was relieved. If I had seen him, I would have run into his arms and never let him go.

Frank was approaching his boat from the opposite end of Dock Street and I waved to get his attention. When we were finally under way I huddled in the back of the boat, clamping my hat to my head as we sped across the bay.

The next few nights at Innisfree were the most difficult I had ever faced there. Not even in my earliest days had I felt so alone, when the enormity of what I had done in buying the place and the strangeness of this wild land had confronted me. Back then, I had nothing to lose, no one whom I had left behind with regret. Now, safely beyond the painful conversation with Tobias, I could allow myself the full measure of my grief.

My usual tactics for coping with distress failed me. I was too exhausted by the pregnancy to throw myself into the frenzy of housework, and even if I had had the energy, there was little to do in November. The garden had been harvested and its bounty already preserved in rows of Mason jars stacked in multicolor arrays in my pantry. The Boat House had been scrubbed and sealed off for the winter since the hurricane. My house was tidy.

I found myself sitting for hours at the dining room table staring out at the water. Some days the sun would set and I'd shake myself from a daze, unaware of how long I'd been there, waiting for a boat I knew would not be coming.

Part of me was relieved that Tobias did not come, did not try to dissuade me from my decision. I continued to be afraid that if he did come, I would not be able to be as strong as I had been the day of the funeral. The further I got from my experience of Tobias at his father's grave, the weaker my conviction that I had done the right thing in freeing him.

I slept. I ate. Ravenously. One thing I did not forget was that I was carrying a baby.

It snowed on the fifth of December. I roused myself enough to shovel a path to the chicken coop and the activity stirred the neglected corners of my being. I gathered the eggs and returned to the house, stomping on the porch to loosen the snow clinging to my boots. After breakfast I searched the linen closet and found the bag from the mercantile with the wool and flannel I had put away unused. It was time to get ready for this child. That day, instead of staring out to sea, I cast on 120 stitches and began to knit a baby blanket.

Chapter Seventeen
Adeste Fidelis

The week before Christmas, Frank Bennett came to fetch me for what was in winter my monthly trip to Edgartown. At the post office I discovered an invitation from Betty Furman, the waitress at the Vineyard Haven Inn, to spend Christmas with her. After my weeks of isolation, I burst into tears with gratitude and called her immediately to accept.

"Wonderful! Can you stay for a few days?" she asked. I could hear the smile in her voice, and assured her that I would.

On the morning of Christmas Eve, Frank made the second trip that month out to Innisfree and brought me to Vineyard Haven. I had baked loaves of date-nut bread rich with pecans and molasses and butter for both him and Betty.

She threw open the door of her cottage with a flourish and enveloped me in a hug.

"I don't know how you do it, out there all by yourself. It's not the life for me. I need to be surrounded by hubbub and other human bodies. I'm so glad you agreed to come!"

She helped me off with my coat and showed me to her cozy parlor. A fire was glimmering in the hearth and a small Christmas tree sat on a table in the corner. I went to it and touched a woven straw star that hung from one of the branches. There were several more, all different.

"My German Oma brought those ornaments from the old country fifty years ago."

"They're lovely."

"Come, you must be famished and freezing after that ride in Frank Bennett's open boat. I've made some soup for lunch."

We settled into a companionable afternoon. Betty was one of the few women on the island who accepted me without judgment and it was a comfort, beyond the warmth and hospitality, to sink into her exuberant embrace. She was full of island gossip and mordant observation.

"People eating dinner at the Inn seem to leave their brains at the dining room door. For some unfathomable reason, they believe that the waitstaff has neither eyes nor ears. Or rather, we become invisible as they play out their little dramas at the table. It's more entertaining than the summer playhouse."

I laughed, for what felt like the first time in months.

In the evening, after a hearty German dinner of sauerbraten and red cabbage, Betty asked me to go to church with her.

"There's a midnight mass at St. Augustine's. Will you come with me?"

I hesitated. I hadn't been to church since the nuns had refused to baptize my daughter.

Betty saw me wavering.

"It's been a while, I'd guess. An Irish lass like you must have grown up in the church. I understand. My own family was devout, too, and as soon as I could, I stopped going to Mass. But now that I'm older, I find myself longing for the familiar comfort of Latin prayers, incense and the lives of the saints. Come. Even if it's just to keep me company on a cold winter night."

I gave in, and we bundled up in coats and scarves and boots and walked arm-in-arm down the street to the church.

The building appeared dark and empty, but when Betty pulled me inside I could see the outline of bodies in the pews and hear the murmur of anticipation. Betty handed me a small unlit candle and led me to a side pew where there were still open seats. A few minutes later a light flamed on the altar and a single *a capella* voice began the "Adeste Fidelis." The single candle flame became two and then began floating down the center aisle, each one lighting the candle of the first person in the row at each pew. The candle flame was passed from one hand to another along the rows until the entire church was ablaze in candlelight.

The choir and the organ joined the single voice as the last candle was lit and the entire congregation soared in song. I sang at the top of my lungs, the familiar Latin words rushing back despite their absence for so many years.

It was then that I felt it. A vigorous kick pushing out from my belly as if it wanted to dance to the joyous music surrounding us. I gasped and placed my hand where I had felt the kick.

"Are you OK?" Betty asked, concern etched on her face. She had been singing with as much spirit as I had, but she hadn't missed the sudden change in me.

I smiled and nodded my head. "Just some gas from the cabbage," I reassured her.

The rest of the Mass was a blur as I half-listened to the nativity Gospel while also waiting intently for another kick, another sign of hope that my baby was alive and well.

The next morning Betty and I opened gifts from one another in our nightgowns and bathrobes and then made French toast and bacon together in her tiny kitchen.

Sticky with maple syrup and lingering over a second cup of tea, we sat at her table by a window that overlooked the harbor. It had begun to snow, great thick flakes that first drifted lazily over the empty streets and then began to fall in earnest, driven by a northeast wind.

"Mac, are you pregnant?" Betty had never been one to sidle up to a conversation.

I put down my cup.

"Is it so obvious?" I asked, looking down at my belly.

"Only to someone who knows you well. Your angularity isn't as sharp-edged as it used to be. You're softer looking, with a fullness to your face I don't remember seeing in the fall. How far along are you?" she asked gently.

"About four months."

"That was the baby quickening last night, wasn't it?"

I nodded. "How did you know?"

"I've given birth to two babies."

"Where are they now?"

"Oh, grown and off into the world. My son is a Marine. My daughter is teaching in Worcester."

"You don't look old enough to have adult children!"

"I started young. Too young!" She tossed aside my compliment. "But what about you? What about the baby's father?"

It was foolish to think that no one would eventually question me about my growing pregnancy. *Just be grateful it's Betty*, I told myself.

"Have you told him?"

My eyes filled with tears.

"I can't."

"Oh, God. Is he married?"

I shook my head.

"Is he dead?"

"No!"

"Then why can't you tell him? Or do you not love him, is that it?"

"I love him as I've never loved anyone else in my life. But if I tell him, he will turn away from the path he should be on. It will destroy his future."

"But what about your future? What about your baby's future? Mae, let's stop talking as if this were a fairy tale about a knight on a quest for the Holy Grail—his 'path,' his almighty 'future.'

Who is he, that you feel you have to sacrifice your happiness for his?"

I couldn't blame Betty for being so direct and practical. It was why I liked her. I wiped my eyes. I realized how desperately lonely I'd been and how much I needed to talk about the baby.

"It's Tobias Monroe."

A spark of recognition lit up Betty's eyes.

"Of course. The Wampanoag you defended; the reason Marcus Gardner wrecked your place. But what is so important about his future that you and his baby can't be part of it?"

"He can't be sachem if he marries me."

"I thought the Wampanoag on the island have been marrying outside the tribe for generations."

"They have. It's just that there's a rising sentiment among the younger members of the tribe that they need to preserve and protect the Wampanoag identity. Tobias' cousin Sadie is one of the leaders. Tribal succession flows through the women of the tribe, the mothers."

"Didn't Tobias have a white wife before? Marcus' sister, right? So why can't he now? What's changed?"

"When Tobias' father died, it was as if something possessed him, filled him with the spirit of his ancestors. He became the sachem right before the eyes of the tribe. Everyone saw it. *I* saw it. That's when I knew I couldn't stand in his way. The sachem can't have a white wife if his line is going to continue."

"Oh, honey!" Betty got up and put her arms around me. "Now that I understand, let's figure out *your* future."

"I've been so numb since I left Tobias. I haven't been able to think beyond getting through the day."

"Well, that's going to change in a few months. First, you can't stay out at Pogue by yourself as you get closer to term. You need to be in town. You can stay here for as long as you need."

"Oh, Betty, I couldn't impose on you like that. Besides, I don't really want a lot of people to know I'm pregnant."

"Are you going to give the baby up for adoption?"

The searing memory of my last pregnancy sliced through me.

"No! I'm going to raise this child on my own. I *won't* give it up."

"Then you have to tell Tobias. As soon as he learns about the baby—and you know he will—he'll know it's his and he'll feel betrayed. You can't make the decision for him whether to give up his role in the tribe or be with you and his child. You, of all people, should understand that."

I knew Betty was right, and I felt chastened.

"That's what happens when you live alone inside your own head. Nobody else is there to speak the truths you don't want to hear."

I reached across the table and squeezed her hand. "Thanks, Betty."

"I know you would have figured it out for yourself. I just pushed you along a little faster, that's all. Now, why don't we get dressed and go for a walk. I've browbeaten you enough."

The snow had stopped and the entire town was shimmering in the pale winter light. Since most people were busy celebrating Christmas, almost nothing had been shoveled or plowed. Betty and I tromped a path through the snow down to the ferry landing and stood at the railing watching the sea.

"I don't know how to begin to tell Tobias. I haven't seen him since his father's funeral."

"Why not stop at his place on your way back to Pogue? Doesn't he live on the other side of the bay, near Tom's Neck?

"I don't really want Frank Bennett to bring me there."

"It can be reached by the road. I could loan you my bike, and the next time you're in town you could return it. If you wait a few days most of the snow on the roads will be gone and you can pedal to the Chappy ferry. The Vineyard Haven-Edgartown bus will let you bring a bike and can take you as far as the Edgartown harbor. Do you think you can manage to pedal a few miles?"

I smiled at her. "I'm not *that* pregnant yet. I think I can still maintain my balance. You have it all figured out, don't you? Whatever obstacle I can imagine to stop me or at least postpone this conversation with Tobias, you have an answer ready."

She smiled back. "I know this is hard for you, Mae, and scary. You don't know how he's going to react. You don't even know how you *want* him to react. But believe me, the sooner you tell him, the better."

Three days later the sun was shining and a slight thaw had cleared most of the main roads of snow. Betty had packed up a basket of food for me to take to Tobias—ham and biscuits and potato salad, along with a couple of bottles of beer. I started out early, and reached the Edgartown harbor before noon. The ferry was on the Chappy side, but I hailed it and it made its way across the mouth of the harbor to pick me up.

The ferryman was a stranger, which was a relief. We made the brief journey back to Chappy without conversation. I pushed the bike off the ramp and pedaled down the main road. All around me was the silence and stillness of a Chappaquiddick winter. Very few houses fronted the road; most were set back in the woods at the end of long drives, and I was alone for the first time in nearly a week. As much as I had appreciated the solace and companionship of Betty, Chappy was where I belonged. I breathed in its peace as I pedaled.

But as I turned onto the road that led to Cove Meadow, the peace fled and I faltered. The road was rutted and still snow-covered in patches, and I could see the tire tracks left by what was probably Tobias' pickup truck. I climbed down from the bike and began to push it, my confidence in what I was about to do ebbing with every turn of the wheels.

I reached his driveway and hoped that the truck would not be there, so that I could turn around and head back to the ferry and forget this whole foolish errand.

But the truck was parked next to the house and smoke was drifting out of the chimney. I steeled myself, leaned the bike against the house, picked up the basket, found my courage and climbed the stairs to the porch.

Silence met my knock and I thought with foolish relief that he might be out on his boat. But then I heard footsteps and forced myself to stay on the porch until the door opened.

"Mae." He spoke my name without emotion—no warmth, no surprise, no questioning.

"Hello, Tobias. May I come in?"

He held open the door silently. Watchful. Wary.

I couldn't blame him. Had I expected him to take me in his arms and welcome me with the passion we had shared before I had turned away from him, sent him out of my life?

I awkwardly put the basket on the kitchen table.

"I brought you some lunch."

"That's certainly not what brought you all the way out here."

"No." I shook my head. "I came because I have something important to tell you."

"I thought you said all you wanted to say back in November. There's more?"

I could not read the darkness in his eyes. Anger? Pain? How was I going to do this?

"May I sit down? It was a long way from the ferry and I tire more easily than I used to."

He pulled out a chair for me and I shrugged out of my coat. I searched his face for any sign of the love he had once had for me, but it was a blank. With despair, I remembered it was the face he wore when he had been arrested and accused of murder—a barrier between him and those who threatened him. Was I now his enemy?

He waited on the other side of the table, clearly unwilling to help me get the words out. I saw no way to ease gently into this conversation—no inquiries about his health or his mother's; no curiosity about whether he had, indeed, taken on the leadership of the tribe.

I plunged in, keeping my eyes on his face. "I'm pregnant with our child."

For the first time since I had arrived, he reacted with more than stony silence. He lifted his head with a sharp intake of breath.

I waited. There was nothing more I could say, except perhaps, "I love you with my whole heart and soul and will love this child as well, whether you acknowledge it or not." But I remained silent. Tobias knew my history. He knew I had said those same words to another man who had rejected both me and my baby.

And then, out of the silence, arose a moan that seemed to come from the depths of his being. I had heard it from him before, not in mourning for his father, but in our lovemaking. He buried his face in his hands and shook with sobs.

I sat frozen for a moment, stunned. Of all the responses I had anticipated, this was not one of them.

Without thinking, I rose from the table and moved to his side. I reached out to stroke his head and he turned toward me, embracing me and pressing his face against my belly. His sobs eventually quieted, but he remained there, as if listening for the heartbeat in my womb. I don't know how long we stayed like that, holding each other, communicating all the longing and loss we had experienced in that wordless embrace.

Finally he stood and took my face in his hands. He kissed me. I could taste the salt of his tears on my lips. Then he whispered in my ear.

"I know we need to talk. But first, I need to make love to you."

"Yes," I managed to answer him before he lifted me in his arms and carried me to his bed.

He made love to me with great tenderness, a counterpoint to the raw force that had driven him the last time we had made love, after the hurricane.

Afterwards, as the early afternoon sun slanted across the bed, he stroked the gentle rise of my belly.

"When will it be born?"

"End of May."

"Why didn't you tell me sooner?"

"I found out the day your father died. I couldn't bring myself to lay another burden on you when you were dealing not only with your grief but also with your decision about leading the tribe. I had no right…"

"You had *every* right."

I shook my head. "At the funeral, I saw you fully, the whole of you that before I'd only caught glimpses of. If I had told you then, I would have been making the decision for you, forcing you away from the tribe before you had a chance to even consider leading them."

"Why tell me now? What has changed?"

"I realized that I also couldn't deny you the ability to make a decision about the baby as well. I was wrong to keep it from you. Forgive me."

"What do you want of me, Mae?"

"I want you with all my heart and soul. I want you in my life and in our child's life. I want you to know this child, love it and be loved as its father. But I don't want you to marry me."

"You won't let go of that still? How can you do that to yourself—bear an illegitimate child!" An edge of disbelief crept into his voice, hovering close to anger. His hand stopped caressing me and he raised himself up on his elbow to look in my eyes.

"Don't you understand?" I continued. "I'm trying to make it possible for you to stay in my life and still remain sachem. As long as you don't marry me, will the tribe still accept your leadership?"

"You and our child are more important to me than my role in the tribe."

"And you and our child are more important to me than what the island thinks of me." What I didn't say was my fear that if Tobias gave up his identity with the tribe as its leader, it would eventually destroy him, and I would bear the responsibility.

"It appears we are at an impasse."

"But we share one thing—we both want what is best for our baby, and that means having you in its life as its father."

"I don't want you labeled as 'that Indian's whore'."

"I'm stronger than the labels the bigots on this island try to stick on me. Aggie Gardner and her harpies can't hurt me—especially when I know I have your love."

"The minute you cannot bear it, I will marry you. You've been hurt too much already."

The memory of Marcus Gardner's rampage and the disdain of people like All Simms flickered briefly between us.

"For every Aggie there are ten people who support us. Remember the outpouring of help to clean up the Boat House. Those people will stand by us."

He took my hand in his and kissed it.

"I will do as you ask and, reluctantly, not marry you. But even though we won't have a marriage ceremony or a legal piece of paper, I want to exchange vows with you. Will you at least grant me that?"

"Yes," I said.

"I'm starving. Didn't you say you had brought me lunch?"

I spent the next few days with Tobias at Cove Meadow. On New Year's Eve we exchanged our private vows before Betty and Henry, but no one from the tribe. That night in our bed, Tobias felt his baby kick for the first time.

I returned to Innisfree in early January, but I was no longer alone.

Every evening like clockwork, the Edgartown cannon announces the sunset, reverberating across the bay just as the last sliver of the sun slips below the horizon. Five minutes after the boom of the cannon, Joe Dubois lights the lighthouse beacon and it begins its illuminating revolutions at the northern edge of the island.

That winter, at the sound of the cannon, I interrupted whatever I was doing and left the warmth and light of the cottage. Tugging on my sweater, I headed outside into the ferocious wind with a lantern, my footsteps flattening the overgrown path to the vantage point on the cliff.

I'd never wanted a widow's walk on the house. The position and height of the cliff above the water had always sufficed. And up until that time, I'd never had need to watch for a particular boat.

The wind whipping my skirt flat against the growing curve of my belly and loosening strands of hair from my braid, I waited each evening on the promontory, my eyes scanning the water for the familiar sail.

When I saw it rounding the cove, I flew down the steps to the beach and held the lantern high as he guided the boat through the narrow channel and turned toward me. Even in the dark, on moonless, shrouded nights, I sensed his hunger and his claim on me, our child and the land upon which I stood.

Chapter Eighteen
Josiah Liam

During January and February, with Betty's sewing and Tobias' carpentry, we created a nursery in the alcove off the parlor at Innisfree. It was filled with sunlight from the three windows that flanked the eastern and southern walls. Tobias built a cradle and lined it with the lamb fleece that had been his as an infant.

"I confided in my mother," he told me one evening as he put the finishing touches on the woodwork.

I looked up, tensed for her response.

"She told me, 'This is a child of my blood, no matter what the old ways decree. I will cherish it.' She made these for the baby." He handed me a pair of beaded moccasins, soft and supple and small enough to fit in the palm of his hand.

I let out the breath I'd been holding.

"She is also grateful to you. I know she is deeply proud that I've become sachem."

"As I am."

"I think you'd like each other."

"Someday."

In March, I left Innisfree and rented an apartment in Hyannis near the hospital.

On May 5th, Josiah Liam was born, named for his grandfathers. I brought him home to Innisfree when he was three weeks old.

Betty had opened up the cottage and stocked it with fresh food. She had a pot roast simmering on the stove, a vase of wildflowers on the dining room table and open arms waiting to hold Josiah as soon as we docked.

After dinner, while Josiah napped in his cradle and Tobias left for Edgartown and errands he mumbled he had to do, Betty and I sat on the porch overlooking the bay.

"Mae, I want to propose something to you, and don't rush to protest until you hear me out."

I had no idea what she was about to say, but I was still in that milky fog of early motherhood when thinking was a luxury for which I had no energy. We had left Woods Hole on the earliest boat to avoid islanders who might raise questions about Tobias Monroe and Mae Keaney traveling with an infant. We had taken the steamer to Oak Bluffs, not the ferry to Vineyard Haven, again because the risk was lower of running into people who would recognize us. Tobias' boat was waiting for us in the harbor. From there we sailed directly to Innisfree. It had been an exhausting trip.

I leaned back in my chair, closed my eyes and listened to what Betty was about to say.

"I'd like you to consider hiring me to help you run the Boat House. Managing a business and raising a child are not incompatible, but they are going to be a challenge. I'd like to help."

Then she shut up.

"OK," I said.

"Just like that? OK? No list of objections about your independence and ability to do it all by yourself? Are you feeling all right?" She pressed a hand to my forehead as if to check for fever, but she was smiling.

"Oh, Betty. I don't know how to thank you. As we traveled here this morning, even with Tobias at my side, I was overwhelmed with what lay ahead of me. I've always been so confident, so determined. But Josiah has changed me. For the first time I was afraid. Afraid that I couldn't protect him, keep him safe, and at the same time provide for him. You have no idea what your offer means to me."

"I think I do, honey. I've been where you are, on my own with kids who needed everything from me. I am so grateful that you said yes!"

"What about your job at the Inn?"

"I'll give my notice today. We can open the Boat House in two weeks. I'll come out on my days off to help get everything set up."

I put my arms around her.

"You are so good to me."

Life at Innisfree took on a new rhythm that summer. Josiah thrived; Betty kept things moving between the kitchen and the dining room with ease and entertained our customers with her outgoing and earthy charm; Tobias arrived every evening at sunset after the Boat House had shut down for the day. On Mondays, when we were closed, Tobias picked up his mother on the other side of Chappy and brought her to Innisfree to spend the day with Josiah while I gardened, Tobias did repairs and Betty went off to town for her day off. It had not taken us long to realize Betty should live out at Innisfree and Tobias had built her a small cottage between the café and my house.

Betty's talents extended beyond the café. She had devised a cover story for Josiah and planted a few judicious seeds when she was still working at the Inn.

"I heard Mae Keaney's cousin died in childbirth. A tragic story. She'd already lost her husband in the war and Mae was the only close relative. She couldn't bear to have the baby go into an orphanage, so she's adopted him. Lord knows how she's going to manage running a restaurant and raising a child, but I guess in wartime you do what you have to do."

It was enough of an explanation to satisfy most people and no contrary rumors ever surfaced. Only a handful of people might have suspected that Josiah was my birth son—Henry, Marcus and Sadie. Both Henry and Marcus had their own reasons for looking the other way.

It was Sadie who worried me, because she had the power to hurt Tobias. Because she lived off-island, I knew it would be unlikely she might hear about Josiah from anyone who frequented the Boat House. Naomi, Tobias' mother, was the only one who could silence Sadie if she ever decided to confront us, and I had to trust that Naomi would protect both her son and her grandson.

It was a time of profound happiness for me.

Our lives continued undisturbed for the next three years. As Josiah grew, Tobias surrounded him with the love of a father. At three, Josiah was already going out with Tobias to fish, his sturdy body nearly disappearing in his bright orange life jacket. He had his own pole, a miniature version of his father's, and was learning to cast from the beach at the Gut.

At night, after I put him to bed, Tobias and I sometimes stood arm in arm in the doorway of his room, in awe and gratitude.

And then, our peace, our family, was blown apart. I had always feared it would be Sadie who would disrupt our lives, but instead, it was my past.

Felicia Bellamy, one of my childhood neighbors on North Neck, arrived at the Boat House in mid-July with an entourage. She had achieved her dream and become a stage actress, and the island was buzzing that one of their own was coming home to appear at the Vineyard Playhouse. I had heard the rumors floating around the Boat House, but had been too busy and distracted to pay them much attention.

Despite my warnings, Josiah had gotten poison ivy and I was busy daubing him with calamine lotion in the kitchen. I heard my name being called in the front of the café.

"Mae Keaney! I heard in town that Mae Keaney runs the Boat House. Where is she?" She was using what I imagined was her stage voice. I had to admit, it commanded attention. I wiped my hands, sent Josiah scooting off to play in the yard, *not* the woods, and pushed open the swinging door into the dining room.

"There you are! Who ever thought you'd wind up here!" She shrieked and held open her arms, expecting me to submit to her embrace. I planted a smile on my face and approached her.

"Felicia! Welcome! But what brings you to the Boat House? " The playhouse was on East Chop, a good distance from Chappy. We'd never had anyone involved in the summer theatre come to eat.

"Why *you*, of course! I wanted to show the cast where I'd grown up on North Neck and then treat everyone to lunch, so I asked the locals if there was anywhere on Chappy where we could get a decent meal. 'Oh, they said, you'll want to head over to Mae Keaney's place.' And I thought, can that be *our* Mae? The Mae who ran away from Boston and disappeared off the face of the earth? I had to find out for myself. And here you are!"

I felt gobsmacked. How would Felicia have known that I had left Boston? She was already gone from Chappy when my family was forced away. But I knew I wouldn't have long to wonder, since Felicia seemed quite prepared to prattle on in her attention-getting way. All heads were turned toward her larger-than-life presence and were listening intently to her every word. She looked every inch the celebrity, dressed in obviously expensive silk slacks and a halter top that were ridiculously out of place in the Boat House.

I moved quickly to forestall any more revelations. I didn't want her disclosing any more Mae Keaney secrets.

"Please have a seat. This table is one of the best for a view of the bay. What can we bring you to drink while you're deciding what to eat? Iced tea? Ginger ale? Coca-Cola?"

She had brought about eight people with her, one of whom was holding an agitated small dog. It took some time to get them settled as we pushed tables together and gathered extra chairs. Betty appeared at my side to take their drink orders and the spectacle subsided for a while. A young girl at an adjacent table approached Felicia for her autograph and Felicia obliged with a flourish.

I breathed a sigh of relief at the temporary respite, but I was uneasy. In all the years I'd been on Chappy I hadn't encountered anyone connected to my family except Henry. That had served me well. But Felicia's arrival and clear knowledge that I had not been in contact with my family was going to have consequences for me.

I went to the kitchen to prepare the sandwiches for Felicia's party and compose myself for the inevitable questions. I had bought myself some time, but that was all. If Felicia was still in contact with my family, she was going to tell them I was here.

I was arranging the sandwich platters on a tray with trembling hands as Betty entered the kitchen.

"That actress has upset you, hasn't she?"

"You don't miss a beat, do you?"

"Do you want me to take care of them so you can slip away?"

"It's too late. Besides, I want to know what she knows about my family and if she is close to them. Because if she's close, she's going to tell them I'm here."

Betty looked at me, her arms folded across her chest.

"I know you've been estranged from them, Mae, and I don't know why. But maybe, especially because of Josiah, it's time to reconcile."

"Please do me a favor and keep Josiah out of sight until they leave. If anyone's going to tell my family about Josiah, it's going to be me."

I picked up the tray and pushed open the door with my hip.

As I served the plates, Felicia touched my arm and beamed.

"I can't wait to tell Kathleen I've found you. You can't imagine what your family has been through wondering what happened to you. They thought you were dead."

I *was* dead, I thought. The Mae they knew died a long time ago. Felicia seemed to have no understanding that I might have powerful reasons for remaining hidden from my family. But, of course, her loyalty would be to them, and specifically to Kathleen. I decided the only thing I could do was accept that I had been discovered. But I didn't have to relinquish the telling to Felicia.

"How is Kathleen? What is she doing?" I tried to sound calm, as if this were normal small talk.

"Oh, she's grand! You know she's married now. Oh, but no, you wouldn't know that. She's Mrs. Ned Bradley. Isn't that a stitch! Childhood playmates and now husband and wife. His father committed suicide a few years after the Crash. That seemed to drive Ned to recover everything they had lost. He's wealthier now than his father ever was. They live on Beacon Hill."

Felicia's words hit me like a punch in the gut and I took a step back from the table to steady myself, gripping the back of Felicia's chair.

"That's wonderful for her," I managed to croak out. "Do you have her address? Now that I know where she is, I'd love to contact her."

Felicia dug into her purse and pulled out a leather address book. She flipped to the "B's" and ran her scarlet-tipped finger down the page.

"Here she is." I handed her the pencil I kept in my apron pocket and she scribbled the address and phone number on a napkin.

Tears welled up in her eyes as she placed one hand on her well-endowed breast.

"I cannot believe that I have been the instrument that has brought you two sisters together. I feel as if it's the most important role I've ever played."

I realized she was indeed playing a role for the benefit of the table, where murmurs of approval emerged over the tuna fish and egg salad sandwiches.

"Bravo, Felicia!"

I tucked the napkin in my pocket, walked through the kitchen and out the back door, where I shed my own tears. Real. Ambivalent. Tortured.

"Mama! Mama! Why are you crying? Do you have a boo-boo?"

Josiah had climbed out of his sandbox and was tugging at my skirt with his grubby hands.

I wiped my eyes with the back of my hand and knelt down to him.

"No, Josiah. Mama's just been chopping onions in the kitchen. You know how that makes my eyes fill up with water. They aren't real tears. But thank you for noticing."

"Silly onions!"

Betty came out of the kitchen at that moment.

"Little man, I need some help in the garden. The cucumbers are running away from the beans and we need to catch them. Can you help me?"

She reached down for his hand and steered him toward the garden. She turned her head back to me.

"The starlet is making noise about leaving and is looking for you to say good-bye. You'd better go inside before she tracks you out here. And wash your face!"

I ducked back into the kitchen, splashed some cold water on my face, smoothed my hair and swung into the dining room.

Felicia was on her feet, looking around expectantly. I think Betty was mistaken. Felicia struck me as someone who considered it beneath her to go in search of anyone to say good-bye. She was waiting for me to seek her out and express my gratitude, not only for finding me but also for honoring my humble establishment with her presence.

"There you are! Well, we must go. Curtain rises at seven and the show must go on! I'll be sure to spread the word at the theatre about your homey place. And I'll be sure to contact Kathleen about my serendipitous discovery."

She kissed me on both cheeks without touching her lips to my face and then waved her companions toward the dock as if she were Mother Goose shepherding her goslings down to the water. Her silk scarf fluttered behind her as she pranced down the boards in her open-toed, high-heeled sandals.

I waved good-bye from the door of the Boat House, but she was already looking out at the bay, her scarf now securing her hair from the tumult of the boat on the open water.

I retreated to the café and began clearing the remnants of their meal from the table.

Later that night, a glass of whisky in my hand, I sat with Tobias on the porch and recounted what had happened.

"I realized after she left that I hadn't asked her about my parents or my other siblings. I think I was afraid to know the answers."

"You mean, if they were still alive?"

"Yes. I especially didn't want to hear it from Felicia."

"What will you do now?"

"Write to Kathleen. What else can I do? Felicia is bound to tell her, if she hasn't already picked up the phone and gushed about her 'discovery' already."

"Have you thought about how much you will tell her? Will you tell her the truth?"

"I don't see how I can do that, now that she is married to Ned. 'Dear sister, your husband is a scumbag, a man who abandoned the girl he got pregnant.' I don't think so."

"Maybe it's best in a letter just to let her know you are alive and well. Keep it simple. Once you see her, if you see her, you can better gauge how much to tell her. And don't apologize."

I kissed him. "Good advice from the man who knows how to keep his own secrets. I'll write tomorrow. Right now I want you to take me to bed and hold me like you never want to let me go. Felicia's visit has dredged up all kinds of memories that I would rather have not disturbed."

The next day a pile of crumpled sheets of paper accumulated in the wastebasket next to my desk as I started and restarted my letter to Kathleen. In the end, it was the fear of what

Felicia would tell Kathleen that finally settled my brain enough to get the words down on the page, address the envelope and hand it to Tobias to take to the post office. I had listened to him and kept the note short and limited to the most basic facts. And then I waited.

Felicia did not visit the Boat House again, although she was scheduled to appear for four weeks at the Playhouse. But neither did I go to see her perform.

I buried myself in the daily rhythm of summer life at Innisfree: breakfast with Tobias and Josiah, weeding the garden while it was still cool, digging up clams at low tide for my chowder, preparing the tuna and egg salads for the lunch rush, then opening the café and crisscrossing the scrubbed and waxed linoleum under my feet between the dining room and the kitchen, keeping up with both the banter and the food as our customers streamed in on their boats. In the evenings, after I'd fed Josiah his supper, given him his bath and put him to bed, I did the books or made out lists of provisions for the next trip into town. I did not want to stop too long, because that is when my thoughts became flooded with a confused array of emotions—regret, resentment, longing, fury. I did not know if I wanted Kathleen to write back or ignore me. Part of that ambivalence I could attribute to my own reluctance to reveal why I had fled Boston. I was ashamed, plain and simple. But I knew in my heart that the main reason I wanted Kathleen to stay in my past and not invade the life I had created on Chappy was Ned Bradley. I felt that he had betrayed me twice—first by abandoning me and our unborn child; but then by marrying Kathleen and thus erecting a barrier between her and me that I could not breach.

I had put aside the longing for my family years ago. I did not believe that they could ever accept and love me again, and I had made my peace with that. But Felicia's arrival had pierced my armor, and I did not know whether I should seal myself up again or throw it all off, exposing my vulnerability in the hopes that my family would at least have compassion for me, if not love.

The one thing I did know was that I was not going to run away again. I had made my choices. I was who I was, loved who I wanted. I was staying, and Kathleen could come or not, but on my terms.

It was Tobias' mother, Naomi, who helped me see that and gave me the courage I would need if and when Kathleen showed up.

We were hanging laundry together while Josiah chased butterflies in and out of the sheets and tablecloths.

"No word yet from your sister?"

"No. In some ways I'm relieved, because I don't know how to face her. And yet, because she hasn't answered my letter, I feel I was right to leave all those years ago. I am still the black sheep who has brought shame to the family and they would rather forget me."

"If you were my daughter, no matter what you had done, I would be flying over the water with open arms if I had learned you were alive and so near."

"Thank you, Naomi. Perhaps my mother would have as well. But I don't know if she is even alive. And if she is, Kathleen may not tell her."

"A lost daughter, a lost sister, especially one who has not only survived but flourished as you have…they will take you back. Give it time. Blood is a powerful life force—not only within us but between us. She may be struggling just as you are. Her fear when you disappeared had probably ebbed to acceptance after all these years. And now, she is torn between the ineffable joy of knowing you are alive and the inconsolable anger that you withheld yourself from them for so long."

"My fear is that her anger will overwhelm her joy, and she will never forgive me."

"Mae, dear child, forgive yourself. Don't abdicate that power to anyone else. You made the choices you needed to make and you have lived with the consequences. No one else has walked in your shoes. No one else has the right to judge you. Whether Kathleen comes or not, whether she forgives you or not, don't allow her decisions to color your belief in yourself. You are loved for the wonderful and unique woman you are."

I absorbed Naomi's wisdom that morning and took a deep breath. I wasn't going to stop living while I waited for Kathleen. When we finished the laundry I ran with Josiah and the butterflies and felt his laughter and indefatigable energy fill me up.

Kathleen did not write.

But one late August afternoon, between the lunch and supper lull, Frank Bennett's boat puttered to the dock and a stylishly dressed woman emerged and began to walk up to the Boat House.

I heard the bell tinkle as the screen door to the dining room opened. I was in the kitchen drying the last of the lunch dishes. I put down my towel and walked out to greet the new customer.

She was alone, silhouetted against the light reflected on the bay below the café. I couldn't see her face at first, in the shadows. But as I approached her, her features took shape with heartbreaking familiarity, and an exclamation of such longing escaped my lips.

"Kathleen!"

"Mae!"

We moved toward each other and embraced. We held each other for several moments, the sheer physical presence of one another awakening our lost affection.

Finally, I drew her to a chair and sat down opposite her.

"You've come! Tell me everything."

She shook her head. "You first. Start wherever—now, then. I don't care. Just tell me about your life."

She didn't demand to know why I had left, although I expected that question would come soon enough. And I didn't ask about our parents. I think both questions had answers we didn't want to hear, and so we postponed them in the first flush of wonder that we now found ourselves sitting in the same room.

I started with the present.

"I have a son, Josiah. He's three and napping right now up at the house."

A flicker of pain crossed her face, so brief that I doubted it at first. She recovered quickly with a gayety I suspected was false. But it had been sixteen years since I had seen her. How could I know what was true or false? How could I know her at all?

"I'm an auntie! I can't wait to spoil him! How long have you been on Chappy? This place seems so remote, but Felicia told me you have a thriving business here. I never thought of you as a businesswoman, but now that I remember, you seemed to take pretty quickly to your job at Jordan Marsh."

She chattered nervously as I described my life at Innisfree, interjecting with the kind of responses one might give to an acquaintance one had just met at a garden party. As if she was exclaiming "How interesting!" when what she meant was "How quaint and utterly unlike anything I would do with my life."

I stopped my story at the moment I had arrived on Martha's Vineyard. I wasn't ready to retrace the steps that had led me to New York. It was Kathleen's turn.

"Tell me about yourself. Tell me about the family."

"Well, you know I married Ned Bradley. You remember him, don't you?"

"When?" I had to know.

"Oh, my. About ten years ago. We don't have any children. Ned didn't…we can't, it seems." She stopped, as if she was inadvertently revealing something she preferred to keep hidden.

Now the look of pain when I mentioned Josiah made sense.

"He's become quite successful…revived his father's manufacturing company…the war and all has been good for business. We've got a house on Beacon Hill. It's a long way from our tenement in Scollay Square, even though it's just a few blocks, if you know what I mean."

I gathered my courage.

"How are Ma and Da and the little ones?"

"Da died of liver disease about two years after you left. The drinking. Ma passed just last year. Cancer. Patrick's a sergeant on the Boston police force. Danny enlisted in the Marines and decided to stay in when the war ended. Maureen made her final vows as a Sister of Charity before Ma passed away."

She spoke with kindness, not accusation, but added, "Ma never gave up hope that you'd come home."

But she didn't ask, "Why didn't you?" Instead, she said, "Tell me about your husband," and touched my left hand. When Tobias and I had exchanged vows he had given me a ring, a simple silver band etched with diagonal lines. Kathleen's ring finger was wrapped in diamonds, a large single stone on her engagement ring and smaller ones circling her wedding band.

I made up my mind at that moment not to correct her and let her assume that the ring on my finger was a wedding ring.

"Tobias is a fisherman, a fixer of all things broken and a wonderful father."

Again, I saw that almost imperceptible flinch.

"Will I get to meet him?"

"Probably not today. He's often out past dark at this time of year."

"Another time, then. Will you show me around?" She rose from the table.

"Briefly. The late afternoon and supper crowd will start arriving soon. This is our busy season."

We left by the dockside door and I led her around toward the cottage. It seemed odd that she wanted to see Innisfree rather than question me about why I had left Boston so abruptly, but I was content to let those inquiries wait until she was ready to ask.

We reached the cottage. The beach roses were spilling onto the lawn in a riot of color; finches and butterflies flitted from the water's edge to the eaves. The house was trim and tight. I felt a surge of pride in what I had accomplished since arriving on the island and I wanted Kathleen to acknowledge it. But she scarcely saw any of Innisfree's wild beauty. She had already climbed the steps to the porch, her back to the land and her hand on the doorknob.

"May I see the baby?"

I raced up the steps to follow her, my finger across my lips.

"Sh-h-h," I whispered. "I don't want him to wake up just yet."

She nodded in understanding but moved into the house, where Betty was darning in the parlor. One of us stayed close by when Josiah was napping. The door to the nursery was ajar and Kathleen headed straight for it, barely glancing at Betty. She slipped into the room before I could even introduce Betty.

Kathleen hovered over Josiah's crib and studied him with such longing that I had to restrain the urge to wrap my arms around him as if he were about to be snatched from me. She didn't move for several minutes, transfixed, as I have often been, by the innocence and heartbreaking vulnerability of my sleeping child.

I gently placed my hand on her elbow to steer her out of the room and she recoiled, disturbed from whatever distant place in memory her mind had gone. Reluctantly she turned away from Josiah.

"What's his name?"

"Josiah Liam."

"You gave him Da's name!"

"And Josiah is his other grandfather."

"He's a brown little nut, isn't he! He must be out in the sun all day when he isn't sleeping."

Once again I pulled back from correcting her. As I wasn't ready to tell her that Tobias wasn't my husband, I also wasn't ready to reveal that my son was half Wampanoag. All in good time, I told myself. I had hidden myself from my family for so long that I could not bring myself to rip away the veil all at once.

I was only beginning to know the woman who had arrived unannounced on my dock, and I did not know yet if I trusted her. She was not the Kathleen I had left behind in Boston any more than I was the Mae who had run away.

"Can I make you a cup of tea?" I asked, to get her out of the cottage.

She looked at her watch. "Oh, no thanks. I told the boatman to come back for me in an hour and it's nearly time."

"Will you come again?"

"I'd like to. I want to hold that baby of yours! And you should come to Boston…"

"After the season is over perhaps. I can't really get away until I close down the Boat House. But come again when you can. Bring Maureen and Patrick next time."

I was careful to name only our brother and sister, not Ned, although I hoped he'd have the sense never to come near me again.

"The little ones barely remember you, Mae, although they do remember the pain you caused after you left. Danny left school to go to work when we didn't have your paycheck any more. And Ma made it impossible for Maureen to do anything else except enter the convent. 'I promised God one of my daughters,' she cried, night after night. She admitted that she had renounced a vocation when she married Da, and that was why she had wanted you to take her place."

"Why Maureen and not you? You were the one most like Ma—beautiful and serene."

"I was already engaged to Ned. We had started keeping company before you left."

The sudden turn in the conversation sent a chill down my spine. I wondered why Kathleen had waited until her final moments at Innisfree to hurl at my feet the consequences of my leaving. The implication that both Danny and Maureen had been forced against their wills to take on the family duties I had forsaken reignited the smoldering guilt that I'd kept tamped down all those years. But the most crushing of Kathleen's revelations was the timing of her courtship with Ned. Before I had left, she had tossed off, as if I should have known.

Frank's boat was waiting at the dock and I could not have been happier to see him. I felt physical pain at Kathleen's recitation of the ills that had befallen my family and I needed to get away from everything Kathleen's presence represented. I also was holding my breath that Josiah would wake up before Kathleen left. The last thing I wanted was for him to climb out of his bed, toddle out to the porch and call out to me as he always did that he was awake. I hadn't been able to warn Betty to keep him in the house if he woke. I had a foreboding vision of Kathleen running back up to the house to scoop him up in her arms. I don't know why that disturbed me so much, but I had the irrational fear that once she held him, she would never let him go.

Kathleen turned to me before she climbed into Frank's boat.

"I can see you've made a life for yourself, Mae, and I'll tell the others. We thought you were dead, and it's a relief to know you're not. But it's also an unanswered question as to why you never let us know. If it hadn't been for Felicia, we might never have found you. Maybe someday you'll tell us why you abandoned us. I'll be back, if only to see that beautiful child. He's the only grandchild, did you know that? Oh, of course you wouldn't. Maybe with him you can make amends."

And then she was gone.

Above me, from the porch, came the voice that had called out too late, thank God, for Kathleen to hear. I ran to Josiah and threw my arms around him.

"Mama," he said, "Have you been cutting onions again?"

Chapter Nineteen
Toys

Kathleen did not return during the summer. But she began sending expensive gifts to Josiah. When the first package arrived, delivered by Frank Bennett, I opened it alone after Josiah had gone down for a nap. It had been addressed directly to Josiah, shipped from a New York toy store I recognized, the kind of place with lavish store windows that instilled unfulfilled longing in the eyes of children on the outside of the glass. I was cautious. I didn't want to deny my son the excitement of a wonderful toy just because I couldn't afford to give it to him. But I also didn't want Kathleen to buy Josiah's affection with Ned Bradley's money.

Betty found me in the dining room saving the twine that had been wrapped around the package. I hadn't opened the box, afraid of whatever extravagance Kathleen had chosen to put between Josiah and me.

"What's this? I saw Frank hauling it up to the house and I didn't remember that we had ordered anything for the Boat House."

"It's not for the Boat House. It's for Josiah."

I still hadn't opened the box.

Betty raised her eyebrows in a question after peeking at the toy store name emblazoned on the box. "It's not like you to buy him an expensive toy."

"It's not from me. It's from Kathleen."

"Ah. Auntie is not above bribery."

"So I'm not just being a jealous fool to think that is what this is?"

Betty shook her head. "No, Sweetie. Especially when she told you that she and her rich hubby didn't and couldn't have kids. She's the jealous one. For all her money and fancy Boston mansion, she doesn't have what you have. What's inside?"

I finally succumbed to curiosity and ripped open the box. Inside were a wooden hobby horse, with a real horsehair mane and tail, and a miniature cowboy outfit complete with chaps, boots, Stetson, holster and cap gun.

"I'm surprised she didn't send a real pony," noted Betty, when we had unpacked everything.

"I can't give him this. Even though he's a Wampanoag and not a Plains Indian, allowing him to pretend he's a cowboy troubles me no end. And I don't even want to think about how Tobias would react."

I put everything back in the box, except for the hobby horse.

"I suppose this is neutral enough. Indians had horses as well as cowboys."

I leaned the wooden horse in the corner and sealed the box.

"What will you do with all that stuff?"

"I can't send it back. That would open up a conversation I'm not ready to have. I'll put it away in the attic, out of sight."

Betty helped me lug the box to the loft and cover it with an old canvas tarp before Josiah woke up.

Watching Josiah's wide-eyed reaction to the horse convinced me I had done the right thing in hiding the rest of Kathleen's extravagance. He galloped around the house all afternoon and took the horse to bed with him that night.

"I have to give him a name," he said as I tucked him in.

"What would you like to call him?"

"Midnight," he said, stroking the horse's dark mane. But he used the Wampanoag word, learned, I was sure, from Naomi. I smiled in relief. Tobias would smile as well. For the moment, at least, Josiah was still ours, his heart not yet claimed by his aunt's efforts to buy his affection.

I wrote Kathleen a thank you note, grateful but not effusive. I had no intention of playing the poor country mouse, happy to scramble for the largesse of her rich city sister. The gifts kept coming through the fall, ranging from a toy car he could ride in to a silver rattle engraved with his name. She did not appear to know what was appropriate for a three-year-old, and consequently the toys careened wildly from too complicated to too infantile. We were running out of space to store them.

The toys, however, were easier to deal with than Kathleen's presence. It puzzled me that she never came back, sending the gifts as her surrogate. But her absence freed me from the questions that were left unasked in August, and I let the silence between us continue.

And then she invited us to Thanksgiving dinner.

I ripped up the letter, threw the scraps down on the dining room table and got up to pace back and forth by the window. The bay was choppy and gray, empty of both boats and birds on the early November afternoon.

Tobias came in from the shed, where he had been tinkering with a generator he had bought to provide us with some electricity. Now that winter was approaching he spent less time on the sea and more at Innisfree with Josiah and me.

"What's this?" he asked, fingering the torn sheets. It was heavy cream-colored notepaper, embossed with Kathleen's monogram. He recognized it immediately.

"What does your sister want that has upset you so much?"

He came over to the window and put his arms around me.

"She wants us to come to Boston for Thanksgiving. Danny is home on leave from the Marines and Maureen has permission from the convent to have dinner with the family. Kathleen is planning a family reunion with Josiah as the centerpiece."

"Do you want to go?"

"No! Yes! I don't know what I want."

"It's because of him, isn't it? The shadow of Ned Bradley is hovering over any possibility of reconciliation with your family."

"I can neither tell Kathleen the truth nor be in the same room with Ned Bradley and pretend nothing happened between us."

"Then we won't go. The Wampanoag don't celebrate Thanksgiving. It's a day of mourning for us, a commemoration of the decimation of the tribe by the settlers, not a happy feast of brotherhood."

His voice had a note of firmness and conviction that, while not totally unknown to me, reminded me that he had grown even more fully into his role as sachem.

Then he softened his tone.

"You know, until you tell Kathleen the truth, you won't be free of the power Ned holds over you and the barrier he represents between you and your family. More than once you urged me to forgive myself for Hannah's death, until I finally listened to you. I'm going to keep encouraging you to be honest with Kathleen. If she can't understand why you left or forgive you, then so be it."

"I don't want to admit that you are right, but deep in my soul I know I'm still hiding from my family. Even though they know *where* I am, they don't know *who* I am. But I'm not ready to reveal myself. Not yet."

I made our excuses to Kathleen, and instead of cooking a turkey dinner, I sat alone at Innisfree with Josiah while Tobias led a memorial service on the beach for his Wampanoag ancestors. Although a few members of the tribe were aware that Tobias had a son with me, we had agreed it was best not to flaunt our relationship. Naomi was seeing to Josiah's education as a Wampanoag, but I wondered as he got older how we would introduce him to the community. Like telling my family the truth about my past, Josiah's future with the tribe was one of those dilemmas I was willing to bury, because I thought I had time.

And then, I didn't.

Chapter Twenty
Blood and Breath

It was Christmas morning when a wave of dizziness came over me and I had to grab the kitchen counter to keep from falling. Then my legs buckled under me and I slid to the floor. I was alone. Tobias had taken his new motorboat to Edgartown to pick up Naomi and Betty, who spent the winter in town working at the one inn that was open. She had the day off and we were planning to celebrate with dinner in the afternoon. Josiah had begged to go with Tobias. He loved to sit on Tobias' lap and hold the wheel. I had bundled him up and sent them off, happy to have him work off some of his Christmas frenzy on the water while I finished cooking.

The dizziness did not abate. I crawled to the sink and pulled out the bucket I kept in the cabinet below just in time to catch the breakfast I vomited up. I hadn't been this nauseated since I was pregnant with Josiah, and a fleeting wish crossed my fogged brain that I might be pregnant again.

My head was pounding with a sharp, knife-like pain, and I leaned back against the cabinet, hoping that Tobias would return soon.

It felt like hours before I heard their voices moving up from the dock. I was soaked in sweat and my legs felt numb.

Naomi was the first to find me.

"Mae! What has happened to you? Tobias, come quick! Mae is hurt."

Tobias was on the back porch removing Josiah's boots and unwrapping him from his bundled layers.

When he saw me, the color drained from his face, but he bent down to pick me up and carried me to the bedroom.

"What happened? Are you hurt?

I tried to recount what had overcome me, but I was in such intense pain that it took my breath away.

Naomi retreated to the kitchen and brewed one of her remedies from a jar of dried spiderwort she kept tucked away on a shelf in the pantry.

I sipped the hot tea but murmured to Tobias I could also do with a couple of aspirin, and he poked around in the medicine cabinet to find some.

"I'm sorry," I managed to whisper. "I don't know what brought this on. One minute I was peeling carrots and the next I was on the floor. I should be OK as soon as the aspirin kicks in."

"Don't worry. Mom and Betty have already taken over in the kitchen. You rest."

I nodded in gratitude and closed my eyes against the pain, exhausted and puzzled. This wasn't a pregnancy. The aspirin finally helped, and I fell asleep.

When I woke up, Josiah was curled up next to me, his head cushioned against my breast and his arm flung across me. His breathing had the steady, untroubled rhythm of a sleeping child, a sharp contrast to my own ragged, distressed gasps for air.

"Feeling any better?" Betty whispered from the chair next to the bed, where she had apparently been keeping vigil.

"Slightly. Headache has diminished, but I'm wiped out. How long did I sleep?"

"About three hours. Dinner is simmering in the oven. We can eat whenever you feel up to it. Or not."

I rubbed my eyes and eased myself out from under the nestled Josiah.

"Give me a hand, will you. I'm not sure about my legs." I slid over to the side of the bed and tried to move my limbs.

"They seem to be working again."

Betty offered me her arm and I stood up, wobbly but better than in the morning. She supported me as far as the parlor, where Tobias was stoking the fire. He jumped up.

"Are you sure you should be up?"

"I'll give it a try. Besides, I need to pee and I didn't think you'd appreciate it if I wet the bed." I smiled, trying to lighten the somber mood that seemed to have descended upon the house.

"I'll help you." And he took over from Betty, holding me with his strong arms as I hobbled out to the bathroom. We now had a flush toilet and Tobias had enclosed the walkway that led to it from the kitchen, but it was still a cold, long walk.

When we got back I sank into a chair at the dining table. Naomi had set it with a red cloth and candles whose reflections shimmered in the windows surrounding the table. I could smell the pungent flavor of venison with apples and onions and I could hear the babble of Josiah waking from his nap.

"Why don't we gather and eat now. I don't know how long I can manage to be up."

Tobias rounded up Betty and Josiah and Naomi and we settled down to the clatter of spoons against serving dishes and the comfort of warm food sliding into our bellies. We all seemed to be trying to make the meal as normal as possible, refusing to allow the morning's crisis disrupt our Christmas. I, especially, kept pushing back the niggling fear that something was terribly wrong. I smiled more than was my nature, chirped my thanks to Naomi and Betty for finishing the cooking, and played with Josiah. It was exhausting, and after about an hour, I knew I needed to go lie down again.

Tobias helped me to the bedroom and undressed me.

"You're burning with fever, Mae."

"M-m-m. I'm so tired. Just let me lie down." I lay back against the pillows, my head too heavy to hold up.

A little while later Tobias returned with a basin and a washcloth.

"I'm just going to cool you off." And he wrung out the cloth and began to wipe my feverish body.

Later that night, I began coughing, my body wracked with a succession of violent convulsions as I tried to clear my lungs. When I took my hand away from my mouth, there was blood on it.

Tobias spent the night in the chair by the bed, sponging my forehead. Betty and Naomi took Josiah to Betty's cottage after they'd gotten the wood stove roaring to warm it up.

In the morning I was no better, and Tobias had made a decision.

"I'm taking you to the hospital. You could have pneumonia."

I was too weak to protest. I knew Josiah would be well-cared for with both Naomi and Betty there, and I allowed them to bundle me up as thoroughly as I had wrapped Josiah the day before.

Tobias raced across the bay and through the Gut, keeping his eyes on the far shore but glancing back every few moments at me, shivering in the stern.

When we reached Oak Bluffs he picked me up out of the boat and carried me to the warmth of the ferry office, where he called for an ambulance.

By the time we reached the hospital I was nearly delirious, barely able to breathe and in excruciating pain. I closed my eyes and my mind to the clamor around me, my body detached, on a gurney rolling down a smooth floor that smelled of disinfectant and my own sickness.

Chapter Twenty-One
Powerless
Tobias

Three times in the last twenty-four hours he thought she was dying—when he first saw her collapsed on the kitchen floor as limp as a rag doll; during the night when her skin was on fire, almost as red as the blood she was coughing up; and then in the boat, when he was pushing the throttle as hard as he could, desperate to get her to safety.

When he lifted her the first time in the kitchen he was stunned by how weightless she was. How had she become so thin without his noticing? He should have brought her to the hospital the day before. He should have recognized sooner how sick she was.

He stood in the hallway staring at the doors through which she had disappeared. They wouldn't let him go with her.

"Are you her husband?" They had asked, and it had taken him a moment to remember that in the eyes of the law, he was not. He had shaken his head.

"I'm her friend," he had said. All the other things he was in her life he kept to himself. *I'm her lover, the father of her son, her protector*. But he hadn't protected her this time, and he felt powerless in the face of whatever had invaded Mae's body and their sheltered, snug existence at Innisfree.

He paced. The winter light slipped below the horizon early and the flickering overhead lamps came on, spreading a cold blue tinge over the linoleum floors. Finally, the doors separating him from Mae opened and a white-coated man emerged.

"Are you the man who brought in Miss Keaney?"

"Yes. Is she going to be alright?"

"She's a very lucky young woman to have arrived here when she did. You're to be commended. She has a severe case of pneumonia. But the hospital has a supply of a new drug, penicillin. We've started her on it and we also have her on oxygen to help her breathe. It will take a few days before she's herself again, but she should be past the crisis by the morning."

"May I see her?"

"She's asleep."

"I won't disturb her. I just want to see for myself, so that I can bring word back to her family."

"You've been waiting here all day, haven't you? Quite a good friend, I'd say. It's not exactly hospital policy, but I'll make an exception. Come with me."

The doctor led Tobias down the hall to a small ward with four beds. Mae was the only patient.

"Five minutes, that's all. And don't disturb her."

Tobias nodded and slipped next to the bed. Most of her face was covered by an oxygen mask, and an IV tube was threaded into her arm, its fluid dripping silently. What he could see of her skin was translucent, the veins pale blue threads just below the surface. Her hair had unraveled from its braid and was spread across the pillow.

She was so still and pale that she looked dead, not asleep, and he choked back a sob. *I cannot lose her.* His hands clenched into fists as if he were primed for a brawl. But there was nothing to punch, no heavy-handed enemy to turn away with his blows.

Instead he turned himself away from this vision of a future without Mae and left the hospital.

He hitched a ride back to Oak Bluffs and hesitated outside the Ritz Café, the kind of dive that would be open on the day after Christmas. He needed a drink, but he also knew he needed to get back to Innisfree to his son, to the women. There was whisky in the house; he could have his drink when he got home.

Chapter Twenty-Two
Miracles

I knew his footsteps anywhere, even in the darkness, whispering across the sterile floor. He thought I was asleep. I hadn't opened my eyes. I was too afraid that I would see reflected in *his* eyes my own death.

Instead, I absorbed the comfort of his solid presence beside me, and when he kissed my forehead before he left, I smiled underneath the oxygen mask.

I was the recipient of a series of miracles, the doctor told me later. It was a miracle that Tobias had brought me to the hospital when he did . . . a miracle that penicillin existed, a discovery that the government had pushed the drug companies to produce as fast as they could during the war, as important a weapon as tanks and machine guns . . . a miracle that within months of the war's end, the drug was made available to everyone . . . a miracle that our small island hospital actually had a supply of the drug on hand . . .and finally, a miracle that my body had responded to the power of the medicine.

I stayed two weeks in the hospital, gradually regaining my strength. Although Betty had to go back to work at the inn, Naomi stayed on at Innisfree to help care for Josiah. Tobias came to the hospital every day, at first just to sit at my side and hold my hand while the penicillin fought off the invasion in my lungs. But once the oxygen mask was off and I was sitting up breathing on my own, he brought tasty bits of food that Naomi had prepared and a drawing from Josiah signed with his own "J."

Although I wasn't feeling robust, I was a long way from the woman who had collapsed on Christmas morning, and I was eager to get out of bed and back home to Tobias and Josiah.

"How much longer before I can be pronounced well enough to be on my way?" I pushed the doctor as he made his morning rounds on the thirteenth day.

"Let's do an X-ray this afternoon to check that your lungs are clear. If that's the case, we can release you in the morning." He flipped closed my chart and moved on to the next patient.

I didn't expect to see him again till the next morning, and was surprised when he showed up in the early evening, a large manila envelope under his arm. Tobias was with me, recounting Josiah's escapades, when the expression on the doctor's face brought our laughter to a halt.

"Are you about to tell me that I have to endure these four walls beyond tomorrow morning? I'm feeling so much better. I'm sure I can get the rest I need at home. It's off-season. All I do in the winter is knit and read and order the seeds for my vegetable garden."

"Mae, I wish that rest was all you need to recover, but that's not why I'm here tonight. We found something on the X-ray. When we took the first X-ray the day you arrived the fluid from your pneumonia obscured anything else in your lungs, but now that the pneumonia has been eradicated, we can see it very clearly."

"See what?" Tobias and I spoke at the same time.

"A tumor. We don't know if it's malignant or benign. It may be the reason you were so susceptible to the pneumonia."

I tried to focus, still a challenge from the fog of sickness. Tobias had shifted his position, moving closer to me, putting himself between me and the doctor as if he could shield me from whatever came next.

"A tumor? What does that mean? Can it be treated? Will penicillin cure it the way it did the pneumonia?" The questions spilled out of me in a torrent, desperate for answers, for certainty.

"I don't know the answers, Mae. And I can't treat you here. We're a cottage hospital. We're simply not equipped for cases like this."

"Where can we go?" Tobias seemed ready to pick me up and take me at that very minute.

"Cape Cod Hospital to start, maybe Boston if they don't have the resources."

"How soon? Can I go home first? I need to hold my son."

"The sooner the better. It's impossible to know how far it has progressed. But yes, go home tomorrow; spend time with your boy for a few days. But I wouldn't wait more than a week or two. I'll call ahead and make an appointment for you with a surgeon."

"A surgeon? You mean she'll have to be cut open?"

I heard the pain in Tobias' voice.

"They will need to do at least a biopsy to determine if the tumor is cancerous. I'm sorry, Mae. This is the kind of news I never want to give, especially to a young woman and a mother."

He left the envelope with us to take to Hyannis. I had to look, to see for myself what he had described. I pulled the film out of its sleeve and held it up to the light, tracing with my finger the amorphous shadow that blotted out more than a quarter of my lung.

"How could I not know this was growing inside me? What did I do, or not do, that caused it?" I felt panic building at a frantic pace inside me.

Tobias sensed it and took the X-ray from my hands. He climbed into the bed and took me in his arms, calming me with strokes of his strong hands as I flailed and raged and sobbed.

"We'll solve this. We'll get you answers. We'll get you help. We'll get you better."

I rocked in his arms until the head nurse arrived with my pills, sympathetic to the news she undoubtedly had already been told but firm in her insistence that visiting hours were over and Tobias needed to leave.

"Mae needs her sleep if she's to go home tomorrow."

I fought the sleep that was supposed to be so crucial. Would sleep make the tumor disappear? I doubted it. I needed to think, needed to figure out how I was going to get across the precipitous ravine that now confronted me, with Josiah and Tobias on the other side. I could not believe that it was insurmountable. I could not believe that I was dying.

I thought with regret of the moment when I *had* wished myself dead, when Catriona had been stillborn. I had believed then that God had taken everything from me and I had no reason to continue living.

Now, my reasons were waiting for me at Innisfree and I was determined to get truly home to them.

Chapter Twenty-Three
A World More Full of Weeping

I spent ten days at home before our journey to Hyannis. Betty had gone back to Edgartown and her winter job at the inn. Naomi had settled into Betty's cottage and established a routine with Josiah as only a grandmother can—equal parts boundless love and gentle, old-fashioned expectations for behavior. I was able to sit by the warmth of the fire wrapped in one of Naomi's woven blankets and enjoy my son. For a woman who had always occupied herself with "doing" all her life, I surprised myself with my ability simply to "be."

We did puzzles, read stories, even napped together, Josiah's robust, growing body fitting itself around mine with comfort and familiarity. His solidity filled my emptiness; his steady heartbeat soothed my own too-rapid pulse. I refused to allow myself the indulgence of slipping into bittersweet thoughts that these moments with my son might be my last.

At night, it was Tobias whose strength and calm shielded me from the terrors that were waiting on the precipice in my dreams.

And then the morning arrived for our trip to Hyannis. Naomi cooked pancakes with blueberry preserves, trying to coax my diminished appetite as she had since I'd been home. I managed to swallow a few bites, trying to remember how much I had savored good food.

We took the motorboat as far as Cove Meadow, where Tobias kept his truck. We were going to need transportation on the Cape and the idea of traveling by bus defeated me. I sank into the seat beside him and didn't want to have to move until we got to the hospital. We took the freight ferry to Woods Hole and, despite the January cold, I stayed in the truck rather than climb to the passenger lounge.

When we finally arrived at the hospital, I braced myself, clutching the X-ray with one hand and Tobias with the other.

I wanted answers. I wanted a treatment plan. I wanted a cure. I wanted hope. That day I got none of those. I needed tests. More X-rays. A biopsy.

I spent the night at the hospital and Tobias stayed with Sadie and Ronnie.

"Are you going to tell them why you're here?" I asked as he prepared to leave me at the end of visiting hours. We had avoided confrontation with Sadie so far, but I knew that eventually Tobias and Naomi wanted Josiah to participate in tribal life and his heritage. I did, too. But fighting Sadie about it right now would take energy that neither Tobias nor I had to spare.

"She doesn't need to know. I'll be back in the morning. Try to sleep, to eat. You need your strength."

The surgeon in Hyannis sent me home the next day to wait for the results of all the tests. He couldn't tell us definitively whether the tumor was cancer until the biopsy was analyzed, and that was going to take more than a week.

"If it is cancer, what are my options?" I prodded him for at least some information, however provisional, while I waited in the limbo of uncertainty.

"Surgery to remove as much of the tumor as we can, then doses of nitrogen mustard. It's a relatively new idea, to treat lung cancer with drugs, but it's starting to show some success."

"What is success? A cure?"

He shook his head. "We don't have a cure for cancer, Miss Keaney. We have measures that can slow the progress of the disease for a time. Sometimes that is months, sometimes it's years. But I cannot promise you how long you will survive and I certainly cannot promise you a cure. I'm sorry. You wanted answers. Let's wait and see what the tests show us. Go home. Put your affairs in order."

He was right. I had asked him for answers and he hadn't spared me, hadn't sugar-coated his assessment with false hope. I somehow found that calming. I wasn't going to waste precious energy chasing some illusory wish that a savior with a scalpel and a syringe was going to make my nightmare go away.

We retraced our journey back to Innisfree that afternoon. Neither one of us had much to say as we sank into our own apprehension of the future and what it would mean. I think we both understood that our individual experience of the days ahead would be very different. And although I knew with certainty that Tobias would be by my side until the end, ultimately I would be making that passage alone. And after I was gone, he, too, would be alone.

We arrived at Innisfree in time for supper. Betty was there to share in the burden my illness had placed on everyone, but also to hear firsthand what we had learned from the surgeon. The house smelled of chicken soup and homemade bread and baked apples, and I tried to appreciate the effort Naomi and Betty had made for my homecoming. But I felt so isolated from everyone, even Tobias. It was more than fatigue, although that is what I told everyone when I excused myself from the table after only a few sips of soup.

I crawled into bed and later, when Tobias joined me, I pretended to be asleep because I could not return his embrace.

I took to heart the surgeon's advice to use the time to put my affairs in order. I had a child to provide for, and the only thing of value that I had was the land that had been my refuge and my salvation. As much as I wanted Innisfree to remain Josiah's home, I knew I would have to sell it. I wrote a note to Marcus Gardner and asked Betty to mail it for me when she returned to Edgartown the next day. In it, I told him I was considering putting Innisfree on the market and asked him to be on the lookout for an appropriate buyer. If I ultimately decided to sell, I wanted it to be to someone who would love Innisfree as much as I did.

I wasn't ready to have a conversation with Tobias about Josiah. I had no doubt that he would want to raise our son. I just didn't know how to protect them both. But I did know that whatever we did had to be unassailable in a court of law. I did not want Josiah to wind up a ward of the state because Tobias and I had never married. I knew I'd need to talk with Henry and planned to go into town later in the week after I recovered from the trip to Hyannis.

But a storm blew in the second night we were home and kept us housebound for nearly three days of fierce winds, sleet and snow. Even if Tobias had been able to get the boat out and across the bay, I knew I would not have been able to tolerate such a ride.

Instead, I made lists. Inventories, instructions, maintenance chores that were due in the coming months. And I began a journal for Josiah of all the things I wanted him to know if I were no longer there to tell him.

On the first clear day after the storm Frank Bennett arrived at the dock with a telegram for me. I tore it open and stared at the block letters forming the message on the thin yellow sheet. "Tumor is malignant. Have scheduled surgery for February 1. Return immediately to Hyannis."

I crumpled the message in my hand, pulled on my coat and boots and walked out to the promontory above the inlet where the pond and the bay meet. Despite the cold, the day was breathtakingly beautiful. The sun glinted off the ice-tipped marshes. All around me the world shimmered. My tears froze on my cheeks and my howls carried across the water like those of a swan who has lost her mate.

Part of my right lung was removed two days later. Any remaining cancer was going to be treated with the nitrogen mustard. The doctors called the treatment "chemotherapy." They didn't tell me that, in addition to killing the cancer, it was also poisoning me.

I spent a month in Hyannis recovering from the surgery and trying to tolerate the drugs. My hair fell out in clumps. On her second visit, Betty arrived with a pair of shears and several colorful scarves.

"Did I ever tell you that I had trained as a hairdresser when I was your age?" she said, wielding the scissors. She spent the next fifteen minutes cropping the straggling remnants of my hair and then washing and massaging my scalp. For those few pampered moments, I forgot my pain and my fear.

After she had toweled dry my nearly bald head, she wrapped it elegantly in a bright pink and yellow silk scarf.

"There. Now you look like Rita Hayworth." She stood back admiring her handiwork and held up a small mirror.

I hugged her in reply.

The surgeon in Hyannis was willing to let me go home two days later after making arrangements with the hospital on the Vineyard to administer my drug treatment. I couldn't bear being away from Josiah, but I also knew I couldn't make too many trips back and forth on the ferry. Still recovering from the assault of the surgery and the side effects of nitrogen mustard, I barely had enough energy to walk across the room, let alone travel across the water twice a week.

Tobias borrowed a wheelchair and stowed it in the back of the pickup truck for the trip home. It was early March and the weather was still blustery and cold. I had pulled a knitted cap over Betty's scarf and was layered as thickly as a child in sweater, coat and gloves, but the frigid air cut through me, robbing me of breath. I forced myself not to panic and remembered to take slow breaths as one of the nurses had taught me one frightening night when I thought I was suffocating.

We made the trip from Hyannis to the ferry landing in Woods Hole with almost no conversation. Tobias was focused on driving as smoothly as possible so as not to jolt my tender body, and I concentrated on counting breaths, in and out, in and out.

Once the truck was on board the ferry, Tobias came around to my side.

"I'm taking you above where it's warm and the air is better. No arguments." To reinforce his words, he slipped his arms under me and lifted me out of the truck. I didn't protest, just buried my head against his shoulder and let him carry me up the steps to the passenger lounge.

He settled me by a window at a table and tucked a blanket around my legs.

"How about something warm to drink? A cup of tea? Hot chocolate?"

"M-m-m, hot chocolate. Thanks." I tried to smile, grateful for these small gestures of care, but more uneasy than I had expected to be outside the familiar confines of the hospital. Toward the end of my stay I had felt as if it were a prison I would never escape. But now, free of its pale green walls and the hushed, rubber-soled footsteps of its nurses, with their endless pills and injections, I suddenly missed the safety of its unwavering predictability. Even though I was heading home—until now a place of sanctuary—it was no longer a source of comfort to me. The place hadn't changed, but I had. The woman who had fearlessly forged a new life for herself out at Pogue was now cowering at the thought of its remoteness and isolation.

I closed my eyes against my fear, like a child who imagines that the danger doesn't exist if she cannot see it. And then I was roused from my dark solitude by the sound of a woman's voice calling my name.

"Mae? Mae is that you? I barely recognized you!"

I opened my eyes and stared at the face of my sister, bent over my seat, the arm of her cashmere coat brushing against the roughened skin of my hands.

"Oh my God! What in the name of the Blessed Virgin has happened to you?"

I could feel the panic setting in and could not speak as I struggled with controlling my breathing. I held up my hand to stop her questions and give myself time to compose myself. I was afraid she was about to sound the alarm and call for help, although I don't think she realized that an ambulance couldn't reach us on the open water. I doubted that the seamen on the ferry would be much help.

At that moment Tobias arrived with two mugs of steaming liquid. A look of questioning at the sight of Kathleen quickly slid into anger when he saw me struggling to catch my breath.

"Get away from her! Can't you see that you are upsetting her?" He slammed the mugs down on the table and pulled Kathleen back into the aisle before moving between her and me.

"How dare you! She's my sister and I have every right to be here with her. Who the hell are you?"

Tobias had turned his back on Kathleen and was holding me, calming me.

"It's OK. Take slow breaths."

Kathleen stood motionless, sputtering but speechless, seeming to finally comprehend that she wasn't going to get any answers while Tobias was calming me and I was trying to breathe.

In the flurry of activity, my cap and scarf had slid from my head, exposing my bare skull. I heard Kathleen gasp. *There*, I thought with relief. *Now I don't have to say the words. She can see for herself.*

"Can you take a sip of cocoa?" Tobias asked, reaching for the mug.

I nodded and took it from his hand. The warm liquid soothed my throat and the sweetness gave me a short burst of energy. The medicine had triggered sores in my mouth and had also increased my thirst. When I had finished a few sips, I put the cup down and adjusted my head covering. Only then was I ready to face Kathleen.

"Sit down, Kathleen," I said quietly, pointing to the seat opposite us on the other side of the table. She slid into the seat and was about to speak, but once again I held up my hand.

"Before you both go off on one another again, Kathleen, this is Tobias. Tobias, Kathleen." They nodded warily at each other.

"If you haven't already figured it out, I'm sick. Cancer." I touched my head. "The medication does this. Kills the hair as well as the tumors."

"Why didn't you let me know?"

"It happened very fast. And there was nothing you could have done."

"I could have taken care of the baby, taken him to Boston while you got treatment."

Tobias stiffened next to me.

"Josiah is being well cared for by his grandmother," he said.

"Why are you here on the ferry?" It was my turn to ask questions. After months of not seeing or hearing from her, it was unnerving to have her show up on this day, on this boat.

"I was planning to surprise you. I brought presents for Josiah."

"Why now?"

"No particular reason," she said, much too brightly. It was unlike the Kathleen I had grown up with to do something as spontaneous as she was describing. I did not push her to find out more, but felt myself sharing Tobias' wariness.

"As you can see, Mae is not up to any visitors right now. It would be best if you took the next boat back to Woods Hole."

"Couldn't I just stop by to see the baby?"

"He's not at the cottage, and Mae needs to get home to rest as soon as possible. I'm sure you want the best for her."

Kathleen looked stung by Tobias' comment.

"Of course I do. I'm her sister."

The steamship horn sounded its warning blast as the ferry turned toward Oak Bluffs harbor, and I could not have welcomed it more.

Tobias stood up. "I need to get Mae below. I'm glad we met. We'll write to let you know how she's doing."

I reached up my arms to him and he lifted me, cradling me the way I had often seen him hold Josiah.

"Good-bye, Kathleen. I'll write when I'm feeling stronger."

She watched us move toward the stairs and then stalked away in the other direction, gathering up the excessive inducement she had brought to buy Josiah's affection.

Once in the relative safety of the truck both Tobias and I expressed relief.

"That woman wants something, and it isn't your good health. Did you hear her? Her first reaction was all about her and how you hadn't 'informed' her. Not sympathy or concern for you, not questions about how you were feeling."

"And her second reaction was all about Josiah and taking him away." We looked at each other, acknowledging the unspoken. She had the power and the money to take him away if I were to die.

"I never want her alone with Josiah." Tobias' voice was firm. But I think we both knew that she didn't have to be alone with Josiah to be a threat to him.

We went to Tobias' house at Cove Meadow. Naomi had moved in from her cottage nearby to care for Josiah. We had all agreed it was best for them not to be alone at Innisfree while Tobias was with me in Hyannis, and, at least for my first days out of the hospital, it was also better for me. There was a phone and town electricity, both comforting if we had an emergency.

I moved slowly up the steps, leaning on Tobias. I didn't want him to carry me into the house, mindful of how Josiah might react. I could hear his excited chatter through the door as Naomi called to him.

"Josiah, Mama is come home!"

Tobias led me into the parlor and to the sofa close to the door where I could be low enough to hug Josiah without stooping or toppling over from his exuberance.

He saw me and ran into my arms, burying himself against my breast. I tried not to pull away from the pressure and leaned in, taking as deep a breath as I could of his scrubbed, sweet little boy smell.

He tried to climb into my lap. Tobias, seeing the wince on my face, lifted him instead to sit next to me, his energetic legs sticking out and not an inch of air between his body and mine.

I put my arm around him.

"I have missed you so, my little man. Tell me what you and Grannie have been doing while I was away."

Naomi retreated to the kitchen to make tea but Tobias hovered. I mouthed to him silently, "We're OK," and smiled with as much energy as I could muster.

I longed to reassure Tobias, to release him from the constant state of watchfulness and protection that had consumed him since the onset of my illness. But I knew he could see through my false bravado, even though neither one of us had spoken the truth that was nibbling at the edges of our fragile haven.

I knew he did not want to leave me alone with Josiah—for fear that our exuberant little boy might inadvertently hurt me; or my energy, already taxed by the journey home, might suddenly fail, leaving me in a heap on the floor. But I needed this moment, unobserved, with my son. I needed to feel normal.

I squeezed Tobias' hand.

"Give me a few minutes with him."

He hesitated, the look in his eyes communicating both the pain of being pushed away and a grudging understanding of my need to have Josiah all to myself.

"I'll be in the kitchen," he murmured. Not far.

I turned to Josiah.

"Tell me everything," I invited him.

He babbled about his rocks and shells and feathers, the odd assortment of beach treasures that he had begun to accumulate from the first days he'd been able to walk along the sand with me at low tide.

"I found a new feather. Grammie said it was from a magic osprey. When I get enough, she'll make me a headdress like Grandpa Josiah's."

Tobias had a photograph of his father in full Wampanoag regalia from the last pow wow before his death. Josiah knew it well, and he knew he was the sachem's namesake.

I kissed the top of his head, the soft hair gleaming in the afternoon light.

"I'm sure it will be a very fine headdress, Blue Turtle."

He beamed at his Wampanoag name.

"A *magic* headdress, Mama. I will put it on and make your hair grow back to your waist."

He touched the bandana on my head. I was learning from my child that there were no secrets I could keep from him.

"Papa carved me a turtle. Do you want to see it?" He jumped down from the sofa and raced across the room to the wooden box that held his toys. During the long hours of waiting while I was in surgery and enduring the chemotherapy, I know that Tobias had stilled his worries with his knife and a block of wood. I expressed surprise when Josiah returned with the turtle, but I had seen it in every stage of its creation.

"It's not blue yet, but Grannie says she can turn it blue when the moon changes." He spoke with awe at his grandmother's power, and I smiled, knowing that Naomi indeed had magic at her fingertips with her berries and herbs.

At that moment Naomi arrived with a tray from the kitchen, more of her extensive array of skills on display—a pot of tea, cornbread and cranberry relish.

"I think your Mama needs to fill her belly as well as her ears with your stories," she smiled, plunking the tray down on a table and pouring me a steaming cup of tea.

I took it in my hands and let the aromatic steam waft up to my face. Rosehips, from the masses of wild bushes that grew along the water's edge and climbed the dunes at Innisfree. I had helped her harvest them myself the summer before. When the liquid cooled I sipped it with my eyes closed. My senses were so diminished that I needed to isolate them in order to experience even a glimmer of sensation. Focusing on the soothing liquid sliding down my raw throat, I tried to find a bit of pleasure in what had become such a world of pain.

"Will you try to eat something?" Tobias' voice was gentle at my side. He knew that I had lost my appetite, and every morsel was an effort. But he no longer shouted at me as he had one evening in the hospital.

"If you don't eat, you can't fight!" He had spoken from his own anger and fear, lashing out at me, begging me to do whatever I must to survive. But I had turned my head away from him, unable to muster the will or the energy even to meet his anger with my own. The knowledge then had been too raw, too new, for me to do anything but flail and cower. Now, a month later—was it only a month?—I had begun to reel in the fear. If it had only been me, the solitary Mae who had roamed the winter moors alone that first winter at Pogue, I knew that I could have easily succumbed to the disease, sliding under its force as I might a wave at East Beach in a pounding storm. But I was no longer alone, bound now to Tobias and Josiah.

I reached for the cornbread and took a bite.

It rained the next day. I would have stayed in bed, enveloped in Tobias' embrace, as I had been through the night. But Tobias had eased himself out of bed in the dim light of dawn, with murmurs of work that had been left undone. Now that I was home and under Naomi's watchful care, I understood he felt able to leave me for a while. He tucked a pillow under my arm to replace his warm and comforting body, and then quietly left. I tried to close my eyes again, but Josiah tugged at the sleeve of my nightgown not long after Tobias left.

"Mama?" he whispered, a tentative and plaintive tone in his voice, as if he didn't quite believe that the strange-looking woman in the bed was really me. Until my arrival home yesterday, he hadn't seen me in a month. While I'd been in the hospital I worried that he had forgotten me. In my darkest moments I was afraid that once I was gone I would disappear completely from his memory. He was just a baby. How could he possibly remember when I was no longer there to hold him or speak to him?

As tired as I was, I pushed myself up on my good arm, opposite the surgery site, and stifled the groan elicited by the sharp pain. I reached out to stroke his cheek.

"Good morning, Blue Turtle."

"Grannie made pancakes."

"I can see that," I said, kissing the syrup on his chin.

"We saved some for you."

"Thank you, Josiah. When I get up, I'll have some."

"Get up now." He pulled my hand, a little boy hungry for his mother's presence. I could not refuse him and crawled from the bed.

"Let me wash my face. I'll come to the kitchen in a few minutes."

He hesitated, still holding my hand, as if he thought I might disappear again.

"I promise. I'll come right away."

He finally let go of my hand, watching warily as I gingerly stepped across the floor and retrieved my bathrobe from its hook.

"Go to Grannie in the kitchen. I'll be in the bathroom for a few minutes."

Holding myself still against the pain and the nausea, I waited until he reluctantly left the room. I gripped the edge of the dresser to steady myself and then slowly crossed the threshold and made my way down the hall to the bathroom. At least here at Cove Meadow it was inside the house.

Beads of sweat formed on my forehead and upper lip and my limbs shook from the effort of walking only a few feet. I lowered myself to the cool tile floor, grabbed the edge of the toilet and vomited.

It was Naomi who discovered me, still on the floor and unable to find the energy to stand. She didn't chide me for attempting to get to the bathroom by myself nor offer words of pity. She simply wiped my face with a damp cloth and lifted me to my feet, her slender stature belying the strength and will that enabled her to help me.

"A little boy is waiting patiently for his mama in the kitchen. Why don't you wash up and refresh yourself. If you look composed, you will feel composed."

It took effort to brush my teeth and wash my face, but I put on a smile as I joined Josiah at the kitchen table.

"I saved the biggest one for you!" he beamed.

I sat down with him and let him put the pancake on my plate. Then I gently grabbed the syrup jug from his eager hands before he drowned the pancake and the entire table.

I ate slowly, nourishing myself, not only with Naomi's food, but with the sight and sound of my animated, energetic little boy.

"I think it's time for Mama's bath, Josiah. You may take your crayons and paper to your table in the parlor."

Naomi had a sixth sense for when I needed a respite. She also had a loving authority that Josiah responded to without protest.

Once he was settled at the child-sized table and chair Tobias had built for him and moved from Innisfree along with his bed and toys, I sank into the tub Naomi had drawn for me.

I floated until the water cooled. My nausea had subsided, and I knew from the experience with the drug treatments that I could expect at least one good day before I had to undergo another dose. I heaved myself up from the tub, climbed out carefully and got dressed. I was determined to expend whatever energy I had with Josiah during the day, and hoped to have at least a little left over for Tobias in the evening.

Despite its rocky start, the rest of the day was a good one, moderated by Naomi's careful oversight of Josiah and me—when we needed to eat, or nap, or play or snuggle with a picture book. If we could sustain this rhythm, I thought I could manage the coming weeks of chemotherapy with a minimum of disruption to everyone else. Now that I was home, I was all too aware of the burden my illness had placed on everyone, and I was determined to lighten that burden as much as I could.

Chapter Twenty-Four
Battle Plan

The comforting shelter of home established by Naomi's wisdom, Josiah's precocious understanding of my fragility, and Tobias' enveloping protection was shattered a few weeks after we had settled into our new routines.

Tobias had gone into town to pick up my mail. He arrived back at Cove Meadow with a deeply troubled face and a thick, official-looking envelope.

"I had to sign for it. It's from a law firm in Boston."

I exchanged a silent glance with him. Kathleen.

I slit open the envelope with the knife I'd been using to peel potatoes. I'd been having a good day and was showing Naomi how to prepare colcannon. The notarized papers inside the envelope slid out onto the kitchen table. I wiped my hands on my apron and picked up the top sheet.

Tobias hung back, but I motioned to him to join me.

"I don't want to read this alone. Come, stand by me. We both know this could be a threat to all of us, not just me."

He put his arm around me and took the letter in his other hand. We bent our heads together to see the words we both had feared might someday try to rip our world apart. As if my cancer had not been enough. Now this.

Kathleen was claiming her intention of taking guardianship of Josiah as next-of-kin.

She had done some snooping—or had hired someone to do it for her—and had discovered that Tobias and I were not married. Somehow she had also gotten hold of my medical records. Armed with both pieces of information, she had petitioned the court, claiming that in my severely incapacitated state I was no longer capable of caring for my child. She had requested that the court remove Josiah immediately "for the safety of the child."

The brutality of the words wounded me more deeply than any scalpel. The sickness I felt in the pit of my stomach was more poisonous than a month of chemo. How could my own sister do this to me? Rob me of my child when I might have so little time left with him. Rob Josiah of the loving father and grandmother who were the only family he knew.

I started to tremble, my body shutting down in fear as my mind absorbed the words. Tobias dropped the letter as if it were in flames and held me tightly to still the shaking and warm me.

"We have to stop her. How much time do we have?" I turned within Tobias' arms to look out the kitchen window, frantic, expecting to find the sheriff on the doorstep, ready to take Josiah away.

Naomi was already on the phone, the letter in her hand.

"Henry," she spoke calmly but with authority. "We have a crisis here and it needs your immediate attention. Can you come to Cove Meadow? Yes, now! Mae is too ill even for a trip to Edgartown. Her sister is trying to take away my grandson, and I tell you now, it will only be over my dead body."

She hung up the phone.

"He'll be here within the hour. Before he comes we need to sit at council. As far as I am concerned, we are at war. This woman may be your blood, Mae, but she has threatened *our* blood and the sanctity of this family. Are we together on this?" She looked at me and Tobias.

I had always known her as a calming and wise presence, but I had never seen her so commanding. With relief, I nodded my agreement. As much as I knew she loved Josiah, the shadow of his mixed blood had hovered over his relationship to the Monroe family and the tribe. To hear her acknowledge Josiah as "our blood" sealed her loyalty. I knew that Tobias and I would not be alone in fighting Kathleen's attempt to steal our child.

Naomi's quick resolve was a salve on the open wound caused by the letter. My trembling subsided and I felt the panic recede.

"Let's sit and talk this through."

Tobias held me as we sat at the table. I knew that his silence was a sign not of defeat or even doubt, but a mask for his anger. Naomi had acted with instinct and fury, rushing to defend us as if the enemy were at the walls of her ancestral village. Tobias' rage was smoldering, a volcano about to spew and destroy everything in its path that would harm Josiah.

"We need a plan," I managed to say after my panic had quelled and I had found my voice.

"The first thing we need to do is marry." Tobias took my hand. "In the eyes of the law. I will not jeopardize my relationship to my son for the sake of the tribe's traditions."

All of the sacrifices we had made, all of Sadie's arguments for the preservation of the tribe's identity, all of the certainty I had once had for Tobias' destiny in leading the tribe, disappeared in that instant when all that mattered was our son. I agreed without hesitation.

"We also need to get Mae's doctors to certify that she is of sound mind. Whatever assumptions Kathleen's 'experts' are making about the effects of chemotherapy on the brain have to be debunked by Mae herself." Naomi was ticking off items on our battle plan.

"When Henry gets here we can have him confirm whether our response will be enough."

"Kathleen has money behind her. All our legal niceties, t's crossed and i's dotted, may not be enough if her husband's power and influence extend to the courts." Tobias knew who we were dealing with and he wasn't going to be lulled into complacency thinking that we could win our case on the strength of the facts alone.

"Do you think Marcus can help us?" I didn't know how far Marcus' influence extended, but he was the judge for our county. If the case were heard here on the Vineyard, I knew no amount of Ned Bradley's money would dissuade Marcus from protecting the people who had saved his life. But if the case were heard in Boston…

"Henry can answer whether it will be our own court that decides the guardianship. And if Kathleen tries to file in Boston, we'll just have to fight her about that as well." Tobias had no intention of allowing Kathleen any advantage.

"I'm concerned about how vulnerable we are here. If Kathleen is desperate enough to have Josiah, she may try to kidnap him if she can't convince the court to name her as Josiah's guardian." Tobias was racing ahead with potential scenarios.

"I don't want to be driven into hiding, always looking over our shoulder that she might be lurking, ready to snatch our son. You once told me I would not be free of the power she had over me unless I confronted her with the truth. I see now that is what I'm going to have to do."

Tobias pressed my hand in affirmation.

"My guess is that Kathleen already knows the truth about her husband. Maybe not the details of his history with you, but in her heart she must have recognized his evil and made a choice to turn a blind eye to it. She's as culpable as he is. And, if this suit is any clue, she is the one who is mentally unstable and unfit to raise a child."

A car pulled up to the house and we all jumped—Tobias to determine who it was and Naomi and I to Josiah's bedroom, where he was napping.

"It's OK," Tobias called out. "It's Henry."

We spent the next two hours reviewing the documents and our options. In Henry's opinion, Kathleen's petition was without merit. First, he assured us that no family court would remove Josiah from my care while I was alive, despite my illness.

"What about the competency issue?" I asked. "Could they convince a judge that I was too damaged by my treatment to care for Josiah?"

"The court would determine your competency, and assign you a guardian if you couldn't make decisions—which would still keep Kathleen at arm's length. But you are your own expert witness as far as your competency, Mae. No judge talking to you would consider you unable to care for Josiah, especially with the family support you have here."

"What about Tobias' rights as Josiah's father, if I were to die?"

"Even though you aren't married, Tobias is still Josiah's closest next-of-kin, especially since he has played an active role throughout Josiah's life. Again, no family court would separate Josiah from his father if you were to die. Forgive me for treading on what may be a sensitive issue here, but I have never understood why you two have never married."

He looked from me to Tobias.

"That's about to change," Tobias spoke with conviction. "Even though I respect your opinion, Henry, the missing element is Ned Bradley's money and power."

"Ned Bradley? George Bradley's son? What does he have to do with this?"

"He's married to my sister."

The confidence and assurance that Henry had displayed since reviewing the documents changed with that information.

"In that case, we need to have everything water tight—no loopholes that a bribed judge could slip through. Would you two be comfortable if I alerted Marcus about this? He may already be aware, if the petition has been filed."

"Of course. We need to keep the hearing on the island, don't you agree?"

"Marcus may be able to help with that. Let's pull together a to-do list, and move quickly."

By the time Henry left at dusk we had our assignments. Tobias and I would get blood tests and start the process for our marriage license in the morning; Naomi was going to plan a wedding; and Henry would gather statements from my doctors in Hyannis and on the Vineyard.

That night we moved Josiah's bed into our bedroom, closed the shutters and locked the doors. We were a family under siege, and no one except Josiah slept.

Chapter Twenty-Five
Ceremony

I was scheduled for chemotherapy the next day. I had never looked forward to these appointments, but the arrival of morning's light brought with it more than my usual sense of foreboding. The treatments were depleting enough when all I had to manage in their aftermath was a smile and a hug for Josiah before I crawled into my bed with a basin. I now needed so much more—energy and clear thinking to outmaneuver Kathleen's phalanx of lawyers; unwavering faith and confidence that justice was on our side; and loving strength to sustain Tobias, whose fear of losing our son was palpable beneath the anger that was fueling him.

I had my own fears—that I would collapse under the added challenges, able neither to fight for my family nor fight for my own life. *I cannot die before Josiah is safe with Tobias,* I told myself fiercely as I pulled myself out of the nightmares that had visited me throughout the night.

We all moved through our early-morning rituals, muffled in our own thoughts. Naomi silently handed me a glass of buttermilk with a beaten raw egg and honey, the only breakfast I'd learned I could hold down on a chemo day. I drank it while staring out at the pond below the house. She'd already gotten Josiah up, dressed, and coaxed him to finish his oatmeal. Normally, she'd leave these tasks till after Tobias and I departed for the hospital.

"Why so early?" I asked her, gesturing toward Josiah pushing a wooden car around his empty bowl.

"Kathleen may be aware of your treatment days. There's no telling what she was able to find out. If she knows you and Tobias are at the hospital, she may come here."

"And you have no intention of being here if she does come."

"You've got it."

"Where will you go?"

"My brother is on his way from Aquinnah in his boat to pick us up. Josiah and I will spend the day in Mashpee at Sadie's."

My eyebrows shot up. The last place I would have named as a safe haven was Sadie's house.

"Why would she shelter my son?"

Naomi turned from the sink, where she was finishing the last of the breakfast dishes. No matter what the crisis, she never left an untidy house. She looked at me, her face once again set in the expression of command she had assumed the night before.

"Because I am a tribal elder and Josiah's safety and identity as a Wampanoag and Tobias' son are the responsibility of the tribe. I told Henry yesterday that I would die before I would allow anyone to take Josiah from us. Overruling Sadie's rigid definition of who is or is not Wampanoag is several notches below that."

She wiped her hands on the dish towel, folded it and hung it on its hook.

"It's time for us all to get ready to leave."

Naomi's brother arrived at the dock before we drove away and I was enveloped Josiah in a hug before he was lifted aboard. As it had been since he was a toddler, being out on the water was a great adventure, and he was too preoccupied with his great-uncle's equipment to focus on our separation."

"Have fun!" I waved as they motored out of the cove.

I climbed back up to the house, grabbed the bag of knitting I hoped would distract me while tethered to my IV, and settled myself in the passenger seat of the truck.

Tobias and I looked at each other. I took a deep breath; he grasped my hand in a reassuring grip and then started the ignition.

In Edgartown we stopped briefly at the town hall to pick up the marriage license application. We planned to get our blood tests at the lab at the hospital. If all went as planned, we'd be married by the end of the week.

Despite my diminished senses, the smell of the hospital assaulted me as soon as we passed through the lobby and pushed open the doors of the cancer ward. The odors of antiseptic and floor wax, and even faint traces of ether, triggered a wave of nausea.

"Catch me," I managed to squeak out to Tobias as I grabbed him with a clammy hand. And he did.

"I hate this," I muttered into his shoulder. "The damn poison isn't even in my veins yet and just the anticipation is making my body protest."

"You are stronger than you know, stronger than this disease." He kissed the top of my bandana-covered head.

All his reassurance and kisses and strong arms around me had not convinced me that I would overcome this latest obstacle in my path. But I straightened up and set my mouth in a grim line.

"Let's get this over with."

I'd had enough treatments over the last month to know they don't get any easier, and this one was no exception. I convinced Tobias to leave me and take care of errands. I saw no point in having him sit with me, his face a mirror of my own, sinking into the pain. He left, reluctantly, and I tried to knit. I tried to sleep. I tried to forget. At the end of the hours-long session I had forgotten everything except the pain.

When Tobias returned, I was curled in a fetal position on the gurney, a basin not far from my head. He gently lifted me and carried me down the corridor, refusing the orderly's offer of a wheelchair. At the door leading to the lobby he stopped.

"Shit," he whispered.

"What?" I tried to lift my head.

"We're going to go out the back door." And he turned about, heading back into the more secluded depths of the hospital. He didn't say another word until we had arrived at a door adjacent to the hospital's laundry. The swish and tumble of its washing machines had a vaguely soothing sound. He deposited me on an empty gurney in the hall.

"I'm going to bring the truck around back. I don't think anyone will bother you here." And then he was gone. My brain was too fogged to try to unravel our unorthodox departure, and I closed my eyes.

When I opened them I was nestled in the truck, a quilt tucked around me, and we were halfway to Edgartown on Beach Road.

"We'll be on the Chappy ferry soon. We're going to stop at Mel Boone's place for a few hours."

"Why?" My mouth was parched and sore, and I could barely manage the single syllable, let alone the torrent of questions that was swirling in my brain.

"Kathleen was in the hospital lobby arguing with the receptionist. I couldn't hear everything she was saying, but I caught the gist of it. She was demanding to see you. 'I know she's here. I'm her closest relative,' she shouted. When she figures out you're gone, I'm afraid she'll come to the house."

"Thank you," I whispered.

Mel Boone's cottage was deep in the woods, about as far from Cove Meadow as one could get on Chappy. The road was rutted and overgrown, which made for a bumpy ride, but I was grateful for how unused it appeared. It was an unlikely path for someone to take who didn't know the island.

Nobody was there—not unexpected in the middle of the day, when Mel would be out trawling or hauling in lobster traps. Tobias carried me in and then went to hide the truck in Mel's shed.

I spent the afternoon in a drowsy trance, sipping water when I could keep it down, sleeping fitfully on an old couch propped up on bricks, and listening to the sounds of awakening new life in this early spring day. Tobias was in the yard chopping wood for Mel as a payment for hiding out at his place, but also as a way of keeping watch. No one came.

At nightfall we ventured back to our side of the island.

The lights were on in Cove Meadow. We could hear the sounds of a meal in preparation and the alternating lilt of Naomi's voice with the gruff baritone of her brother George. I was assured, at least for that moment, that all was well.

Naomi stopped her banter with George as soon as she saw us in the doorway. Tobias had doused the lights on the truck as we had approached the house to hide our arrival. Without words, her face expressed both concern and relief.

She had expected us to be home when she returned from Mashpee, but she didn't question us. Josiah was under the kitchen table playing, but he scampered out as soon as he saw my legs. At least Tobias hadn't had to carry me into the house, but I was more than ready for my bed.

"Come cuddle with me, little man, while Grannie finishes cooking supper."

Playing finger games with Josiah I could hear the murmurs in the kitchen, Tobias recounting his discovery of Kathleen at the hospital and questioning his mother about any signs around the house that she might have come here as well.

"Mama! You're not paying 'tention." Josiah took my face in his hands and turned it toward him. I smiled and tickled him, trying to focus my thoughts on him and away from my uneasiness.

When Josiah was finally asleep after supper and I had successfully kept down a cup of Naomi's nourishing chicken soup, we adults gathered in the parlor. I stretched out on the sofa with my feet in Tobias' lap. He massaged my calves.

"I can't keep running away from Kathleen, hiding Josiah and myself. I feel like I'm allowing her to drive me from my home, from my sense of safety and security, from what I need to survive. I can't go through another day like today. I just want enough strength to confront her, make her see what she is doing to us."

"I agree that Kathleen needs to be confronted, Mae. But not until you and Tobias are married. Remember what Henry said. You are too vulnerable without that marriage certificate." Naomi was understanding, but firm.

"If you weren't sick, you'd be battling Kathleen with every ounce of your energy. We know that. Let us fight for you," she added.

"I know how exhausted you are and how much you need to rest. I've watched you endure these treatments for the last month and am in awe of your courage and tenacity. But I need to ask you to hold on for just a few more days. We can't stay here, not with Kathleen on the island. Every minute you and Josiah remain here is another opportunity for her to sweep in and grab what she wants. I saw and heard her in the hospital this morning. She was unhinged, out of control. Any attempt to confront her would only push her over the edge. I don't trust her. No rational talk will get through to her. I need to get you away."

"I can't tolerate a boat ride, Tobias."

"This one won't be far. We'll go to Cuttyhunk, but we'll leave from Menemsha. The members of the tribe there will protect you. On Friday, George will bring Marcus over to marry us. He's agreed to sign off on the marriage license so we don't have to wait."

"It sounds like you have it all planned out."

"I know how you feel about having control taken out of your hands, Mae. But this time I need you to listen. I *beg* you to listen."

I looked around at the faces surrounding me. Not my blood, but people who loved and cared for me and my son.

I nodded, and leaned back against the pillows, trying to quell not only the nausea but also the fear and pride that were pushing back at the very people trying to help me.

"We'll leave at 3 a.m. to drive to Menemsha and meet up with George. He's going to motor over there now."

"Come with me, Mae, and you can tell me what you want me to pack for you and Josiah. We need to find a suitable wedding dress in your closet."

I appreciated that Naomi was not allowing our flight to overshadow the significance of our wedding, but it also crushed me that I could not even summon the energy to pick out a dress.

"You are not just fleeing from Kathleen, Mae. You are fleeing toward Tobias and your future together." She stretched out her hand and pulled me up. With her arm around me, we went back to the bedroom.

As Tobias had promised, we left Cove Meadow in the middle of the night. Both Josiah and I were wrapped in warm coats and Naomi's heaviest blankets. I felt every bump over the uneven roads but gritted my teeth and practiced telling myself that pain was just one more sign that I was still alive.

George was waiting at the Menemsha dock and we took off immediately, even before the other fishing boats had loaded their ice or fired up their engines.

Dawn was creeping along the horizon as we pulled into Cuttyhunk harbor. Josiah had slept the entire trip and was just waking up as George and Tobias threw the ropes to waiting hands on the dock.

A donkey cart was waiting at the end of the pier. If any cars or trucks were kept on the island, they were nowhere in evidence. We traveled inland to a hidden settlement with a couple of cottages. A wood fire was burning in the largest house and the cart driver hopped down to give me a hand climbing out.

"Louise has breakfast waiting for you all."

Naomi carried Josiah and I leaned on Tobias as we trooped into Louise's kitchen. I wished I could have appreciated the comforting aroma of baked bread and frying bacon, but all I wanted was a bed and a cup of tea. Naomi, ever vigilant, handed Josiah to his father and led me toward the back of the house.

"Let's get you settled. Louise, could brew a cup of tea for Mae?"

I collapsed into a bed that had been freshly made up, its crisp sheets still faintly fragrant, whipped dry by sea air.

"Do you think you can manage some toast?" Naomi asked, as Louise arrived with a tray laden with a fat teapot, a mug, and a jar of honey. I shook my head. "Maybe later. Just some tea now and some aspirin for my head."

I took a few sips, swallowed the pills Naomi held out to me and drifted, finally, into a sleep accompanied by dulled pain and grasping dreams that pulled me in opposite directions. Light and dark. A child's voice and a hollow void.

I slept, off and on, until the next morning.

I woke to the smell of chamomile and mint—it was the tea I had drunk when I was nursing Josiah and the fragrance pulled me out of my conflicted dreams and into the sweet memory of my baby boy, nestled against my breast.

"I thought you might want to start the day with some herbal tea," said Naomi. "When you're ready, there's a warm bath waiting for you."

I sipped the tea propped up in Louise's bed and through the window caught a glimpse of Josiah romping in the grass with Tobias, who was catching him and whirling him in the air. It did me enormous good to see them moving with such abandon, able to forget all the somber shadows that had encroached upon our happiness even if for a few moments. It was a jolt of very good medicine, unlike the chemo that was a double-edged sword. I smiled, and the very act brought me joy.

The bath Naomi promised expanded the sense of well-being that was suffusing through me. I felt wrapped in a cocoon in this hidden corner of a remote island, protected not only from Kathleen's grasping threat, but also from the amorphous enemy of my disease. One of the more insidious characteristics of the cancer had been its lack of boundaries. I could not see its edges, not even the faint line of a horizon in the distance that might have given me hope, a parched sailor adrift in an endless sea of pain, uncertainty and disorder.

But this morning, as the steam rising from the lavender-scented water eased my breathing, I closed my eyes and listened to my son's laughter and the bustle of a household preparing for a wedding. *My* wedding.

When I emerged from the bath it was Betty who slipped into the bedroom to help me dress. I embraced my stalwart friend.

"When did you get here? How did you know?"

"I came with Marcus on George's boat this morning. Marcus stopped by late yesterday to fill me in. I had to come. I've brought you a few things—the traditional 'old, new, borrowed, blue.' I've been saving them."

She pinned to my slip a thin blue ribbon that held a tiny gold cross.

"Josiah is letting you borrow this," she smiled as she fastened the cross to the creamy silk. It was his baptismal cross, a gift from Betty as his godmother.

Then she whipped a pair of stockings out of rose-colored tissue paper.

"Real silk!" she said with a flourish. The cool, smooth fabric felt like a caress against my skin, so battered and damaged by the chemo.

The dress Naomi had packed for me hung on a hook on the back of the door. Someone had washed and ironed it. It was one of the few items from my life in New York I had not left behind. I'd barely worn it in my years of island life, but I must have known I'd need it one day.

"It's perfect," Betty purred as she zipped it up the back and then helped me button the tiny, fabric-covered buttons on the sleeves. I twirled around, my arms outstretched, when she was done. The bias-cut skirt swung out around me in a graceful arc, and I reached out to Betty both to steady myself and to feel the strength and warmth and love that was embodied in my friend.

She embraced me, and I could feel the tears on her cheeks.

"I don't want to crush the dress or ruin your make-up, but I want you to know how beautiful you look and how happy I am for you today."

I kissed her. "Thank you. For everything."

A knock on the door was followed by Naomi's voice. "May I come in?"

Betty opened the door to arms full of voluminous lace.

"I found a woman in Plymouth who tatted and I had her make this up for you." Naomi held out a veil as delicate as a spider's web and arranged it on my head.

"This should keep it from sliding off," she said as she placed a wreath of wildflowers and ivy on my head.

"Come, look at yourself." She took my hand and brought me to the dresser, where a large mirror hung in a carved frame.

"I barely recognize myself," I smiled. The woman staring back at me was not the gaunt, fearful woman who had been inhabiting my body for the last four months. In her place was someone who reflected a glimmer of radiance and hope, like a candle burning in a window welcoming strangers.

I turned to the two women who had been my rocks, my fortresses. I reached my hands out to both of them.

"Let's go have a wedding."

It had been many years since I had imagined myself as a bride. Ned's abandonment had set me on a path that diverged far from my girlhood dreams; and when Tobias' love had finally released me from my solitude, I had tamped down the sparks of longing to be a wife for what I had once believed to be a greater good.

So this moment of anticipation as I stepped out of the house with Naomi and Betty was totally new to me. I trembled, not from the physical weakness that had beset me since I became ill, but from the exhilaration of finally allowing myself the freedom to dream of becoming Tobias' wife. There wasn't going to be much time between "becoming" and "being." I looked across the lawn to where a small circle of folks were gathered under a blossoming apple tree. I didn't know most of them, but two faces held meaning for me.

Marcus stood in the center, his judge's robe bringing a formality to the simplicity of Louise's country garden. I suppose he could have married us in a suit. The marriage would have been equally valid. But like the veil Naomi had ordered for me—how many months ago?—Marcus' robe honored us. It said, this is an important moment and we will mark it with the care we take with every element.

Off to the side, talking with some of the older tribal members who had come together to protect Josiah and me with this refuge, was Henry. I knew he had secured Marcus' support in expediting our marriage license. But I also knew that he had come not only as our lawyer, but also as our friend. He was also my one link to the past, the only one here who had known me as a child. That connection seized me so powerfully that I broke away from Naomi and Betty and moved toward him, calling his name.

He came quickly to me, took my hands in his, and said, "Mae, you are beautiful!"

"Henry, I have favor to ask you. Will you give me away?"

He caught his breath and looked at me.

"I'd be honored. There is nothing I'd like more."

He took my arm and tucked it into his.

Naomi had slipped away for a moment, but she returned with flowers in one hand and Josiah in the other. She passed me a bouquet brimming with early spring flowers—crocuses and hellebore and snowdrop anemones—tied with a wide yellow ribbon.

Josiah had also had a bath that morning and was now scrubbed and combed and dressed in a pair of short pants held up with red suspenders and a pressed shirt with a red bowtie. In his hand was a metal sand pail. When I looked to see what was in it, suspecting a frog, he flattened his hand over the top.

"Don't peak! I'm the wing bear."

Betty stifled a chuckle as she smoothed his cowlick and mouthed the words "ring bearer" to me, pointing to the velvet box in the bottom of the pail. "Indeed you are, little man. I think it's time for us to lead your Mama to the apple tree."

A single drum and flute had begun a cadence.

We formed a small procession with Naomi at the head. Tobias' cousin Ronnie approached her and she took his arm as he led her to Marcus and the assembled guests. I knew that Tobias had asked him to be his best man, and I scanned the others for Sadie but did not see her. I pushed aside her absence. It was not going to cast a pall on this day.

I hadn't seen Tobias since he'd been playing with Josiah in the morning. But as Naomi approached with Ronnie, he emerged from behind the apple tree. He bent down to kiss his mother, who whispered to him.

Then he looked up, first at Josiah swinging his pail and then at me.

I stepped forward with Henry, leaning into him at first, not trusting my body to be strong for me. But as Tobias watched me, I focused on the transformation taking place before my eyes. His face, so accustomed to masking his emotions, especially in these last months of terror, was suddenly unprotected. In those unguarded moments as I approached him, I saw longing and fierce protectiveness, my warrior and my wise man. My love.

The closer I got to Tobias, the less I relied on Henry's firm support, until Henry turned to kiss my cheek and place my hand within Tobias'.

At that moment, I felt life surging through me—defiant, passionate, willing to fight for every breath left to me. I walked to Tobias on my own and, pledging to love him for the rest of my life, vowed to myself that I would do everything I could to make that life a long one.

Chapter Twenty-Six
My Breath is Mixed into His Breath

Naomi had thought of everything. Not just the flowers and the veil, the license and the music. She had prepared a feast in Louise's barn, with deviled eggs and cranberry bread, a roast turkey and a baked him, and wedding cake covered in butter cream frosting half an inch thick.

In the late afternoon, when the last toast had been offered and only crumbs remained on the cake platter, she gathered up Josiah and with a twinkle in her eye told us the donkey cart was waiting to transport us to our honeymoon.

We looked at one another and Tobias shrugged. "I know nothing."

"Louise's brother has a cabin further inland, overlooking the marsh. It's yours for the night. A fire is already burning in the woodstove and your clothes were sent over earlier. Go. Enjoy your first night of married life. And may there be many more."

She kissed us both and sent us off for our first night alone together since I'd collapsed with pneumonia at Christmas.

We arrived at the cabin just as the skies opened up with a steady rain that beat a tattoo on the roof and splashed rhythmically into the marsh. The sound formed a comforting backdrop, a low hum like an active hive, where there might have been a hollow silence.

We had not spoken on the ride over, each of us folded in, exhausted, overwhelmed not only by the whirlwind of the last 48 hours, but by the enormity of the last four months. Tobias stoked the fire in the cast-iron stove as I wrapped myself in a thick shawl. Darkness, compounded by the rain clouds, was descending upon the cabin.

"I'll find a lantern. Are you hungry or thirsty?"

I shook my head.

When he returned with the light casting a small circle on his face I saw once again the weariness and the wariness that had been erased so briefly during the ceremony earlier. He set the lantern down on a low table in front of the sofa. I patted the empty spot next to me.

"Come sit with me."

He settled onto the lumpy cushion and put his arm around me. I nestled against him, his familiar leanness my bulwark in the rough seas of the past winter.

"What do we do now?" I asked, my mind still locked in the solitary reverie that had visited me on the road to the cabin.

"I thought I would take you to bed and ravish you now that I've made an honest woman out of you."

I smiled and turned my face to kiss him, a kiss of both gratitude and longing.

He stroked the side of my face.

"My mother tried very hard today to give us a wedding with all the trappings of normalcy."

"Yes, she did," I agreed, waiting for the "but." He did not disappoint.

"But, despite the veil, and the apple blossoms, and the toasts and the three-tiered cake, it lacked what every married couple expects."

"A future," I acknowledged, pulling slightly away from him. As I did so, my bandana slipped. Instead of straightening it to cover my bare skull, Tobias lifted it away.

"You are beautiful without it," he said, as he looked at me.

"As we rode over here, away from the tumult of well-wishers trying to pretend that everything was wonderful, I had a chance to think for the first time in days, instead of merely reacting to every threat that loomed. I came to a decision."

I waited for him to continue, wondering if his thoughts had led him in the same direction as mine.

"But first, I need to ask you something. Are you happy to be my wife? Put aside the necessity for our marriage, if you can. I know you would do anything to protect Josiah. Apart from Josiah, is this what you want for *you*?"

I did not hesitate.

"Yes. With all my heart. I didn't know it until I saw you waiting for me under the apple tree. The knowledge of how much I loved you flooded through me, pushing aside the fear and the pain."

A guttural moan emerged from his throat, as if he were unleashing the caged animal of his own fear and pain. He pulled me toward his heart in a powerful embrace.

"We may not be able to change the outcome of your illness any more than we can alter the course of a river that has cut through a canyon for thousands of years. I don't want to pretend it's not there, the way Naomi suspended reality today. But I also don't want its shadow hovering over us, stealing from us the moments of true happiness we may still have together."

"That's what I want, too. No more and no less. I want every minute with you to count. When that final moment comes I want no regrets that I didn't live fully the life that remains to me."

He lifted me in his arms at that moment.

"Then let me take you to bed, Mrs. Monroe."

Chapter Twenty-Seven
An Island Child

We left Cuttyhunk the next morning, when the rain had stopped and the sea was calm enough to motor directly to Cove Meadow. I was midway between treatments, which had been good timing for the wedding and our wedding night. The surge of energy I had felt during the ceremony and the honesty Tobias and I had expressed at the cabin sustained me in ways I had not experienced since becoming ill. If ever there were a time when I would need my strength, the next few days turned out to be that time. I remembered Ma telling me something the night we learned the Bradleys had lost everything in the Crash and we were about to be turned out of our home.

"God doesn't give us what we cannot handle. If we look deeply enough inside, we will find what we need, hidden perhaps by the illusion of ease, but ready to fight for us if we know how to call it forth."

I had long ago abandoned my faith in God, but not my faith in my mother's wisdom.

Waiting for us at the house was a messenger with a court summons. Kathleen had succeeded in getting a hearing to declare me incapable of caring for my son and to award her guardianship of Josiah.

"Let her try," Tobias shouted defiantly to the sky and the woods and the sea.

Kathleen had not succeeded in forcing the hearing to be held in Boston. We would be in our own courthouse in Edgartown, and I knew that both Henry and Marcus had used their influence to keep the proceedings on the island. But the timing of the hearing was the day of my next chemo appointment, as if she had used my treatment schedule deliberately to put me at a disadvantage. A puking, exhausted woman was hardly going to appear capable of managing an energetic four-year-old.

"We should ask for a postponement until you've recovered from your chemo session," Naomi suggested.

"No. That would only reinforce the perception that I am incapacitated. I want to go ahead with the hearing. I know we are ready. I'd rather postpone the chemo a day."

"Is that a risk, to disrupt the timing?"

"I see more of a risk of losing Josiah if we try to delay. I want to go into the courtroom strong, not sick. I can do this."

The next day, unannounced, a court-appointed social worker came to the house. She was an off-islander, dressed in a peplum suit, pumps and a hat, as if she were traveling to the city and not an island cottage on a dirt road.

Tobias was out fishing; Naomi was in the kitchen shelling peas. I was on the back porch pulling laundry off the line while Josiah sprawled at my feet building a wall of wooden blocks and then knocking them over with a rubber ball and lots of sound effects.

The woman, of course, came to the front door. I heard Naomi's voice as she answered the knock. She offered no warm welcome, only a firm demand to see the woman's authorization to set foot on our property. We had felt ourselves under siege for so long that any stranger was suspect. Satisfied, Naomi led her through the house to the porch. Forewarned, I had straightened my kerchief and smoothed my skirt. The bandage that covered the black-and-blue bruise on my arm where my IV was inserted at every session was hidden by my long-sleeved shirt, but I tugged down on the cuff anyway.

I greeted the woman with a firm handshake, determined not to display even a flicker of weakness.

"Would you like some lemonade?" I offered when we sat in the parlor. "It's a warm day to be on the road."

She declined, opened her file and began to pepper me with questions about Josiah's birth, health and "child development milestones." I don't think she had any children of her own, and I wondered how she'd be able to assess Josiah's well-being or my capacity as a mother if all she relied on was a sterile set of measurements established by some bureaucrat at the State House. She seemed only to care if he had walked, talked and learned to use the potty at appropriate ages. What I wanted to tell her was how fascinated he was by the natural world, noticing the minute striations on the inside of a seashell or identifying the call of an owl when he took a night walk with Tobias. At four, he could already read the wind, retell the Wampanoag creation legend of the island, and mix up a batch of blueberry pancakes with berries he had helped his grannie to pick. He could carry a tune, swim in the pond and watch a colony of ants for hours as they carried grain after grain of sand out of their tunnels.

"He's an island child," I said, fiercely proud of his accomplishments. "Like his parents."

"The question is whether he will adapt quickly to the city—whether he has been prepared for a life with more advantages."

Naomi's cool hand found its way to my trembling one just before I was about to explode.

"Josiah has all the advantages a child needs—a loving family, a safe environment in which to test his wings and the stability of a community in which he is a cherished member." She spoke calmly but with the steel of conviction that tolerated no contradiction.

"Yes, well. It will be the court that decides what is best for him. I'd like to speak to him to complete my assessment, and then see the house and the grounds. I noticed when I came in that you have no fence between the house and the water."

"Josiah learned to swim when he was three, and he has also learned that he's never to go to the water's edge alone. Island children understand at an early age the power and danger, but also the wonder, of the water. You may certainly talk with him, but either I or his mother will be in the room."

The young woman had clearly never faced anyone as intimidating as Naomi before. She backed down from her officious stance and accepted without objection that she was not going to be allowed to be alone with Josiah.

Her "interview" with him was brief and stilted. I was curious if she had ever spoken with a child this young before. Dressed as she was, she couldn't get down on the floor with him, and she only asked questions that he could answer with a "yes" or "no." She didn't invite him to tell her about his favorite toys or what he liked to do best. It was Josiah himself who finally asked a question of her.

"What kind of feather is that in your hat? I have an osprey feather just like my granddad had in his headdress. He was the sachem. That means chief. Was your granddad a chief, too? Do you want to see my feather?" He got up to retrieve it, but she stopped him.

"No, that's OK, Josiah. I have to be going soon."

She touched the feather that curved so artfully from her stylish hat, I'm sure without a clue that it had once come from a living creature.

She sniffed her way through the house, which was as spotless as it always was, thanks to Naomi. If she was looking for signs of neglect at worst or simply the paraphernalia of a sick room that might pose a danger to a child, she found none. My pills were locked away out of sight, I slept in a standard bed and I had no need of a wheelchair or a chamber pot.

When she finally got into her car and drove away, Naomi and I retired to the kitchen for a stiff drink.

"Henry will tear her to shreds in the hearing," she said, lifting her glass to mine with a satisfying clink.

Chapter Twenty-Eight
Warrior

The day of the hearing was hot for late May, but because I'd struggled to keep warm all winter as my weight had dropped, I welcomed the stifling temperature. I felt wrapped in the balmy air, another cocoon to hold at bay one of the irritants of my illness. I had learned that cancer isn't one gaping maw of pain. There is that, of course. But accompanying the enormity of cancer, were a hundred minor vexations that I found myself swatting away like a plague of deer flies in July.

But the heat that was a comfort to me was making Josiah cranky. Although he would not be in the courtroom, the summons had stipulated that he be present in the courthouse. He would wait in the judge's quarters during the hearing. Neither Tobias nor I was at ease if he were not with one of us, but we both needed to attend the hearing. Leaving Josiah with the judge's secretary was not enough reassurance of his safety. Until we were secure in the decision of the court we were still cautious. Kathleen's obsession might still drive her to kidnap Josiah, even as we appeared before the judge. We wanted someone with him whom he knew and who would also protect him as we would. Betty readily agreed to watch over him.

I had dressed Josiah in his wedding outfit, but the discomfort of the heat was making him fuss with the bowtie. In exasperation I untied it.

"You can go without it during the ride to Edgartown, but it goes back on when we reach the courthouse. Daddy is wearing a tie today, too."

Betty and Henry met us on the steps of the courthouse, and Henry led her and Josiah to the judge's quarters via a back hallway. We did not want Kathleen to get even a glimpse of him.

Tobias took my hand and squeezed it as we watched them walk away.

"Ready?"

I squeezed back, and we climbed the spiral staircase together, its graceful curve leading directly into the large open room at the top of the courthouse. Naomi, her brother and several of the tribal elders were waiting for us on benches on one side of the gallery. Marcus was also there, in quiet conversation with my doctor from Hyannis.

"All your forces have gathered to defend you," murmured Tobias.

"To defend *us*," I corrected him. "Our family."

I thanked everyone quietly and then glanced around. On the other side of the wide room, on a bench near the front, I found what I was looking for. Kathleen had her back to me, huddled with three men in expensive suits and highly polished shoes. Although it took me a moment to recognize him, I knew the heavy-set man with the florid complexion was Ned Bradley. He was no longer the athletic, sandy-haired young man who had walked into the Jordan Marsh bakery fifteen years before, looking for a blueberry muffin and finding me.

I wondered how many drinks he'd already had this morning, when it was only eleven.

I turned away. Of course he would be here. Even if it was Kathleen alone who wanted guardianship of Josiah, she must have known she would have to present a united front with her husband. I had expected this, mentally. We had talked about it, Tobias and I, and I had prepared myself. I was not going to allow Ned Bradley to rattle me. Too much was at stake. But emotionally I felt the punch in the gut he had delivered when he had thrust the hundred dollars in my face and told me to "get rid of it." It, our unborn child.

Tobias sensed my rising panic. I had told him once it was the hunter in him, that he could detect my mood shifts so easily.

"Steady," he whispered, slipping his arm around my waist. "You are a fortress. A warrior. He cannot harm you or Josiah."

He turned my face to his and anointed my cheeks as if he were streaking them with war paint.

"Every warrior is afraid right before the battle. Use the fear to fuel yourself. Get angry with it. Fight this as you have been fighting the cancer." He kissed me, hard.

I'd never been to a court proceeding before. "This is a hearing, not a trial," Henry assured me. "The judge is here to decide what will be in Josiah's best interest—not Kathleen's, not yours. But Kathleen has a very weak claim. Josiah has been in your care his entire life and has been clearly loved and nourished. She is making a very unusual request in seeking guardianship in the *anticipation* of the loss of his mother. She may have some cockamamie psychologist to back her up, but the court doesn't like to set unusual precedents, especially when it comes to children. Besides, Tobias is a closer blood relative than Kathleen, and, as your husband, he is Josiah's legal as well as biological father. Even if he were absent, Naomi has a stronger claim as his grandmother than Kathleen does as his aunt. In some states, even the tribe would have a stronger claim if there were no immediate family. What all of this means, Mae, is that you and Tobias have a very strong chance of walking out of here with your parental rights upheld and a restraining order to keep Kathleen away from Josiah. As far as I have been able to ascertain, cancer has never been cited as a reason to remove a child from his mother. Drug addiction, mental illness, yes. But not cancer."

Marcus had been even more blunt. "Frankly, I'm astonished she was even able to get as far as a hearing. I can only attribute her success in getting this far to her husband's money and political connections in Boston. But I know the judge who's been assigned. Walter Bishop is not going to allow any nonsense in his courtroom."

Despite their reassurances, the simple fact that we were even in this courtroom this morning meant the decision was still open, and Kathleen believed she had the power to leave here with our son.

I was surprised at the level of disorganization when we first arrived. Papers were pulled from folders and brought to the clerk; murmured conversations took place as knots of people gesticulated on both sides of the aisle. The judge was not yet in the room, and as we waited, it occurred to me that he might still be in his chambers and therefore with Josiah. Would he perceive Josiah's crankiness as the sign of an unhappy and neglected child? Did this judge have any experience with small children? My mind was racing with a number of alternatives and I forced myself to take a deep breath.

Remember that you are a warrior, I told myself, and touched myself where Tobias had marked me with his strong hands.

And then one of Kathleen's lawyers approached Henry, who listened intently, nodded and then came over to speak to us. In a low voice, with his back to Kathleen, he told us, "They seem to be realizing how weak their case is. Kathleen is offering to drop her request for guardianship while you are still alive, in exchange for you naming her as Josiah's guardian in your will. Hold your fury, as I did. I needed to make the appearance of bringing the offer for you to consider. I assume you refuse?"

Tobias was rigid with rage. "Does this woman not understand that Josiah has both a mother and a father, a grandmother, a tribe? Does she believe we are ignorant of the law because we don't live in a mansion on Beacon Hill?"

Now it was my turn to be the calming influence. I placed my fragile, blue-veined hand on his arm, willing the strength back to him that he had passed on to me earlier.

"We categorically refuse, Henry. As far as I am concerned, she will never even see Josiah again." My voice was as strong as it had been on our wedding day, when I had pledged my vows to Tobias.

He nodded with an "atta-girl" smile and delivered our answer. I did not even glance across the room at my sister.

At that moment, the court officer announced the judge. We rose, the shuffle of several pairs of feet on the wooden floor accompanying the judge's climb to his seat behind the bench, and the hearing began.

As Henry had predicted, our case was strong, well-documented and supported by the testimony of my doctor and—surprisingly—the prim social worker. She testified that she had not found any issues with Josiah's home situation that even suggested less-than-adequate care.

"He's an intelligent, imaginative child with advanced language skills," she stated when asked for her assessment. Naomi and I looked at one another with smiles in our eyes, if not on our mouths.

The surprising moment of the hearing occurred when Kathleen herself took the stand. Later, Henry acknowledged that it was the crowning blow, a serious mistake on the part of her lawyers. But he guessed that they had risked it as a final, last-gasp attempt to turn the hearing their way.

She was agitated when she began, and rapidly descended into an incoherent rant of need, resentment and detachment from reality. By the end, she was accusing everyone of conspiring against her—her husband for refusing to give her children of her own, me for abandoning the family and leaving her to cope with our parents' despair, Tobias for turning me into his whore, and the entire community of Martha's Vineyard for keeping her from her "right" to Josiah. She was shrieking, white-faced and unreachable.

The judge finally turned to her lawyer and ordered him to calm his client or he would have her removed from the courtroom.

I wish I could have felt pity for my sister, or have found some corner of my heart to understand her pain. But I could not. It was all I could do to hold myself together against my own pain as I waited for the judge to make his decision. I was grateful that he did so quickly and forcefully.

"I find unconscionable what has taken place here today and what the Monroe family has endured in this threat to their wholeness. It is clear to me that Mrs. Bradley has no capacity to parent Josiah or any other child, and I strongly urge that she be found help for her delusions. I appreciate her desire for a child, but stealing her sister's son, as this surely was her intention, will never be sanctioned by this court. This hearing is adjourned. Mr. and Mrs. Monroe, you may come with me to collect your son, who is a precocious and delightful young man. And I totally agree with him that today is too hot for a tie."

We followed Judge Bishop through the door by the bench. Behind us, amid the scraping of chairs and the gathering of papers, I heard Kathleen's voice, indignant and unbelieving.

"He can't do this to me. That baby belongs to me. He'll be sorry. Wait till the governor hears about what happened here today."

And then, as sharp as a slap across the face, Ned's voice.

"Oh, shut up, Kathleen. This escapade of yours has already cost me a fortune, and I'm not wasting any more favors by calling in the governor. Let's get the hell off this island. All it does is leave a bad taste in my mouth."

Ned had never once acknowledged me or even looked me in the eye during the entire hearing. His sullen boredom with the whole process had been palpable and his dismissive words to Kathleen only spoke out loud what he had been communicating to everyone in the room, including the judge.

The door closed behind us as we entered the corridor to the judge's chamber, and as far as I was concerned, the door between Kathleen and me was not going to be opened again.

I had my last chemo treatment at the end of June. The X-rays showed that the tumors had shrunk and no new tumors had formed.

"I'm cautiously optimistic," declared Dr. Bradford in Hyannis.

No clean bill of health, no guarantees. But it was a reprieve, no matter how brief.

"I want to spend the summer at Innisfree," I told Tobias as we returned to the island on the ferry.

We moved back out two weeks later, opening up the house and sweeping out not only the dust and mouse droppings that had accumulated over the winter, but the memories of illness and uncertainty that it had witnessed. I planted my vegetable garden. Tobias hung a swing for Josiah and repaired the roof. Josiah added to his rock and shell collection. And Naomi began weaving his precious osprey feather into a headdress that he would wear for his first Pow Wow in July, when he would formally be given his Wampanoag name.

It was Tobias who announced that Josiah would attend the Pow Wow.

"We did everything right to declare to the white community that Josiah is my son. It's time for me to acknowledge him to my—and his—people."

Epilogue
August 1947

My hair has begun to grow back, a cap of soft curls that Betty massages with Breck shampoo in the kitchen sink every Monday morning.

Afterwards, I sit on the back porch, letting the sun and the bay breeze dry it as I fill the pages of my ledger book. The entries are no longer lists of provisions for supplying the Boat House with sandwiches and pies. Betty has taken over that task, along with managing the café.

Instead, I am composing a letter to my son, a diary of our life here at Innisfree. It is sometimes no more and no less than a description of a hummingbird flitting from one scarlet beach rose to another, or a sleek merganser dipping its graceful neck below the surface of the shimmering bay to catch a fish.

I hear Josiah's laughter as he pumps his legs on his swing. I watch at sunset as Tobias' boat skims into the pond on the incoming tide, its sail taut and a bucket of bluefish brimming on the deck, ready to be fried with potatoes and onions for our dinner. I feel Tobias' kiss on my neck and his warm hands around my waist as I close the book and go inside.

We are home.

DISCUSSION QUESTIONS

1. Eudora Welty, in her essay "On Place in Fiction," wrote, "The truth is, fiction depends for its life on place." How important is the setting of *The Boat House Café* to your understanding of the story? How do the wildness and isolation of Innisfree shape Mae's perception of herself and her relationships—with Tobias, with her customers and with the town?

2. The once vibrant culture of the Wampanoag was nearly invisible on Chappaquiddick by World War II. Even as a child in the 1920s, Mae had barely been aware of the tribe, except to avoid the burial ground on North Neck. How does her understanding of the Wampanoag evolve and why is it so uncomfortable for her initially?

3. Although Mae's life in New York was deeply unsatisfying—"a necessity, not a choice"—at one point after her return to Chappaquiddick she wishes for the anonymity she once had in the city. Given the insular nature of island society and the expectations for sexual morality in the 1940s, was Mae's decision to defend Tobias brave or reckless? Would you have spoken up for him?

4. The keeping of secrets is an important theme in the story—Mae's shame in the life that took her so far from her mother's expectation that she would enter the convent; Tobias' reluctance to reveal to Mae his previous marriage; Mae's withholding of her pregnancy. How do these secrets impair the relationship between Mae and Tobias?

5. Do you agree with Mae's decision to keep her pregnancy from Tobias so that he will take on the leadership of the tribe? Do you think any other motives colored her choice to raise her baby alone?

6. Do you think Mae was justified in not returning to her family or letting them know she was alive? After she was reunited with Kathleen, should she have reconciled with her family?

7. What did you think of Sadie's rigid attitude against Tobias marrying Mae? Could you understand or sympathize with her position?

8. The nature and meaning of family ties is another theme in the novel. How does Mae, so determined to survive alone without help, come to an understanding of her own need for connection? What are some of the different forms of "family" that emerge over the course of the story?

ACKNOWLEDGMENTS

I am indebted to several people whose knowledge and generosity of spirit helped to shape the story of Mae Keaney and Tobias Monroe.

First, I am deeply grateful to Judy Self Murphy, who offered her beloved cottage on Cape Pogue to my family for a magical decade and whose love of that special place inspired me to write this book.

I also wish to thank Alma Gordon-Smith, Sachem of the Chappaquiddick Wampanoag, and Margaret Oliveira, member of the Chappaquiddick Wampanoag Tribal Council, for their willingness to share with me their tribal history and traditions.

Thanks also go to the knowledgeable staff of the Dukes County Courthouse: the Honorable Lance J. Garth, Associate Justice, Retired; John Hanavan and David Oliveira, Court Officers; and Joseph Sollitto, Jr., Clerk of the Courts. They each provided rich details of the history and structure of the courthouse and gave me an opportunity to explore and absorb its special character.

I am also grateful to A. Bowdoin Van Riper, Library Assistant at the Martha's Vineyard Museum, whose enthusiasm for this story had him delving through dusty archives to unearth the "telling detail" that helped me to recreate the Martha's Vineyard of the 1940s.

Grazie mille to Julie Winberg, who endured long car rides listening to me hammer out the plot and who served as the reader of my early drafts. After the research was done and the story written, special thanks to Ann DeFee, who combed through my words with diligence as my editor, honing the tale till it had a very fine edge.

And finally, a huge thank you to my husband, Stephan Platzer, who waited every evening for me to recount the next installment of the story, and who encouraged me with his keen and perceptive reactions.

ABOUT THE AUTHOR

Linda Cardillo is the award-winning author of the critically acclaimed novels *Dancing on Sunday Afternoons* and *Across the Table.* After graduating from Tufts University with a degree in American literature, she worked as an editor of college textbooks and then earned an MBA at Harvard Business School at a time when women made up only 15% of the class. Armed with her Harvard degree, she managed the circulation of a magazine during its successful start-up, founded a catering business and then built a career as the author of several works of nonfiction, from articles in *The New York Times* to books on marketing and corporate policy. She later went on to teach creative writing before her debut novel, *Dancing on Sunday Afternoons*, launched Harlequin's Everlasting Love series. For ten years she and her family were privileged to spend part of every summer at Cape Pogue on Chappaquiddick Island.

Visit Linda's website at www.lindacardillo.com; like her on Facebook at Linda Cardillo, Author; or follow her on Twitter @LindaCardillo

Read an excerpt from Book Two of *First Light*

The Deep Heart's Core

Linda Cardillo

BELLASTORIA PRESS

Books that nurture the soul

Elizabeth Innocenti
Innisfree
2005

The weather was overcast and threatening rain as Elizabeth packed the Jeep with the paraphernalia and provisions she had accumulated. When it was time for her to go, her brother Sam's entire family lined up with her son on the porch. The cousins had dragged Matteo out there, explaining it was time for the ritual known as the "Hammond Wave." It was Grannie Lydia who had initiated the wave, standing on her front porch and vigorously waving farewell whenever anyone in the family departed. As children, Elizabeth remembered that she and her brothers always rolled down the windows in their car and extended their arms out to their grandmother. They knew she didn't go back inside the house until the car was out of sight. Elizabeth was touched by Sam's family carrying on the tradition and initiating Matteo. She saw his arm raised in salute as she rounded the corner and turned onto Beach Road.

Despite the dismal weather, a boisterous group of teenage boys in brilliantly hued baggy shorts was crowded onto a stone bridge spanning a channel between the marsh and the sea. One by one they did cannonballs from the railing into the water below, each one trying to outdo the others with the height of his leap and the magnitude of water displaced when he landed. A group of admiring girls in bikinis watched from the bank, screaming and stepping back from the splashes. Across from the bridge a van with a striped awning was selling hot dogs and cotton candy.

Elizabeth smiled at the tumult of the American seaside, and could even, reluctantly, imagine Matteo taking his place on the railing. Debbie had been right to encourage her to let him stay a few weeks with his cousins instead of accompanying her to Innisfree.

When Elizabeth reached Edgartown she pulled into the Stop & Shop to pick up the last of the perishables she would need. Once she was out at the cottage she knew she wouldn't want to leave. The supermarket was a madhouse of tourists impatient to get their deli orders filled so that they could extract every precious second out of their week-long beach rentals. Elizabeth escaped from the crowded store with her purchases, packed them into the cooler in the back of her Jeep and dumped a couple of bags of ice on top of everything. It might take up to two hours to get from Edgartown to the cottage, depending on the wait for the Chappy ferry that plied across the mouth of the Edgartown harbor to Chappaquiddick Island. The ferry trip itself took less than five minutes, but it only carried three cars.

As she expected, the queue was long, extending beyond Dagget Street and back onto Simpsons Lane. She pulled behind the last car and forty minutes later arrived at the dock, the first in line for the next boat. The harbor was churning with activity—small dinghies with oversized outboard motors darting past luxury yachts, the ferry plowing nearly sideways through the current and booming a warning to smaller boats. At the pier adjacent to the ferry a trimaran that took tourists on harbor cruises announced its next sail over a loudspeaker. Everywhere Elizabeth looked, she saw the hustle of a waterfront summer resort, with vacationers frenetic in their search for the next adventure or the latest t-shirt.

As soon as the last car drove off the incoming ferry, the pilot waved her forward and Elizabeth crossed a clanging metal ramp onto the boat, a flat-bedded open craft with benches along both sides for walk-ons and room for three tightly parked vehicles.

At the Chappaquiddick side of the harbor, Elizabeth led the short caravan of vehicles behind her off the ferry and onto a narrow paved road. After she passed the small cluster of people waiting to board the returning ferry, Elizabeth saw only a couple of cyclists peddling. The cars behind her turned off onto side streets and she was on her own. The road meandered past an apple orchard, an improvised roadside stand with white plastic buckets filled with crimson peonies and dahlias for sale, and a few barely visible houses set back beyond meadows or woods. After the cacophony of Edgartown, this sparsely populated rural neighborhood seemed to belong to another time. When the road curved sharply to the right, Elizabeth slowed and, instead of following the turn, drove straight ahead onto a packed dirt road that lead directly to the Dike Bridge that linked Chappaquiddick to the narrow barrier island that was Cape Pogue. When she reached the bridge, she stopped at a small sandy parking area and stood on the sloping bank of Pucha Pond, scanning a horizon that offered only sky, water and sand. She heard nothing but the gentle lap of water against the sturdy wooden pilings that supported the bridge.

She dug a tire gauge out of the glove compartment that she had remembered to purchase at the hardware store and lowered the air pressure in the tires as she had learned as a teenager. She had checked the tides before she left Oak Bluffs and was glad she was crossing the beach at low tide this first time out on her own. There had been times in her youth when stormy weather had driven the tides high on the beach and she'd had to ford stretches where the water was over the wheel wells or back up and resort to a narrow and overgrown trail in the middle of the island. She knew that years of erosion had more than likely altered what she remembered, but she was eager to move away from the tourists starting to fill up the parking lot in spite of the overcast weather. She wanted to get out onto the trail.

She climbed into the Jeep, backed away from the pond and crossed the bridge. She made the turn after the gatehouse and felt the car straining through the soft sand. But with a lurch, she managed to pass the first hurdle and guide the Jeep into the shallow tracks that lay ahead.

The three miles to the cottage through the Refuge took forty minutes to traverse, a constantly changing landscape punctuated by scrub pine and beach roses, undulating reeds, sea vistas through breaks in the dunes and—ever present—the birds. Elizabeth noted that, as in years past, there was neither a single structure nor sign of human presence on the whole route.

She finally pulled off the beach, stopped to open a wooden gate that marked the boundary between the Refuge and the Hammond land and steered the Jeep up the rutted drive to the house. She wound past a grove of red cedars, bent and twisted by a century of wind. On her left, sleek black mergansers preened on a sandbar in the middle of the pond. As the drive curved up a short incline, the grey-shingled cluster of buildings came into view, perched on a promontory at the junction of the pond and Cape Pogue Bay. The image was at once heart-stopping in its familiarity—the source of idyllic childhood memories—and disturbing in the reality now seen through adult eyes that had been too long away.

In her memories and in her hunger for a place of refuge, Elizabeth had held onto Innisfree and its environs as "a paradise." But in the dull, metallic light of this late June morning, Elizabeth was forced to acknowledge the dilapidated structures, the rusting propane tanks stacked against the house, the weathered and splintering

Adirondack chairs scattered on the rough and uncut grass, the scraggly shrubs struggling to gain a foothold in the sand. The house stood in stark isolation on the point, clearly battered by years of Nor'easters and bearing an aching, lonely witness to Lydia's absence.

Elizabeth sat in the car, mute with sadness at what had become of this precious place. Even the hand-painted wooden "Innisfree" sign that had once hung over the front door was missing, apparently torn loose by some ferocious wind. She pulled her sweater tightly around her, but the chill she felt was not just coming off the water. She had journeyed here needing a respite, expecting Innisfree to envelop her in its magic. Instead, it struck her that it was as needy as she was.

A flash of lightning illuminated the sky across the bay, rousing her to the realization that she had a carload of stuff to unpack. She worked quickly to get everything inside the main house before the downpour that had been threatening finally descended, pounding the roof with the rat-a-tat of a snare drum. The air inside was stale, the cobwebs thick. Sam had managed to get out to the property earlier in the month when she had sent word she was coming, but he admitted to her he'd only had time to deal with the basics of opening the house for the summer—removed the plywood that protected the windows during the winter, ordered propane and hooked up a fresh tank, primed the pump and made sure she had fuel for it and for the generator. Elizabeth wandered through the stuffy rooms, absorbing both the familiar and the forgotten as she took stock in the murky light that struggled to make its way through clouded, dirt-spattered windows. She confirmed that the stove and the gaslights worked, which reassured her. But when she turned on the faucet in the kitchen it shuddered and spewed a thick torrent of rusty water. She left it running, hoping it would finally clear up. She was relieved she'd loaded a few gallons of bottled water into her cart when she'd gone shopping, although at the time it seemed extravagant. When she opened the refrigerators on the porch, she was hit with a wave of nausea from the black mold climbing up the walls. The decline and desolation around her appalled her. How long had it been since anyone had lived here?

On the wall between the kitchen and the living room she brushed her fingers over the hundreds of notches that had recorded the growth of every generation of children who had summered at Innisfree. The first row, closest to the kitchen door, listed Elizabeth's mother, Susan, and her two brothers, John and Andy, marching up the wall from the time they were toddlers until they reached their teens. Parallel to them were Elizabeth, Chris and Sam and all their cousins, John's and Andy's children. Her last notch was dated the summer before she left for Italy. Next to her generation were her nieces and nephews. Kneeling down close to the floor she searched for one mark she remembered making when she had last been at Innisfree. She found it. Matteo, at age three, who had wriggled in protest at being asked to stand still for a few seconds. Even then he was tall, she marveled. Like his father.

While she was crouched at this level she was able to see with dismay the accumulated layers of grime and the evidence of small inhabitants that had wintered over in the relative protection of the house. In all the years she had come to the cottage in the past, it had always been prepared for her. Plumped up pillows on the window seats had beckoned her to curl up with a book; frosty pitchers of lemonade in the fridge and fresh-baked vanilla crescent cookies had waited on the counter; starched curtains had fluttered in the steady sea breezes wafting through open windows. She leaned back against the wall, struggling to remind herself she was no longer a child. After the ease with which she and Matteo had been absorbed into the rhythm of Sam and Debbie's home in Oak Bluffs, she had assumed that she'd find the same comfort at Innisfree—even more so, given her memories. She had built up Innisfree in her mind as her salvation all through the spring. It had been her talisman against the gloom and weight of grief under which the villa had been buried. Everything would get better once she was here, she had promised herself. She had believed Lydia's words fervently, that she would heal here.

She'd made a terrible mistake in coming. The deteriorated condition of the house only added to her sorrow and her sense that all she cherished—Antonio, Lydia and now Innisfree—were irrevocably lost to her. As she sat in the middle of the house she recognized that it had begun to be reclaimed by the wildness it had confronted for nearly a century. And then there rose a keening from somewhere deep inside her that was as primitive as the wind howling outside.

When she was spent, her face streaked with dirt as she wiped away her tears with dusty hands, it was late afternoon. The storm front had not moved on, but seemed to have settled itself over the bay for a long stay, battering the windows on the western side of the house with sheets of water that paralleled her own weeping. She pulled herself to her feet and lit one of the kitchen gas lamps to dispel the encroaching darkness. She supposed she ought to eat something. She was resigned to spending the night here, given the duration and strength of the storm and the knowledge that it was now fully high tide. But after that, she didn't know what she was going to do.

She couldn't function beyond the simplest tasks. She opened a can of tomato soup and sliced some bread; after she ate she pulled some sheets and a comforter from the cedar chest where Lydia had last packed them away and made the bed in Lydia's bedroom. She'd always slept in The Linnet, the girls' sleeping cottage, but it was separated from the main house and getting across to it would soak her. She felt the need to cocoon herself. She remembered one of her mother's stories of riding out a hurricane at Innisfree when she was five. The lavatory was also an outbuilding, although reached by a covered walkway that was connected to the back porch. Lydia wouldn't let the children venture out of the house even to go to the bathroom for fear they'd be swept off the porch, and had improvised a chamber pot in the master bedroom closet. Elizabeth didn't think her situation was that drastic, but didn't relish needing the toilet in the middle of the night. She made a trip, brushed her teeth and returned to the house to close up for the night.

Once in bed, she drew the faded quilt up to her chin, gathering herself tightly against the chill and the damp. Despite her emotional exhaustion, she found herself acutely aware of every sound—the staccato metronome of her own pulse, the whipping of the ropes against the flagpole outside, the rattling of the loose windows and the rhythmic surge and recede of the waves against the beach below the house.

She finally slept, but woke abruptly around 3 a.m., her body aware of a dampness that was far more tangible than the moist air that had surrounded her since she'd arrived. With a moan Elizabeth realized that the bed was soaked from rain that had worked its way through the roof.

She grappled for her flashlight, threw off the soggy covers and padded in her bare feet to the kitchen to find a bucket. On the way she discovered more water where the French doors to the patio had blown open and rain had poured into the living room.

She rummaged under the sink and grabbed a dishpan for the bedroom leak. Flashes of lightning illuminated the way back. She pulled out a stack of towels from the linen closet and started mopping up after she secured the French doors and pushed the bed out of the way of the leak.

Stripping the bed as the storm howled around her reminded Elizabeth of the nights when Matteo had been a bed wetter sobbing in his parents' doorway, and she had dragged herself out of warmth and sleep to make everything right and dry for him.

She tossed the wet linens in a laundry basket on the back porch by the washing machine, too tired in the middle of the night to get the damn thing running. The mattress was too wet to remake the bed. Instead, she found more blankets in the cedar chest and curled up on the couch, exhausted, discouraged and cold.

The sound of banging on the front door of the cottage, followed by shouts, roused her from her cramped sleep in the morning. The sun was just visible at the eastern edge of the pond as Elizabeth wrapped the blanket around herself and stumbled to the door.

Through the glass she saw a man in the khaki uniform of the Refuge rangers. His face, not much older than hers, was one that had spent a lot of time in the sun, and his thick black hair was pulled back into a long ponytail held by a thin strip of leather. Elizabeth cautiously opened the door.

"Is something wrong?" Elizabeth was still waking up. Had he come to warn her of flooding? Wild birds on the attack? What else could possibly have brought him here at such an ungodly hour?

"Ma'am, may I ask you what you are doing in this house?"

"Trying to sleep until a few minutes ago. Why?"

"As far as I can tell, you are trespassing. Unless you can show me some authorization from the Hammond family allowing you to be here, like a lease, I'm going to ask you to get into your car and vacate the island."

"I don't need a lease to be in my family's home. I'm Elizabeth Innocenti, the Hammond's granddaughter!" After she had said it, she realized the name Innocenti would mean nothing to him, had no relationship to Innisfree in more ways than he would understand.

"May I see some ID please?"

The ranger stood firm in the doorway, his gaze sweeping over the disarray—soggy towels and animal droppings on the floor, the rumpled couch, and through the doorway to the bedroom, the stripped bed pushed askew. To someone just arriving on the scene, unaware of her miserable night during the storm, the house looked ransacked.

She pulled the threadbare blanket more tightly around her, feeling vulnerable in her thin nightshirt. Not only had it not kept her warm during the night, but now it offered her scant protection from the watchful eyes of the unyielding man in the doorway.

He was one more reason that she had made a mistake in coming to Innisfree and she wanted him to be gone. Realizing that the identification she had with her—her passport and her Italian driver's license—would not connect her to her grandparents, she swept her eyes over the room for some shred of evidence that would satisfy the arrogant and self-important intruder. With relief, she silently thanked Lydia for the bookshelf cluttered with family photographs. Both at her home in town and out here at Cape Pogue, Lydia had amassed a collection of pictorial mementos that chronicled the family as thoroughly as the growth chart carved into the wall. Elizabeth strode across the room and grabbed a framed photo from the shelf. It had been taken the last time she'd been at Innisfree, when the entire family had gathered to celebrate Lydia's 75th birthday. She returned to the door and thrust it at the ranger.

"That's me at my grandmother's birthday about ten years ago," she said, pointing to her younger self, her fingers grazing the image of

Antonio next to her, his arm casually draped across her shoulders. Matteo was in her arms. She willed herself not to break down in front of the stranger. "Are you satisfied now that I'm not a squatter?"

The ranger took the photo from her and studied it, his eyes passing from the Elizabeth standing before him—sleep-deprived, as ravaged and unkempt as the house itself—and the polished, contented woman in the photograph surrounded by the sprawling Hammond clan in clearly happier times. Elizabeth watched with relief as his eyes registered a connection between the image and her exhausted self.

"Sorry to have bothered you," he said, handing her back the photo. "Just trying to keep an eye on the place as a favor to Mrs. Hammond. The old-timers on the ranger staff passed on the word that your family hasn't been out here much since she went into the nursing home. I won't be bothering you again. I've got more than enough to keep me busy on the Refuge without acting as a private security guard. Especially when it's not appreciated."

He left as abruptly as he'd arrived, striding across the lawn with a casual confidence and climbing into a dark green pickup truck with the Cape Pogue Refuge seal. The mergansers rose up in a flurry as he shifted into gear and drove off, turning toward the northern tip of the island when he reached the end of the driveway.

Caleb Monroe
Cape Pogue Bay
2005

Caleb Monroe hadn't recognized Elizabeth Todd when she opened the door at Innisfree. Too thin, too pale, too agitated. She looked like the off-islanders who flocked to the Vineyard in the summer, with their designer sunglasses and stiletto sandals jaywalking across Water Street. She didn't look like the spunky little girl he remembered tagging after her brothers and him when they'd explored the island as children, nor the out-of-reach teenager he'd later only peripherally been aware of as he and Sam and Chris Todd had drifted apart. He'd heard that she had married some Italian and was living over there. What she was doing alone at Innisfree was beyond him.

It appeared that Elizabeth hadn't recognized him either, which didn't surprise him.

He had put women like Elizabeth Todd behind him a long time ago, women he'd known in New York when he'd followed many of his classmates there after college. He'd grown weary of people finding it surprising that he'd gone to Dartmouth. If you're Native American, they assume you're either an ironworker, a dealer at a casino or a drunk. But he knew he never would have gone to Dartmouth if he hadn't found the book on the shelf in the living room at Innisfree.

His grandfather Tobias used to be the caretaker for the Hammonds until he got too old to be wrestling with propane tanks and repairing the roof every spring after Nor'easters tore half the slates off. When he went out to the cottage, Tobias used to take Caleb with him. While his grandfather tinkered with the pump or replaced broken windows, Caleb and the Todd boys scrambled over the moors. As he got older, Caleb worked alongside Tobias, especially at the beginning and end of the season. The October of his senior year of high school they were closing up the place—shutting off the gas, boarding up the windows. Caleb was supposed to be doing a walk-through, making sure all the valves to the stove and the lamps were closed. He did as Tobias expected, but it was also an opportunity he couldn't pass up to explore. It had been awhile since he, Sam and Chris had hung out, especially after he had gotten a job at Cronig's Market. For many summers, he had only seen the family from a distance when he'd be motoring over to the Gut in his father's Whaler to fish after work.

Being inside the house instead of watching it from the water intrigued him. In the living room was a bookcase, filled with books on celestial navigation, crossword dictionaries and three rows of paperback novels that had curled from the dampness of the salt air. A book had been left out and he was going to put it back on the shelf—tidying up was part of what Tobias did at the end of the season before affixing the plywood to the windows that shut out the light and the weather. But Caleb turned it over to read the back cover and discovered that the author was a Modoc Indian and the head of Native American Studies at Dartmouth. He stuck the book in his back pocket, promising himself he'd return it to the bookcase in the spring when they opened up the cottage.

Caleb didn't sleep that night until he'd finished the book, a story about three Native American women whose lives had nothing and everything to do with his. Then he did something he'd never done before—he wrote to the author. He didn't really know what he wanted when he did, but the author recognized something in Caleb that he hadn't discovered yet—an unsatisfied hunger to understand himself through his people, the Wampanoag—native to the island and parts of the Cape.

A year later Caleb was welcomed as a student at Dartmouth, which was intent on fulfilling its original charter to educate the "Youth of the Indian Tribes in this Land…." It was a heady adventure for a boy whose only experience off-island up till then had been as goalie on a traveling soccer team that played games in southeastern Massachusetts. The four years in Hanover, New Hampshire, were like a juggling act in a Wild West show, except that instead of keeping tomahawks in the air, he was balancing Pow Wows and Ivy League football games, computer science and Native American oral literature. When Caleb left

Dartmouth, he was bifurcated—stripes of war paint on his cheeks and a green-and-silver striped tie around his neck.

New York was not a good place for an island boy who needed to feel the wind against his skin to know which way to turn. He quit his job and joined the Navy, which turned him into a cryptologist and sent him to the Middle East.

He was good at it.

He had come home six months ago after his second tour of duty was up because his mother had sought his help. It was temporary, she said. Give me a few months after all the years you've been away. Tobias was dying. Caleb's father had lost his job and wasn't looking for another one.

Caleb hadn't intended to stay. In the spring, Tobias was still able to go out in his boat on the bay. They spent the time together with not much talk, some fishing and a couple of beers nursed over the course of the afternoon. As Tobias descended into the maw of his disease, what little he said was only in Wampanaak, their native tongue. Caleb watched his once robust grandfather, the man who had taught him to sail and clam and hunt, to listen to the silence and recognize the minutest fragments of the world around him, shrivel into an empty pod. His breath, when Caleb bent his ear close to his grandfather's lips to decipher the sounds he was trying to make, stank of the decay that was eating him from the inside.

But whatever was eating at Josiah, his father, Caleb hadn't begun to understand. He wasn't drinking or beating his mother, of that he was sure. Grace would not have kept something like that hidden. But the sadness and anger that had descended upon him and upon their home was palpable. Like Caleb, Josiah was a veteran. He'd fought in Vietnam. You'd have thought that would give them a bond. But it hadn't. Growing up, Caleb had always been closer to his grandfather. And now, with his mother begging him to do something, he was helpless.

He should have left. But like a lot of men around here in the off-season, Caleb drifted. There's not much call for cryptologists on Martha's Vineyard, but he'd seen enough of war. He knew he wasn't going back into the Navy. But he also didn't know what else he could do.

It was Caleb's cousin, Simon Banyard, who told him about the job at the Refuge. They beef up the ranger staff during the summer to handle the influx of tourists. Not folks who summer out at Pogue—there's only a handful of houses up by the lighthouse, all owned by long-timers who love the land and the isolation and keep to themselves. It's the day trippers who come over to Chappy for the beach and the fishing who swell the population on the Refuge a hundredfold and who need to be reminded to deflate their tires and take their garbage out with them.

Caleb spent his days—or his nights, depending on his shift—patrolling the trails and the beaches. He didn't do the tours. The Refuge had been his childhood backyard, long before the land got put into trust. He knew every cranny and cove, every clam bed and fox den. But he wasn't an entertainer. He left that to the crew-cut blond guys who cajoled the sunburned and the bored into noticing the sandpipers and the plovers as they traveled over the dunes or led a caravan of kayaks through the waters of Pucha Pond.

By sunset, the tourists were gone. When he went out at night to the Gut to fish, he shared the beach with only a handful of men who'd learned to cast, like he had, from their grandfathers. No one talked. The only sounds were the whip of a line and the ripple of a slow tide on the rock-strewn sand. It suited him.

Look for *The Deep Heart's Core* in early 2015.
For more information, go to
www.bellastoriapress.com.